KATE

AN ENEMIES TO LO

KATE LAUREN

A Recipe for Disaster

This is a work of fiction. Names, characters, places, and incidents either are the product of the author's imagination or are used fictitiously. Any resemblance to actual persons, living or dead, events, or locales is entirely coincidental.

Copyright © 2023 by Kate Lauren

All rights reserved. No part of this book may be reproduced or used in any manner without written permission of the copyright owner except for the use of quotations in a book review. For more information, address: thewriterkate1@gmail.com

First paperback edition November 2024
Cover illustration by Jessica Lynn Draws
jessicalynndraws.com

ISBN 979-8-3757-9254-5

KATE LAUREN

Track One: Iris - Goo Goo Dolls

Track Two: I Think I Like You - The Band Camino

Track Three: There She Goes - The La's

Track Four: Lotus Inn - Why Don't We

Track Five: There's Still A Light In The House - Valley

Track Six: Thunderstruck - AC/DC

Track Seven: Shut up - Grayson Chance

Track Eight: Welcome To New York (Taylor's Version) - Taylor Swift

Track Nine: The City - Lauren Zocca

Track Ten: Starving - Hailee Steinfeld, Grey, Zedd

Track Eleven: Crash My Car - COIN

Track Twelve: Honeybee - The Head And The Heart

Track Thirteen: I Knew You Were Trouble (Taylor's Version) - Taylor Swift

A Recipe for Disaster

KATE LAUREN

This book is dedicated to those who wonder if fictional men exist—they do…I promise you.

A Recipe for Disaster

One

IRIS

In the fall of each year, a competition is held in Miami, Florida, called The Art of Cooking. It's a prestigious event that calls upon the three most decorated chefs in each state to compete for an ultimate cash prize of $100,000 and the honor of being named "America's Ultimate Dining Experience"—a title that would surely take my restaurant to the next level.

I'm Iris Hammond, owner and head chef of The Sweet Red, which you'll find perfectly located off Pineapple Street—one of three adjacent streets in Brooklyn, New York, named after a distinctive tropical fruit.

My thriving small business and personality mimic just that of a pineapple. From the outside, we're unique. Pineapples, with their distinctive sharp leaves and vibrant colors, and myself, with my naturally red hair, freckles and blue eyes.

We can also stand our ground. Pineapples, with their notoriously mixed reviews on whether they belong amidst a savory or sweet dish. And me, being a female business owner on the brink of New York, doing my best to make it in an environment where I know that at any second, I can be easily replaced.

Nonetheless, pineapples and I are synonymous with one

A Recipe for Disaster

another. We have an objective to always blur the lines—and allow those to see beyond reason. Yet, on the inside, we're sweet, fresh, and sure to leave you returning for more. An experience that is *rarely* unwanted or undesired.

Next, you'll find Orange Street, home to Lore Llyod—my best friend, self-taught dessert connoisseur, and business partner for the past five years.

Like an orange, Lore brings the vibrancy, brightness and that piece of zest into my life that I often can overlook. With Lore, I've transformed The Sweet Red from your basic restaurant into a high-class staple for those in the Brooklyn region—by serving high-quality and unique dishes at a fractional cost to our competitors.

As the years have passed, Lore and I have worked tirelessly to engage in various competitions. We've won some, ranked in all, and done our due diligence to get our name out there—making us one of the most decorated establishments in Brooklyn.

However, this year, unlike the ones prior, has proved to be more challenging to receive this notary invitation, all thanks to the recent opening of The Closed Cook. An establishment that you'll find on the last of the fruit street triad—Cranberry Street.

In only a few short months since The Closed Cook opened their doors, *this* cook has nearly closed her own. Our business has plummeted since the local paper called The Closed Cook "the newest high-class dining experience to hit the Brooklyn scene." And if the restaurant wasn't awful enough, the owner and head chef, Dakota Foster, makes this situation completely unbearable.

Let's just say, unlike myself and my restaurant, both sweet

and delightful in nature, Cranberry Street is a perfectly suited name for Dakota, who is entirely unpleasant and leaves you with a sour, bitter taste in your mouth.

How do I know this?

Well, all I have to do is think back to three months ago. The first day of the new competition season and the first time I met the renowned *Dakota Foster*.

Three Months Ago

"Our first competition of the year!" Lore squeals as we walk through the banquet hall, following the signage that leads us to the check-in line. "And right here in New York City! Where else could be a better place to start?"

I eagerly nod in agreement. After a short break, we're back and better than ever, and frankly, I couldn't be happier. Competing is what I do best.

Scratch that.

Cooking is what I do best.

But spending a good portion of my life honing my craft doesn't make me immune to those same rollercoaster of emotions that transpire every time we arrive at a new competition.

Pre-comp jitters are the worst. Here's the best way I can describe them. Think about that feeling when you climb the first hill of a rollercoaster. You're going up, and in your mind, you know that the drop is coming—you've signed yourself up for it, strapped yourself in, and within a few seconds, it's going to happen.

Pause right there.

That's the feeling.

That's the emotion.

The anticipation always seems to be way worse than the drop itself.

But oddly enough, over time, I've found comfort on the uphill. That weird, unsettling feeling. I've realized that it's not the climb that scares me. It's the inevitability that what must go up must always come down.

That's what I hate.

The downward feeling.

I've grown into someone who avoids the downfall. I've felt it before and never want to feel it again. Instead, I hover, I float, and I live my life in what I call the *in-between*.

"This is the year, Lore." I clutch onto her arm firmly to dismiss my anxiety. "This is the year we'll get invited to The Art of Cooking Competition. I can just feel it!"

Lore smiles enthusiastically back at me. "It has to be," she agrees with a nod of her head. "We were so close last year. There is *no* way we don't get that invite this—"

A buzzing interrupts her mid-sentence.

"Sorry." Lore pulls her phone out of her back pocket, her eyes darting toward the screen. "It's Elias," she reveals, her thumb hovering over the decline button. "I'll just call him back."

"It's fine." I release my grasp from her arm. "Answer it. You wouldn't want to keep your *fiancé* waiting, now would you?" I playfully cock a brow. "I'll sign in for the two of us. Go."

"You're the best." Lore wastes no time accepting the call and moving her way out of the line. "Hey baby, we just arrived…" I hear the first few words of her conversation before she disappears out of sight.

Lore and Elias.

They've been together for 18 months, and just a few weeks ago, Elias decided to pop the question.

Now, let me preface this by saying that I love Elias. He's funny, intelligent, charismatic and loves my best friend with all of his heart. But I'd be lying if I didn't have my own selfish reasons for wishing he'd waited just a tad bit longer to propose.

I know, I know. Who am I to stand in the way of someone else's happiness?

Truthfully, since the proposal the two of them have re-entered the honeymoon phase. Lore has been distracted and consumed with wedding planning, which, with full transparency, I'm a sucker for—but I've just got other priorities at the moment.

1. Getting into The Art of Cooking Competition
2. Doubling our yearly revenue.

and

3. Being the best resturant in New York City.

That's it. That's all I want right now.

Three things that I hold onto as the line continues to crawl forward, prompting me to peer down at my watch.

We're late.

Not by much, mind you, but like my dad always told me, "late is late."

"C'mon…" I tap my foot impatiently and glance over my

shoulder, even though it's hardly been a few minutes since Lore left. The worst part about attending these culinary competitions has got to be the routine check-in process, which includes, but is not limited to: dreadfully long lineups, an endless amount of paperwork, extensive costs—and don't even get me started on the travel. Travelling is absolutely the worst.

"Next!" A voice at the vacant table ahead gestures for me to step forward.

"Good morning!" I singsong, leaning down to sign in both mine and Lore's name on the check-in sheet.

"Morning!" A middle-aged woman cheerfully responds. "Can I grab your name?" She looks up from her laptop with tired eyes, yet a full smile.

"Iris Hammond," I tell her as she types into the keyboard. "I'm here with my business partner, Lore Llyod. We're with The Sweet Red."

"Wait…" The woman pulls her hand back as her brows furrow in thought. "Did you say 'The Sweet Red'?"

I nod in response as her lips curve into a smile.

"I've been there before with some of my friends!" she exclaims giddily. "We rented out the restaurant for a bachelorette party. Maybe you remember us. The bride's name was Jessica."

"Jessica?" I repeat, trying to re-hash my memory—the name's not ringing a bell.

"Jessica Smith," she chimes up again in an attempt to clarify. *Yeah, that narrows it down a lot.*

"I…uh…" I stutter, my hand finding its way towards my ear as I twist my earring in discomfort—something I usually do when

I don't know what to say.

Carefully, the woman leans across the table, gesturing for me to follow. "We, uh…" She lowers her voice to a whisper. "We're the ones that brought the three male strippers to the restaurant. You had to call an ambulance because Sebastien fell."

Despite her attempt to keep things hush, I can't help but burst into laughter at the reminder of that memory—although at the time, having to call 9-1-1 because a male stripper managed to fall off one of my tables and break his arm was less than humorous.

"Oh my goodness. How could I forget?" I snicker. "You guys enacted the *no climbing on tables* policy."

The woman lets out a hoarse laugh. "I'm glad we made such an impact."

My laughter trails off as I continue filling in the form. "Did Jessica get married?" I can't help but wonder. "I remember that the wedding was supposed to be in—"

The sound of someone loudly clearing their throat from behind me causes me to lose my train of thought. I hardly look over my shoulder, waiting to hear someone speak, but no voice follows, guiding me to continue.

"Sorry." I shake my head. "As I was saying, did the wedding go okay? It didn't rain, right? I know that was something she was worried about—"

"Ahem." The voice from behind interrupts me yet again, only this time I turn around, tilting my head.

"I'm sorry," I say, hands impatiently on my hips. "Am I—"

"Don't be." A tall frame gently pushes past me to find a spot at the check-in table before I can muster out so much as another syllable. "I just need to sign myself in."

"Excuse me?" I blurt out in annoyance. "It's not your turn yet."

The man shrugs nonchalantly, reaching for a form with no regard. "You were taking too long."

I fold my arms across my chest in a huff. "Maybe you should learn to wait your turn and not overwhelm…" I look down at the clerk's name tag. "Dear Beth here." I gesture in her direction. "Did your mother not teach you a thing or two about respect?"

"It's okay," Beth interjects before the man has the chance to, visibly taken back by my shift in demeanor—whereas I'm visibly taken back by the way her eyes have since glazed over as she looks up at him in adoration. "Would you mind filling out this form too?" She shifts her attention back towards me, handing me a few extra pieces of paper before her gaze returns to the man whose presence has completely overwhelmed my space.

My eyes narrow as I take in his appearance. His dark brown hair is perfectly combed back, yet a few strands have managed to escape across his forehead. Regardless, I waste no time adding his face to my mental list of people with no basic understanding of manners, yet a complete understanding of how to use a hairbrush.

His strong yet slightly rounded jawline is complimented by a faint layer of facial hair, his lips a rosy shade of pink. He's stupid handsome—gorgeous, in fact. All the more reason why I choose to dislike him that much more.

"Thank you, *Beth*." He slyly smirks at her, a huskiness cascading through his voice. "I really appreciate you being so *lenient*."

A flushness falls over Beth's full cheeks as she bashfully looks away, asking him for his name ever so softly.

"It's Dakota," he tells her without skipping a beat. "Dakota Foster."

Beth types his name into the computer, batting her eyelashes as she looks back up at him. "Perfect. It says here that you're competing alone. Is that right?" she asks, handing him some additional forms to fill out.

"That's right, *Beth*," he emphasizes her name again, reaching for a pen and obnoxiously clicking it open. "That's very observant of you."

Beth rests her hands on either side of her face, admiring his expression. "People tell me that all the time, actually…that I'm observant."

Dakota shoots her a groan-worthy wink. "I bet they do."

Much to my dismay his sarcastic and snarky attitude seems to go right over poor Beth's head. I'm not so easily convinced. While she giggles away, my lips have never been so straight in my life. I can see right through Dakota Foster as if he's a piece of paper held up against the sunlight.

I'm certain he thinks he can get away with whatever he wants with a charming smile and a "rules don't apply to me" attitude. Unlucky for him, I won't let that fly. No way, no how.

Now, my cheeks are equally as red as Beth's, but with a sense of anger—not affection. My pen sinks into the paper much firmer as I suppress my frustration and continue writing my information onto the page. I'm confident my name will be embedded into this plastic fold-out table for the rest of eternity.

Once I finish, I let out a breath, unclick the pen and hand my

A Recipe for Disaster

completed forms over to Beth, who's clearly disappointed that her job description doesn't entail staring at Dakota all day long.

"Do you have the allergy form?" I try to conceal the irritability in my voice. "I need it."

"The form?"

I flash her a look.

"Oh, yes." She swivels around in her chair. "Let me grab that for you." As she does that, I briefly glance over to my side, analyzing the awful penmanship of a man with no respect, no patience, no—

"Here you go." Beth hands me the form. "What was the allergy?" she requests, pulling a clipboard out from her side. "I need to include it on my tracking sheet here."

"Peanuts," I respond. It's the same allergy I've had my whole life and one that, when it comes to any competition, I'm sure to make a note of. "It's severe. If you can make sure that I won't come into contact with it during the competition, that would be greatly appreciated." I grant her my best smile, holding my head up high as I stick my "hello, my name is" tag onto my shirt.

"Noted." Beth's pen vigilantly moves along the page. "Is there anything else I can help you out with?"

Before I can respond, we both take into account that in the span of our conversation Dakota has managed to fill out his forms, straighten the papers into his hands, and is continually tapping them against the table.

My eyes dart over to his repetitive motion, where I catch not only the sheer size of his hands—but also that of a small tattoo that pokes out from his sweater.

What is that? I'm left deciphering the faint lines through my questionable line of vision.

A moth?

A dragonfly?

A butterfly?

"Anything else I could help you with?" Beth repeats once more.

I come back to reality.

"That's everything," I tell her, swallowing hard. "Thanks, Beth."

I'm just about ready to walk away when the words, "sorry again about the stripper," escape Beth's mouth.

As I freeze, I can't help but notice the way Dakota's eyes light up. I can see how he's trying to process that those words just left Beth's mouth—and worse, the fact that that sentence was directed towards me.

I grow intrigued by what he's thinking, but have to remind myself—who cares? We've only had a brief interaction, but that's all I needed to know that Dakota Foster's mind is probably filled with cobwebs and too much hairspray that's seeped through his skull.

"Oh, it's alright." I try to mitigate the situation as Dakota snickers like a child, covering his mouth in delight. "You have a good day now, *Beth*," I join in on the exaggeration, letting out a huff as I finally march away from the table in an attempt to find Lore.

I only make it a few steps when a deep yet concerningly recognizable voice calls out to me. "Hey!"

A Recipe for Disaster

I slowly turn around at the sight of Dakota's strong arm lifting my black bag into the air—the one I'd just left at the sign-in table.

"Forgetting something?" He raises a suggestive brow.

Pursing my lips, I slowly inch my way back over to him. Yet, as I go to take the bag back from his grasp, he childishly lifts it into the air.

I shoot him an unamused glare and attempt to reach for it again, only for him tor repeat the same action.

"Are you being serious?!" I lift onto my tiptoes and snatch the bag from his hand. As our skin makes contact, a sizable knot forms in my throat.

"What?" Dakota's eyes peer down at me with a glimmer of trouble in his eyes, one that I refuse to entertain. "I'm just joking around."

I pull the bag over my shoulder and gulp down this conflicting emotion.

Is it frustration?

Anger?

Why can't I tell?

All I can tell for certain is that rather than saying anything else, Dakota's eyes are hyper-fixated on my chest.

Is he staring at my tits?

Seriously?

I'm seconds away from blasting him into oblivion when he diverts his eyes back up and into mine. "Interesting placement," he remarks. "I wouldn't have thought that that would be where you'd put a name tag."

"Huh?" I question, dropping my eyes down to my chest. As I do, I notice that for some inexplicable reason, I've stuck my name tag below the deep V of my shirt.

What is wrong with me?

"Iris." He says my name for the first time. "Nice name," he compliments before ruining it. "Just like an eyeball. Your parents must really like anatomy, huh?" He deviously smirks.

"Like you're one to talk." He ignites a fire inside of me. "What are you named after, huh? A state? I'm debating whether I should call you North or South Dakota."

"Aw." He pities me, folding his muscular arms across his chest. "Didn't you say that your restaurant is called The Sweet Red? That wasn't very *sweet*, now, was it?"

I clutch my purse with one hand and place another on my hip. "I'll have you know that I am *incredibly* sweet, kind, caring and a whole lot of other things."

Dakota runs a free hand across his stubbled face, scanning me up and down. "A 'whole lot of other things' is definitely right," he retorts, flinging his jacket over his shoulder. "Now, I'd love to stay and chat," he adds with a sarcastic roll of his eyes. "But I've got to get going. I've got a competition to win. I guess I'll see you around, *neighbor*."

It takes him being a few strides away before I can process his final word.

Neighbor?

"I'm sorry." I don't realize I've caught up with him and clutched onto his arm until it's too late. "What do you mean by '*neighbor?*'"

Dakota doesn't immediately brush off my touch, but it doesn't matter. I take the liberty to do so myself.

"Oh, did I forget to mention? I just opened up down the street from you. The Closed Cook." The words fall effortlessly out of his mouth. "That's my restaurant."

"*You?*" I say in disbelief, as the name not only rings a bell but unleashes a million sirens in my mind. "You're the new place on Cranberry Street?"

Dakota looks up in thought, gesturing a finger in my direction. "I think you meant to say the *best* place on Cranberry Street."

"No." I cross my arms in front of my chest, shaking my head with certainty. "No, I most certainly did not! You're painful, do you know that? Besides, that location is cursed. Everyone who opens up there is in and out within a year. So good luck, because you're sure as hell going to need it!"

"I guess, we'll see about that," Dakota sneers, attempting to walk away, but I stop him again.

"Wait." I can't help but shake the lingering question in my mind. "How did you know where my restaurant is?"

"Iris!" Lore walks back over to me before he can respond. "Are we all set to go?" she asks before gleaming up at Dakota, pausing as if she's expecting an introduction that I refuse to give.

"Let's go." I pull on Lore's arm, darting as far away from Dakota as possible.

She shakes me off as we reach the hotel check-in counter. "Ouch!" she cries. "What's going on? Why are you so upset? And who was that?" The question trail never seems to end.

"Trouble," I barely have the words to respond. "He's a whole lot of trouble."

A Recipe for Disaster

Two

DAKOTA

Six Months Earlier

Before I arrived in New York City, I was only certain of two things.

First, that moving out of Colorado would be the best decision I'd ever make. It was a decision that I didn't take lightly, mind you. I'd just left behind a stable nine-to-five job to move across the country, in hopes of pursuing a dream that, deep down, I'd always known I should've from day one.

My parents thought I'd lost it, and my sisters thought I was making a mistake, but my brother believed in me—and I'd be damned if I let him down any more than I already have.

Getting out of Denver was the only logical choice. Being there was a constant reminder of everything I'd lost. Choosing to stay was doing nothing but setting me back in this grieving process. Everything was a reminder of him.

Everything.

Our family.

Our friends.

The town we grew up in.

I could barely drive down the street without passing the exact spot where it all happened—reminding me of how shitty of a person I'd been and how great of a guy he always was.

This leads me to the second thing I'd been certain about. That I, Dakota Foster, am one lucky son-of-a-bitch. The man who, in their last attempt to break free, fled to the unfamiliar streets of Brooklyn, in hopes of searching for the perfect location to open my first restaurant and fulfill my brother's last wish.

"So, what do you think?" my estate agent—Craig Daniels, the one I'd hired shortly after my arrival, asks as we stop in front of what must be the tenth vacant storefront today.

"Weird street name," I can't help but comment.

Craig's thick brows furrow together in unison. "What do you mean?" He seems partially offended. "What's wrong with it?"

I gesture to the street sign that hovers above us. "Cranberry street?" I scoff, tucking my hands back into my pocket. "Don't you think that's a bit…odd?"

Craig runs a hand through his speckled gray hair—I'm confident I've been the root cause of that in only the week we've been working together.

My mother always called me "difficult," but I think the word "particular," is better suited. I've always known what I wanted. I'd just never acted on it. Now that I've finally taken the leap to make my dreams a reality, all must go to plan—and to do that, I can't let anything set me back. Definitely not some ridiculous street name.

"You've got to be kidding me." Craig lets out an exasperated sigh. "Do you even know where we are, Dakota? This is the fruit street triad, for crying out loud!" He scolds me as if I should've known all along.

I cock an eyebrow.

Triad?

Meaning, there's more?

Craig continues. "The fruit street triad consists of three streets. Pineapple Street, Orange Street, and last but certainly not least, Cranberry Street." he cheers with an abundance of enthusiasm—one I'm trying to find within myself.

"*Yippee*! Cranberry Street—the best fruit of them all." I fill my words with a false sense of excitement, causing his eyes to light up in delight.

"See, you've got it!" Craig doesn't sense the raging sarcasm in my voice. Very few people seem to. "Can't you see? We're in the heart of Brooklyn, Dakota? Don't you think that this would be a perfect spot for you to open up your first restaurant? C'mon, it's absolutely perfect!"

As much as I hate to agree, he's not wrong. From where we're standing, we can practically see the Brooklyn Bridge. Plus, if what I read on the information pamphlet before we arrived is true, the lease for this place seems fair enough. Not to mention that the restaurant location is majorly populated by a perfect mixture of both residential and commercial customers.

But that's not even the best part. The picturesque scenery is beyond what I was expecting. In fact, it's perfect. Whatever that means, exactly. Except for the name. *Cranberry Street.* The name is the only thing that mildly annoys me, which, if I'm being honest, isn't all that difficult to do.

All I can think about is how it's going to sound.

"Hey, come on down to my restaurant. We're located on Cranberry Street!"

I let out a breath. My establishment needs to speak to high-class meets middle-class dining. A place where anyone can casually go for a drink after work, watch a sports game or even arrive in black tie attire and feel like they fit right in.

That's what I want—diversity and flexibility. Not to sound as if I'm on an episode of a children's television show.

If I'm being really picky, it's not like cranberries are a great fruit, either. Especially when compared to pineapples and oranges—my competitors' street names.

Realistically, other than making some jelly around the holidays, what do you really use cranberries for? And if someone wants to argue that cranberries make a good juice, you're either a gynecologist like one of my sisters or are missing your taste buds.

"Listen, Dakota," Craig's voice pulls me out of my escalating thoughts. "The area's already got some great food vendors—one of which is the most decorated establishment in Brooklyn!"

His words spark my curiosity as I fold my arms across my chest, tilting my chin in interest. "Go on." I tell him.

Craig smirks. "I've been to the restaurant a few times. It's a great place, and lucky for you, it's two streets over, so enough distance so that when your restaurant kicks ass, there's some room for that rivalry to begin!"

I can't tell what irks me more. Hearing the words "kick-ass" come out of a sixty-something-year-old man's mouth or that there is already stiff competition around here.

Besides, this might actually be a good thing. If the area is

A Recipe for Disaster

already known for its elite dining, I won't need to do the brunt work of building up a reputation around here. If anything, by joining this neighborhood, I'll just enhance it.

"Well, don't just stand there." Craig punches a code into the lockbox and pulls it away. "Come on in and have a look for yourself."

As he swings open the creaking door, I follow him inside and flip on the light switch. Immediately, the two of us are met with a space that has been visibly vacant for quite some time.

Dust lingers over every square inch of the room as if no one has occupied this place for months.

But, in my eyes, all that matters is the character, the structure, and the bones of the establishment, and from what I see as I carefully scan the room—this space has all of that.

The bar in the center of the dining room is modern, comprehensive and with live edge countertops.

The booths that outline the restaurant's perimeter are grand, with deep brown leather seating that overlaps either side.

The solid oak floors appear as if they were installed in the '60s, as the faintest creek follows with each subtle step.

The restaurant is rustic, timeless and radiates a look that I'd always dreamt my first restaurant would entail. I'm sold before I even step foot into the kitchen. When I do, I'm astonished. The appliances are brand new, and precisely what I envisioned.

You'll flourish here, I tell myself. *Here, you'll become the best in Brooklyn.*

"So? What do you think?" Craig asks, securing the lock right back onto the front of the door as we make our way back outside.

"It's great, isn't it?"

"I mean, as much as I hate to admit it, Craig. You've sold me. This place is perfect," I agree, forcing a smile to his cheeks, only to dissipate it with my following few words. "But could you explain to me why it's clearly been vacant for so long? I mean, it's every restaurant owner's dream. I'm surprised it's even available for lease right now."

Craig allows for a long-winded pause, pulling his sunglasses out from his jacket pocket before he slips them over his face. "Let's take a walk, shall we?" he prompts.

I nod, following alongside him as we make our way two blocks north, stopping once we reach the center of Pineapple and Hicks Street.

"Dakota," Craig pauses. "Do you remember that restaurant I told you about earlier?"

The competition. "How could I forget?"

"Well..." He gestures just ahead. "There it is."

My eyes follow his hand as I see the words "The Sweet Red" cascaded in a cursive font over what I'd call an overly decorated storefront.

The Sweet Red has a complete pergola-style patio where string lights hang from side to side. A colorful assortment of flowers rests atop each table which is carefully lined with bright tablecloths and mix-matched furniture.

The restaurant is an eyesore that makes sense...if that even makes sense.

But it's not that that makes the establishment unmistakable from the others on the street. It's the flood of people that take

A Recipe for Disaster

make their way in and out of the storefront every few seconds.

"You see," Craig chimes back up. "The Sweet Red is what I'd best describe as..." He lingers his speech, looking up in thought. "A *challenge*."

"'A challenge'?" I suck in a breath. "In what way?"

"Within the last two years, The Sweet Red has driven three restaurants out of business—the storefront on Cranberry Street *always* being one of them."

It takes a second for his words to register, and as they do I try to accept how this angelic-looking restaurant with the word "sweet" in its name, has turned everyone else sour.

"I'm serious, Dakota," he says bluntly as I look at him in disbelief while another four people enter the restaurant. "The lady that owns this place doesn't mess around. She knows her stuff."

At the same time as Craig finishes his remarks, a woman in a chef's jacket and jeans—a combination I immediately question—steps outside.

"Speaking of which..." He lowers his voice and tone. "That's her."

Without having to follow his now pointed finger to confirm, I know that without an ounce of doubt, I'm already looking at exactly who I need to be. No one stands out in that mixture of people besides her.

It's only *her*.

Her hair is redder than the sunburn forming on my arm from this unusual spring heat beating down on me—and the way her jeans curve around her hips makes me want to take back my comment about the interesting outfit combination.

Now, it's my new favorite.

I gulp, hoping to resolve the dryness that has formed in my throat. I'd always thought crushes were stupid and for children. Yet, the fact that I need to shift my eyes away from her to stop this ridiculous fluttering in my stomach is downright embarrassing. I can hardly look away for a second until my eyes demand that I look back at her.

"*Iris*." I hear her name for the first time. "Her name is *Iris Hammond*. Maybe you've heard of her before." Craig probes.

I shake my head. I know I haven't. If I had, I surely wouldn't have been able to forget.

Craig lets out a stifled laugh. "Well you better get familiarized, especially if you want to move in just down the street. Iris competes in cooking competitions both in and out of state. She's built up a real reputation around here. How do you think The Sweet Red has become so highly decorated?"

I have to bite down on my lower lip to suppress the smirk I can feel forming. My competition and I unknowingly have something in common. Although I'd never traveled much out of state to compete, it had quickly become one of my favorite things to do back in Denver. It was a hobby that, since the accident, I'd seemingly lost the courage to get back into.

"And you know all of this, how?" I analyze his face.

"Because I'm a massive foodie. I always keep up to date on all the competitions." Craig explains as Iris steps back into the restaurant, leaving me with a conflicting sense of longing and loathing.

A Recipe for Disaster

I hardly needed a second glance to come to terms with the fact that she has to be one of the most beautiful women I've ever seen in my life. The Delilah to all my temptations, yet a threat to the exact reason why I've come to New York City. One bat of her eyelashes, and I'm sure I'd fold.

The fact is, Cranberry Street is perfect for me. There is no way that I can let Little Miss Red add a fourth bankrupted restaurant to her belt. There's just no way. I've gone through too much and come too far to go down without a fight.

I'll find a way to make this work.

I always do.

"Wait!" Craig's voice goes back up an octave, causing me to flinch in surprise. "Didn't you mention yesterday that you once competed? You did, didn't you?"

I reluctantly nod my head, forgetful of the fact that I did, in fact, tell Craig that back home, competing was what I did for fun on the weekends.

"Oh, this is so good." Craig rubs his hands together in what I can't tell is thought or excitement.

Maybe it's both.

"Dakota, you should do it again! The first competition of the season starts in a couple months. The best part about it is that it's going to be right here in the big apple!"

I roll my eyes discreetly, annoyed by all the subliminal fruit references. However, time and time again, Craig's ideas aren't half bad. They say if you can't beat them...*join them*. Give them a taste of their own medicine. Maybe, that's the only way to make all of this work.

"You know, Craig," I slyly comment. "I think you might be onto something."

"Ah, there's the spirit!" Craig pats me on the back like a proud father. "I knew you'd pull through, Dakota. So, what do you say? Are you up for the challenge? Do you think that you have it in you to take on The Sweet Red?"

As the response looms on my lips, Iris re-emerges from the restaurant. For a moment, I'm certain she's peering over at us. I allow myself a final glance in her direction before I force myself to turn away and accept the third and final thing that I know will take me to the top:

Revenge is a dish best served cold.

Carefully I glide my thumb along the tattoo that lines my wrist, another reminder that nothing will stand in the way of making my dream a reality. Not the challenge. Not the risk. Certainly not a girl.

"Let's start the contract," I say with assurance. "The Closed Cook is coming to Brooklyn."

A Recipe for Disaster

Three

IRIS

Present Day

"Travis! These tables aren't going to serve themselves! Let's pick it up, Twinkle Toes!" I shout through the kitchen, repeatedly tapping on the service bell I'd purchased just so that Travis could hear when an order was up.

Yet, unlike Pavlov's dogs, Travis can't seem to comprehend the fact that the sound of the bell equals an order is ready, and an order is ready equals it's time to serve it to the customers.

It's a simple request, considering it's what I pay him for.

"Twinkle Toes?" Lore squirts a dollop of whipped cream on top of her infamous strawberry cheesecake, flashing me the side eye in combination.

"He took ballet when he was little." I peer over the counter, hoping my stepbrother will come into view. He's tough to miss. He's six foot two, at least 240 pounds of pure muscle, and has a complete mop of shaggy blonde helmet hair that I constantly tease him for.

Annoying Travis is my favorite pastime, after all.

"Travis!" My voice inflates as I watch the kitchen door swing open, only it's not Travis. It's Melody, our other server, who at a whopping five foot one, is incredibly hard *not* to miss.

"It's just me." She barely reaches up to grab some plates from the service window, making room for me to add the next table's meals, which I've just finished plating.

I flash her a sympathetic smile, knowing that, as usual, she's picking up the slack for Travis's poor work ethic. "Thank you, Melody. But where's Travis?" I aggressively slice into a steak that I'd just let rest. "I've been calling out his name for ages."

"Where do you think?" she asks rhetorically. "Like usual, he's busy talking up some brunette by the bar." She huffs, rolling her eyes as she organizes the plates onto her tray.

"You've got to be kidding me. That mother—"

"I've got it, Iris," Melody interrupts me. "Just let me cover his tables for now. We're so swamped that I just want to get people fed and out of here as quickly as possible. We've got at least ten people on the waitlist right now!"

"Ten?" I repeat back to her in disbelief, brushing my hand over my forehead as yet another ticket comes through.

Although it's stressful, I've always loved the five o'clock rush. It's that time where everyone has finished up work for the day and has decided that the grumbling in their stomach can no longer be ignored—leading them straight to me.

"Why is it so busy all of a sudden?" Lore inquires from behind, taking the words right out of my mouth.

"Word on the street is that The Closed Cook actually listened to their name tonight and closed." Melody smirks in delight, as do I.

Everyone around here has seemingly caught onto the fact

A Recipe for Disaster

that The Closed Cook is our number one rival, and any jabs they take at them become a gold star in my book.

"For good?" I join in on the shit-fest, as I finally plate the steak.

"One can only wish." Melody walks out of the kitchen as Travis stumbles his way in. "Watch it!" she sneers, forcing him to apologize profusely as he reaches the counter in a sweat.

"Where are my plates?" He tightens his apron around his waist, seeking an answer in my straight face given that the window is completely empty.

"They're in front of our guests, Travis. You know, where they're supposed to be," I remark. "And speaking of where things are supposed to be, where should you be, huh?"

"Well, I should be at the bar—"

"Wrong!" I push two new plates toward his chest, taking him by surprise.

Now, I know I'd said that Travis hadn't learned how to pair that the sound of the bell means that the food is ready. But I can say with certainty that Travis has learned that when I have my notoriously raised eyebrow and stern expression, it means no more fooling around.

"Table six, Twinkle Toes." I place another two plates into his struggling grasp. "And no more canoodling with my guests. You hear me? Or else I'll have to write you up."

Travis shoots me a playful stare, reminding me I can't fire him despite how much I've tried over the years. Our family ties make it impossible. "You've got it, Cliffy!" I hear him shout as he exits the kitchen, bumping into Melody once more on his way out.

"Cliffy?" Lore smirks over at me as she torches the top of a crème brûlée, unphased by the drama that working in a kitchen always seems to possess.

I stubbornly point to my mop of red hair as I turn back around to sauté some vegetables in a pan.

Lore lets out a sizable laugh as she makes sense of Travis's comparison to me and a big red dog. "I'll have to give him that one." She snickers. "That was pretty good."

I groan in annoyance, trying to ignore Travis's jab and focus back on Melody's referral to Dakota's restaurant. "Why do you think they're closed tonight?" I turn to Lore, hopeful she has the answers I'm searching for.

"Who cares?" She shrugs, placing the crème brûlée on the window. "Their closure tonight is our gain. See it as a win."

I nod, trying to accept her answer, but I can't help but shake the fact that The Closed Cook hasn't once been *closed* since they'd opened a few months ago. Why now, on a Wednesday night in the middle of September? It just doesn't make any sense.

I plague myself with my habitual curse of always needing to know everything. Lore is right. I should be taking tonight as a win. Since Dakota opened The Closed Cook, he's proved to be precisely what I thought he'd be—*trouble*.

Not only has he given me competition for the first time in years here in Brooklyn, but he's also participated in all the culinary events that have taken place this season.

That's right—he's competed in every single one of them, and to make matters worse, he's done equally, if not a tad bit better than me in terms of ranking.

It's a terrible feeling, one I can imagine I've made many others feel over the years. But it's not the losing part that stings the most. It's how I can feel The Sweet Red's invitation to The Art of Cooking Competition slipping out of my grasp and into his. That's what keeps me up at night.

"Iris?" Melody snaps me back into reality as she stands ahead, waiting for me to hand her the next few plates.

"Sorry!" I brush a bead of sweat off my forehead, handing them to her. Even thinking about Dakota steers me off my game—he's a menace without trying. I need to snap myself out of this, and I need to do it quickly.

I find comfort in comparing The Closed Cook to a new exchange student that comes to your school. For the first little while, they're the top shit. Why? Because they're new! Everyone wants to be their friend, know them, and associate themselves with them. But eventually, like everything in life, there's an expiry date. At some point, you can't just rely on the fact that you're new and different. You have to establish yourself and create your own name—and if you don't, you will fall behind.

Unfortunately, the "new" phase hasn't yet worn off Dakota's restaurant. All I can do is hope that the clock is ticking on that one.

Tick, tock.

DAKOTA

As a kid, I used to love birthdays. Emphasis on the words "used to." As of today, I've decided that I officially hate them. I hate them more than anything.

Birthdays in the Foster household meant one thing: major parties with a theme. My parents had always been big on themes.

The perk of having two older sisters, or as Dallas and I used to call them, "the party planning committee"—meant that the themes would go all out. Not to mention, the added advantage that everything seems to get a little more amplified when you're an identical twin.

That's right: the two of us were born five minutes apart.

When I think back, the birthday that stands out the most to me was when we turned eight years old. Dallas and I had a *Power Rangers* themed party—decked out with everything imaginable in the colors yellow, red, blue and green because at the time, Dallas refused to admit he was in love with the pink one. Therefore, she got discluded.

From ages nine to 12, our parties consisted of paintballing, rock climbing, going to monster truck rallies and even white-water rafting. Let's just say Dallas and I went through an adrenaline junkie stage.

Our thirteenth birthday was the first party where inviting girls became the top priority above all else. The theme for that year was getting a girlfriend.

I was a late bloomer at that point. All of my friends had, at minimum, kissed a girl or at least had their first girlfriend, whereas I was still at the admiring stage.

It was on that night that Dallas was determined that I'd have my first kiss, forcing us all to play spin the bottle. I'm certain the bottle was rigged because it landed right on Pamela Davies the

A Recipe for Disaster

second I spun it—the prettiest girl in our eighth-grade class, and the only girl I was hoping it would land on.

Dallas couldn't hold back a stupid roaring cheer when it happened, prompting our friends to do the same. I never did think I'd have my first kiss in front of a crowd of people, let alone while they all chanted "kiss, kiss, kiss."

Dallas never let me live that one down. Not the kiss, but the fact that he caught me making out with Pamela later that night behind the pool house we had out back.

As the years went by, our birthdays got more casual, and after we turned 21, the only theme was getting drunk and partying—well, that was until we finished college, and all of a sudden, life's theme, birthdays included, became *work*.

It's September fifteenth—our twenty-eighth birthday. My theme this year? Forgetting that my birthday exists.

I've been ignoring my parents' and sister's calls all day because I refuse to let anyone say "happy birthday" to me. Dallas and I had a rule that we'd always say it to each other before we'd let anyone else. Where is that rule now?

I've said it to him. I've said it so many times as I lay here staring up at the Brooklyn Bridge, waiting for him to say it back, that it doesn't even sound real anymore.

Today marks my first birthday without him, and because of that, it didn't feel right to do anything other than seek refuge on this park bench and feel sorry for myself.

I know Dallas wouldn't have wanted this. Frankly, being the businessman he was, he'd probably be pissed right now, knowing just how much money and food is going to waste—considering I decided to close the restaurant tonight.

I don't care. It's been six months since I arrived in New York City and three months of working full steam ahead. Throughout that time, I haven't let anything stand in my way. Not the stress of launching my own restaurant, not the responsibilities of managing not only an establishment but a whole team of employees, and especially not Iris, who consistently proves to me that keeping up with The Sweet Red is no easy task.

The girl is like a God-damn roadrunner, the way she effortlessly manages her restaurant while finding time to travel around the country for competitions.

I've done my absolute best to keep up with her in any capacity that I can, and miraculously, I have. The Closed Cook has been more successful than I ever could've imagined.

Competing has helped me spread the word about the restaurant and get the occasional win. But I believe that deep down, my debut success of The Closed Cook is because Dallas has been looking out for me. He wanted this for me, so he's making it happen.

I glide my hand over my wrist as I carry out that thought, brushing away the dampness that fills my eyes. "Get it together, Dakota," I tell myself firmly as a cool breeze washes over me, guiding me to finally sit up.

I lift my back up from the bench, straining my core as I force my legs to stand for what feels like the first time in days.

Thankfully, my apartment is just off Henry Street, only a few blocks away, and adjacent to The Sweet Red—meaning that I pass by Iris's storefront on my walk to and from work every day.

A Recipe for Disaster

It's a not-so-gentle reminder that keeps me in check when it comes to my ludicrous plan to fight fire with more fire. It's draining, to say the least, but it's the only way to get to where I want to go while holding out on an easily permeable emotion that she evokes.

Lust.

With each step alongside the sidewalk, I find myself closer to my apartment, yet as I approach my street, I can't help but stop at the sight of The Sweet Red that now heaves with crowds of people. The line has practically wrapped down the sidewalk. I catch a glimpse of their servers pumping food out to tables at record speed.

"Hey!" Someone calls out to me, their voice full of New York impatience. "There's a line up 'ere. You oughta wait your turn!"

It takes me a moment to realize that I've pushed myself to the front to peek inside. "Shit." I take a step back. "Sorry about that, man," I apologize, yet his face tells me he doesn't give two shits. I think I might have a thing or two I need to learn from him. I, too, shouldn't give two shits about what's going on inside The Sweet Red tonight.

The truth is, Iris hates me. She's made that abundantly clear since the day we met, and in every minor interaction we've had with one another ever since. I've been a jerk, but that is the point. They say don't hate the player, hate the game…but hating her seems to be the only way that I can match her at this game.

I step away from the storefront, weaving my way through the crowd until I reach my apartment, throwing off my jacket and peering over at the clock that hangs on my wall.

11:59 PM.

"Happy birthday, Dallas," I say for a final time as the clock strikes midnight. "Happy birthday."

Four

IRIS

At The Sweet Red, I follow a strict routine before the restaurant can officially close shop.
1. Clean up the kitchen.
2. Clean the dining room.
3. Stock the pantry.
4. Stock the serving stations.
5. And prep.

Do as much prep as possible.

These simple yet mundane tasks disregard any sense of exhaustion that one may feel after a 14-hour shift—because, if there is one thing I've learned as a restaurant owner, no one will do the work for you.

No one.

An operation can only exist with preparation. I'm reminded of that as Lore and I each sprawl across an empty booth, both exhausted and slumped out of our minds.

Get back to work, Iris. I try to listen to that nagging voice in my mind, making an attempt to sit up, but ultimately lie back down.

Okay, five more minutes.

"Iris?" Lore sighs as she rests her head beside me.

"Yeah?" I dart my eyes over to her.

"Do you mind if I go home?" Her words come out as a pained groan. "I'm really not feeling good."

I take the liberty to sit up, stretch my arms out and search for any sort of motivation for what lies ahead. After all, at the end of all of this, I've got myself a date with a king-sized bed and half a night's worth of sleep.

Exciting.

I place a hand on her shoulder in concern, noticing her pale and tired face . "Lore, you realize you don't have to ask me, right? We're in this together. This is *our* restaurant."

She brushes her hand along her clammy forehead. "That's precisely why I have to ask you. We're partners. I can't just leave you to do everything."

I help steady her on her feet as we stand. "Don't even sweat it. Melody is still here, and Travis better still be. So, you go home and take it easy. And if you're not feeling any better tomorrow, don't worry about coming in. I've got Auston and Freddie on deck bright and early," I rhyme off the names of our other two kitchen staff. "We'll be okay."

"Are you sure?" Lore asks again, clutching onto her bag. "I don't want you to be upset."

"I'm not upset!" I guide her towards the door. "Go! Get some sleep. I mean it."

Lore smiles through tired eyes. "Goodnight, Iris."

"Goodnight," I watch her exit the restaurant before I make my way back into the kitchen.

"Would you mind giving me a hand?" Melody requests as she

pushes the last set of dishes through the washer.

I nod. "You do know you're a lifesaver, right?" I collect some clean dishes that have passed through the dishwasher and place them back onto our shelves. "Thanks for staying behind. I hope you know how much I appreciate it."

Melody flashes me a playful smile. "It's what you pay me for, right?"

I stifle a laugh. "Right."

I was 21 when I first opened The Sweet Red—a young buck, paving my way into the food industry. I knew that there would be a lot of late nights, long hours and a ton of responsibility—all considering the success and sustainability of The Sweet Red lands on both my and Lore's shoulders.

Since we opened, Lore and I have developed a system that works for us. I focus on all the main menu items regarding stock, inventory and delegation of the kitchen staff; Lore oversees the dessert side of things.

Let me tell you, Lore's desserts aren't just any ole' sweet treat. She makes some of the most delicious creations in all of Brooklyn.

"So, did you hear the news?" Melody asks as I finish stacking the last of the plates.

"News?" I tilt my head in her direction. "What 'news'?"

"You haven't heard?" She places her hands on her hips in surprise. "One restaurant in New York already got an invitation to The Art of Cooking Competition!"

Melody's revelation catches me off guard. Around the fall of each year, The Art of Cooking Competition begins their recruiting process. I assumed that since it's only mid-September, we were still a few weeks out, not already at the invitation stage.

I immediately stop what I'm doing. Nothing is more important than gathering every possible detail about this. "Which restaurant?" I ask eagerly. "Who got it?"

"Tavern House," Melody says, prompting some relief to wash over me. It's no surprise. Tavern House gets invited every single year. They're consistent, to say the least—I hate them for that.

"Oh, stop stressing!" Melody instructs as she moves over to the counter to roll some cutlery into napkins. "New York State still has two more invitations to be sent out. Remember that."

I sigh. "And you really think out of the thousands upon thousands of restaurants in this state, The Sweet Red will be one of them?"

Melody pauses, staring at me as if I have grown another limb. "Yeah, Iris, that's exactly what I think. We've got one of, if not the most, popular restaurants in Brooklyn, and you and Lore won what—six culinary competitions this year?"

"Four." I can't help but correct her. Six is how many times Dakota has won, and each time, he'd shot me a stupid half-assed wink or mouthed to me, "better luck next time."

He's an asshole. An asshole that knows how to cook—that's probably the worst thing about him. That, or the fact that he looks like a *GQ* model as he makes a soufflé.

It's beyond frustrating.

"Relax," Melody reassuringly rubs my shoulder. "This has been your best year to date. I'm sure your invitation will be in the mailbox before you know it! No need to stress."

I take a deep breath in, calming my nerves. Melody has always had a way of comforting me with her words. She's a fourth-year psychology major at NYU, so it's no surprise that she is likely using her brain power on me. I don't mind, though. I'll graciously be her test subject before she starts Med school.

"Thanks," I say, prompting a faint smile to fall over her rosy cheeks. "You know, I'm really going to miss you when you're gone next year."

"Well, don't take me off payroll just yet." She wraps up the final piece of cutlery. "Becoming a psychiatrist isn't cheap, you know. Besides, you'll have Travis when I'm not here anyway."

"Ugh." My eyes roll to the back of my head. "I love you, but I also hate you for leaving me with Travis as our head waiter." I allow my head to fall into my hands. "Speaking of which…" I snap my head back up. "Where *is* Travis?"

"I don't know." Melody shrugs in laughter, finding amusement in my melodramatic ways. "He told me he was doing an inventory check in the storage room." She picks up the cutlery bin and tucks it underneath her arm.

"Inventory check?" I repeat back to her. "But I did one earlier. Why would he need to…"

I stop mid-sentence, prompting Melody to raise a suspecting eyebrow.

"I'll be right back." I march over to the storage room, almost certain I know exactly what I'm about to walk in on. "Travis!" I shout as I work my way through the kitchen. "Travis!" My voice picks up yet again, only this time with more conviction.

A loud moan followed by a "shh, shh, she'll hear us," echoes through the hallway, guiding my strides directly in front of the storage room door.

"What the hell?" My hands ball up in a fist as I pound on the door repeatedly. "Travis! You have three seconds to get out of there!"

"Three!" I start the countdown.

"Two!" My hand hovers over the doorknob.

"One!" I swing the door open, and much to my surprise, there's Travis, yet, he's standing completely alone, clothed, and with a clipboard in his hand, acting as if he was just hard at work.

"Oh hey, *Iris*," he draws out my name. "I didn't hear you there. How's it going?"

I scrunch my nose in annoyance. "Who's in here?" I demand, scanning the room to see where he could've hidden a girl.

"I am," he sarcastically responds. "See?" He uses his hands to gesture up and down his body.

I place my hands on my hips. "Yeah, I know you are, idiot! What was that noise? Who were you having sex with in here?"

"Sex?" He places his hand atop his chest as if I've just shot him with my words. "Now *that*, that is a wild accusation to make, Cliffy, especially considering I'm a virgin."

I scoff. If there is one thing that I know about my stepbrother, it is that he's definitely not a virgin. This wouldn't have been the first time I would've caught him balls deep in some random girl from the bar.

He's a total frat boy, true and true, but as much as I hate to admit it, we do get a good crowd of people coming into the restaurant—since rumor has it, we have a "hot" waiter.

So, as much as it annoys me that my dad pushed me to give

little ole' Travis a job as he finishes his way through college, he does generate a consistent stream of customers who want a whole lot more than to taste my food.

Travis retracts his words as if I'm a kettle ready to pop off. "Oh, calm down, Cliffy." He steps towards me. "I was just messing with you. I promised that I wouldn't have sex with someone in here again."

"*Again?*" I hyper-fixate on a keyword in his statement. "You said you wouldn't have sex with anyone in the bathroom again. I didn't know that you'd had sex with someone in here!"

"Oh, did I say again?" He guides me out of the room. "Must've just been a mindless slip-up. Don't worry, Iris, I was just kidding. It was all a joke. You know what? You need to go home. Get some rest. You seem tired."

I pause as we reach the kitchen. He's acting weirder than usual, but he has a point. I am tired, and lucky for him, too tired to deal with his shenanigans tonight.

"You're right," I tell him. "I should go home, but I have one question first before I do."

He releases his arm from around my shoulder. "Shoot."

"Should I be concerned that you moan like a girl?"

"I don't moan like a…" He seems offended, yet cuts his frustration short as the satisfaction from the landing of my jab washes across my face.

I knew that would sting.

"You know what? What you should be concerned about is the fact that you don't trust me!"

I roll my eyes.

Travis is the same guy who, as kids, was tasked with babysitting my betta fish while I was away at summer camp and dumped the entire container of food inside. "He looked hungry," he told me when I found my fish upside down after two weeks away. How can I trust Travis if he can't even care for a betta fish? Mind you, he was eight at the time, but I'm still unsure if his now twenty-one-year-old mind works any differently.

"You've got to have some trust in me, big sis." He nods. "It'll be good for you."

"Step-sis." I always correct him. We're not brother and sister—never have been and never will be. "And fine," I cave. "You want trust? You've got it. Tonight, I'll trust you to close up shop. How does that sound?"

"Wait," Travis stutters, his face flush. "I didn't mean I wanted that trust right now. Maybe another night, or even—"

"Goodnight, twinkle." I exit the kitchen, tossing the restaurant key in his direction as I head back into the dining room, where Melody has since secured her jacket around her waist and is toying with her bag.

"Is everything alright?" she asks in concern.

"If you mean, am I about to make the biggest mistake of my life and let Travis lock up tonight—then yes, things are *great*."

Melody lets out a sigh, one that I can't tell is of relief or stress. "Are you sure you want to let him do that?" she questions, a sense of nervousness in her voice.

Definitely stress.

"You know, I'm trying this new thing called trust," I tell her.

"Trust is good." She nods in approval as we work our way out

A Recipe for Disaster

of the front door and towards our cars parked out front. "*Trust* that your invitation is coming soon too," she reminds me.

"I will," I smile "Goodnight, get home safe—"

"See you later, Travis!" A tall brunette slips out of the restaurant's side door, her hair tousled and dress astray before she makes a bee-line down the street, leaving Melody and me to stare at one another—her, in confusion and me, in disbelief.

How did he manage to hide her without me seeing?

"Do I even want to ask?" Melody questions.

"*Trust* me." I shake my head. "You don't."

Five

IRIS

Did you know there's a world record for who can waste the most gas in a week?

Oh, you didn't?

Well, that's because it doesn't exist.

It's an award that I've granted myself to make up for the fact that the only thing my daily trips to the mailbox have delivered is an utter sense of disappointment—not the invitation I've been so desperately waiting for.

"I'm headed out for a bit," I call over to my sous chef, Auston, and line cook, Freddie, who, have worked tirelessly since our busy night last week given that Lore has called in sick ever since.

It's been tough without her here. She says she thinks she has the stomach flu, but I've never heard of one lasting a whole week.

Nonetheless, Lore has never called in sick once over the past few years. She's the most reliable and consistent friend/co-worker I've ever had. Cutting her some slack is the least I can do.

The only real problem with being a business owner is that you can never really have a "day off", especially when you have employees that rely on you for a source of income. Being self-employed has been much more challenging than I'd ever anticipated, but it's also the most fulfilling thing I've ever done—the oxymoron of my life.

"And where exactly are you headed?" Auston pries, his interest in my whereabouts visible all over his face.

"Just to the mailbox," I tell him bluntly, trying my best to give him no indication that I want our work-with-benefits relationship to be anything more than explicitly what it is.

His face drops as he pulls on another ticket that comes through. "But you just went this morning," he questions. "You're really going again?"

"Yes, Auston." I'm tired of being nagged. "I need to see if I got—"

"The invitation," he finishes my sentence for me. "I know, I know. You need to relax. It'll come, sweetie, don't you worry."

I'm not quite sure how I feel about the word "sweetie" leaving his mouth, but that's the last thing I need to be concerned about. Auston will get the message soon enough.

Hopefully.

"I'll be back soon," I dryly respond as I maneuver through the kitchen and exit towards my car.

Since I've grown up in New York City my entire life, busy traffic has never phased me, but do you want to know what does?

Parallel parking—the ultimate sin of driving a car.

And as luck would allow it, the only way I'm checking my mailbox is if I parallel park.

Great.

Let's be honest. How many people really know how to parallel park? I only learned so that I could pass my driver's test, and even then, it took me three attempts to get my driver's license.

During my first attempt I was going too fast and didn't realize that I needed to slow down to make a turn. Poor Tony, the first man I did my test with, had a heart attack when I whipped around a corner at almost 40 miles per hour.

On my second attempt, I forgot to check my blind spot, resulting in me *almost* hitting another car while changing lanes. It was a mistake that Maureen docked me significant marks on.

But Stan, good ole' Stan, after twenty minutes of being in the car with *Liability Hammond,* somehow gave me a pass. He'd said I "needed a lot of work," but I was "just passable."

So "just passable," is how I describe my ability to drive.

"Okay, pull up close to the car in front of the spot you want to go in, put the car in reverse, then start to crank the wheel," I talk myself through the instructions I've come to memorize for these exact moments.

"Crank it, crank it, crank it," I whisper, and holy shit, I'm actually doing it. "Crank it the other way," I say out loud as the car starts to shift into the spot so seamlessly that I wonder if culinary was the right profession for me after all. Maybe I should've been a *Formula One* driver.

My body jolts in surprise as my bumper collides with the car behind me.

Shit.

Immediately, my foot slams into the break, jerking the car forward as I shift my gear into park and rush out of the car.

"I am so, so sorry!" I carefully analyze the black bumper before me as a tall figure steps out of the vehicle in my peripheral vision. "I'm 'just passable' when it comes to driving. I'll pay for any damages, I promise!" I find myself on the ground as my eyes inspect the car much more intently.

To my relief, as I scan I can't see anything. Not a dent, not a scratch, *nothing*. I sigh, grateful that today might very well be my lucky day.

All it takes is one thing to change that.

"Isn't it just reassuring to know that they give out licenses to those that are 'just passable'? I sure as hell feel much better with that tidbit of information."

I slowly lift my head up from the bumper at the sound of a familiar, agitating voice belonging to the man that not only towers above me, but is smirking down with a false sense of amusement.

Dakota.

DAKOTA

I've learned several things since my big move to New York City.

The first is that everyone around here talks incredibly fast and with a twang—especially in Brooklyn.

It's not "how do you take your coffee?"

It's "what's ya *cawfee* order?"

"Would ya like a *watah* with that too?"

"This is my *sista*, Danielle."

And with the twang comes the infamous sayings. Let's name a couple of my favorites, shall we?

Eh,' I'm walking *'ere.*

Get outta 'ere.

I swear to my motha.

And the word *fuck*. Simply fuck. Everything is fuck this, fuck that, fuck *to* you, me, and everyone. It's great, really. I love to fuck—I fit in almost immediately.

And last but certainly not least, New York City has some of the worst traffic in the world, with some of the most questionable drivers. The blue sedan that's just smacked into my car while attempting to parallel park has made that abundantly clear.

Eh, that's my caah!

"God dammit." I let out a huff of frustration. Submitting an insurance claim is a perfect way to start my Monday morning. *Lucky me.*

I reach for my phone while simultaneously grabbing a pen and paper from my glovebox. This idiot better have insurance.

As I step out of my car, I watch as an *abundance* of red hair drops to the ground, profusely apologizing as she inspects my bumper.

This is not the New Yorker that I expected.

It's Iris.

It's been a few weeks since I'd last seen her at a competition in New Jersey, where I'd ranked second, and she ranked third—a spot she was thoroughly unimpressed to be in. We didn't speak to one another, but the looks we exchanged said it all.

Screw you.

Screw you back.

I've reached a point where I can just look at Iris and get under her skin. The way her expression has gone from an apologetic suburban lady to a Karen who just got the wrong order at their family dinner confirms it.

"*You…*" She rises to her feet, crossing her arms in a huff. "Of course, it's you!"

"Nice to see you, too." I lean up against my bumper, matching her foul expression. "Well, I suppose it would've been nicer if you didn't just hit my car."

She rolls her soft eyes. "I didn't just hit your car, *Dakota.*"

Dakota.

There's something that always fazes me when she says my name. Why does she always have to make things so complicated? She's back in those same jeans, this time with a loose-fitted top and her hair tied up in a bun—and still, she manages to burn me alive with one single look.

It's infuriating.

I should be upset. She just hit my car. Instead, I'm pleased we've ended up in this situation.

"Is there a reason why you're looking at me like that?" She catches me in a daze, her voice full of impatience.

I snap myself out of it, placing my hand on my wrist as I attempt to think fast. "Oh me?" I resort to, to buy some time. "I'm just waiting."

"Waiting?" she repeats with a cock of her brow. "Waiting for what?"

"Oh you know…" I kick the pavement beneath my feet before looking into her eyes. "Just for when your nose is going to grow, considering that was the biggest lie I've ever heard."

Nice save, Foster.

"You're a jerk!" She grinds her teeth, ready to take another jab when I take a subtle step forward.

"Now, now." I attempt to settle her. "That isn't any way to speak to someone whose car you just hit. Is it?"

"'Hit' is a strong word." She raises her hands in defense. "I lightly tapped your car. Our bumpers just merely kissed. See?" She points to the lack of damage that was caused. Truthfully, I know there wasn't. I just wanna see how far I can push her.

Frustrating Iris seems to be the only way to keep her at a distance; lucky for me, I don't have to do much. Just the thought of me breathing seems to do that for her.

"You know, my car didn't want to kiss your's." I peer down at my phone, pretending as if I'm about to make a call. I hope she thinks I'm calling the cops, but I'm actually just opening up my *Wordle* of the day.

"Want to kiss mine?!" I take a second to glance up at the sound of her panic-stricken voice. "It's a car, Dakota! Cars don't have…you know what? Forget it. You're not worth it." She shakes her head.

Fuck.

I think flustered Iris might very well be the hottest Iris. The way her cheeks light up in fury. How she stomps her feet and brushes her hand through her messy hair…it makes her even more vexing to be around.

"Can we just pretend that this didn't happen?" she pleads. "There's is no evidence that your car was damaged in any way. Now, if you'll excuse me, I need to get to that mailbox!"

She nudges her shoulder into me on her way by, expecting

some sort of impact, when in reality, her shoulder barely reaches my bicep.

I tuck my phone into my back pocket as she passes. "Waiting on something?" Curiosity gets the better of me as she reaches the mailbox just ahead.

She doesn't shoot me a single glance as she fiddles with her keys. "That's none of your business, Foster," she barks. "Besides, is there a reason why you're still here? Don't you have other people you can torment?"

So, she does find me tormenting.

"I'm sorry, I didn't realize you owned this street? Am I not allowed to check my mailbox as well?" I retort.

Her eyes narrow before she turns back to the lock.

I only parked my car here to get to the gym. I had no intention of checking my mail. But since I've realized that my slot is so conveniently located beside hers, now seems like the *perfect* time.

I search through the million keys on my keychain as Iris swings open the door to her slot, pulls out a white envelope, and tears it open.

"Oh, my goodness!" She lets out a sudden blood-curdling scream as her eyes scan the words in front of her. "I can't believe it!"

Her outburst overwhelms my senses as she slams her mail slot shut.

Something else I've learned about living in New York City is that you don't turn your head at any outbursts if you're a local. That's how you know this city is used to the chaos.

"Could you be any louder?" I ask, using a pile of envelopes

that I've retrieved to cover my ears.

As I do, Iris freezes in place, her ecstatic state turning sour as I watch her eyes divert to the envelope in my hand. "What is that?" she asks slowly.

"What is what?" I taunt, pulling the envelope away from my ears and holding it in front of my eyes so that I can see.

Holy shit.

"You got invited as well?" The disbelief radiates through her voice as I take a second to process the fact that the envelope in my hands looks awfully familiar to the one in hers, with the words: The Culinary Committee of The United States written in cursive.

Is this what I think it is?

"What does it say?" Iris leans in, her breath practically over my shoulder. "Let me see!"

I take a reluctant step back, her presence being all-consuming. "That's none of your business," I spit her words from earlier back into her face as I temptingly peel open the letter and lift it so that it's just high enough so that she can't see.

"You're such a jackass," is the last thing I hear her say before I start to read.

Dear Dakota Foster,

As head chef of The Closed Cook, we are pleased to invite you to the 73rd annual The Art of Cooking Competition in Miami, Florida, from October 6 to 11. This prestigious culinary event will showcase some of the best culinary experts in the country. You are one of them!

Do you have what it takes to be America's next greatest chef?

We hope you'll find out.

A Recipe for Disaster

The Culinary Committee of The United States.

"You've got to be kidding me." I lift my head up from the page to see Iris shaking hers in disbelief, staring down at her phone, where I can see that she's pulled up The Art of Cooking webpage—clearly so desperate to retrieve an answer that I'd refused to give, despite it being abundantly obvious.

As her eyes scan across the screen, mine do the same.

Competing for New York:

Tavern House.

The Sweet Red.

The Closed Cook.

"I can't believe this," she groans, locking her phone and throwing it back into her bag. "How did this happen?"

If I'm being honest, I'm asking myself the exact same thing. Before I started competing again, I knew nothing of The Art of Cooking Competition. I only found out it existed when I overheard Iris raving about it back at a competition in Chicago.

It wasn't until I got home from that trip that I started to look into it, realizing not only what a big deal this event is to chefs across The United States, but what winning a competition like this could do for a restaurant. The cash prize is merely the cherry on top.

I groan at the subsequent part of my thought. This neighborhood is rubbing off on me, and I don't like it. I've never thought so many fruit idioms in my life.

"I guess that means I'll see you in Miami." I shoot Iris a devilish smirk, knowing that that is probably the last thing she wants to hear coming from of my mouth. "May the best chef win."

She scrunches her nose in frustration, crossing her arms and storming back to her car. "You're going down, Foster!" she shouts with conviction. "You're going down!"

Six

IRIS

"I have big news to tell you!" I sit across from Lore, who I've somehow managed to drag out the house for dinner, even though I can visibly see that she's hardly been able to eat anything this entire week.

"Iris," she groans. "Couldn't you have told me over the phone? I feel awful."

I grow sympathetic to her state. I've never seen her sick like this before, but at the same time, if anything would brighten her spirit, it's this news.

"No, Lore," I decide to carry on. "This is life-changing news. News that deserves to be spoken in person face to face. You need to *see* these words come out of my mouth."

She shifts in her chair, rubbing the back of her neck.

And all at once, her demeanor suddenly catches me off guard. "Hey, speaking of news, I have some news that I want to share with you first," she anxiously admits.

"What? You do?" My first thought is that perhaps she's already seen the announcement on the website. Are we both about to blurt the same thing out to one another?

"I do…" She slowly sips on her water.

"Okay!" I sit up enthused, reaching inside my purse to pull out the letter I'd gotten from the mailbox earlier.

I'm practically bursting at the seams to tell her we made it. We did it! We finally got into The Art of Cooking Competition, and better yet, we're leaving in two weeks. It's not a ton of time to get everyone up to speed in our absence, but if there's one thing to be known about Iris Hammond, it's that she's always up for a challenge. That, and she likes to think in the third person.

"I'm pregnant," Lore interrupts my thoughts with her confession.

As if someone has just burst a bubble around me, the color drains from my face. "What?" I have difficulty understanding the two words that fell out of her mouth. "What did you just say?"

"I'm pregnant," she repeats. "Eight weeks, to be exact."

"You're…" I can barely spit out the words. "You're…"

"Pregnant," she repeats again. "I know. I'm just as shocked as you are."

"Lore," I begin. "When did you find out? How long have you known?!" My mind races with questions that I can't stop from spewing out of my mouth, even though I know that my first words should've been, "congratulations, I'm so happy for you."

"I found out the night I left work early," she tells me. "Elias was worried about me when I got home and insisted on taking me to the emergency room. They ran some tests, and the next thing I knew, I was told I was pregnant. I'm sorry for not telling you sooner." Her voice drops. "I've been so sick this whole week, going to doctor's appointments and just trying to wrap my head around all of this."

A Recipe for Disaster

"Oh, Lore." I reach out to place a hand on hers, feeling remorseful for my less-than-conventional response. I've never been good with surprises. "First of all, you don't need to apologize. I do. That was not the reaction I imagined you were looking for. I'm just surprised, that's all. But Lore! I'm so happy for you and Elias."

"Thanks." She flashes me a tired smile, squeezing my hand in return. "I appreciate it."

A silence falls between us as I shake my head in disbelief. "Wow. I can't believe you're going to be a mom! What's going to happen with the wedding plans, though?" I can't help but wonder.

"You know what?" Lore pulls her hand back, resting it on her forehead in stress. "Enough about me. What is this 'life-changing' news that you've dragged me out here to say?"

Is this news really "life-changing" in retrospect to hers? Lore is having a baby, for crying out loud. I'm merely nourishing mine. In no way are these two one and the same.

I've always dreamt of starting a family of my own one day, but The Sweet Red has surmounted that thought with its ability to occupy not only my time, but my love life, too.

It's hard to balance a relationship when my working hours are the opposite of your typical nine-to-fivers. Weekends and evenings are always taken up, and if I'm being honest, no one has made me want to try and make it work—hence why Auston's been a temporary solution.

"So?" Lore chimes in again as my vacant stare and silence grant her no indication of what I was just dying to say. "What's the news?" She probes yet again.

I peer down at the letter that rests carefully in my bag before pulling it out and placing it on the table before her. "Have a look at this." I push it in her direction.

With a raised eyebrow, she picks up the envelope.

"Open it." I prompt her. "Go on, open it."

As her eyes scan over the words on the page, it's as if I'm rereading it for the first time...not that I've memorized it or anything by now…

"Dear Iris Hammond and Lore Lloyd. As head chef's at The Sweet Red, we're pleased to invite you to the 73rd annual The Art of Cooking Competition in Miami—"

"We did it!" I let out a squeal, uncaring of the turned heads that scowl in response.

"You did it, Iris!" Lore looks up at me as she places the letter back down on the table. "There's no way this would've been possible without you. You know that, right? I've just been along for the ride, but you've been the driver."

A sense of warmth floods my chest. "I just can't believe it finally happened," I manage to speak. "All these years, all these goals, they're finally paying off."

"They will pay off, I promise you." She smiles, joining me in my excitement until her face shifts.

"What?" I can't help but ask. "What are you thinking?"

She looks up in thought. "If Tavern House got the first invite, and we got the second, then I wonder who got the third?"

I clench my teeth together as I'm reminded of my earlier encounter with...no, I refuse to repeat his name and allow him to spoil this moment.

"Yeah, I wonder who?" I sarcastically remark with a roll of my eyes.

Lore lets out a half laugh. "I know that look," she speaks. "I'm missing something, aren't I? You know who got the other invite."

I clench my fists underneath the table, my knuckles turning white as I crane my neck from side to side in an attempt to relax my tense body. "Unfortunately…" I shake my head in dismay. "It's Foster."

"Dakota Foster?" The glass Lore once held up to her lips drops down to the table, nearly spilling everywhere. "You've got to be kidding."

"Oh, let me tell you, I wish I was." I place my head in my hands. "Can you believe it, Lore? This guy barely competes in all the same competitions as us and miraculously gets invited. It's taken us *years* for us to get to this point. It's rigged!"

Lore lets out a pained sigh, tapping her fingers along the table. "Not to play the devil's advocate or anything, Iris…" Her face turns empathetic. "But Dakota does know how to cook, and The Closed Cook does serve delicious food."

"I know, I know." I don't realize I've agreed with her claim until it's too late. Candidly, I've never tasted anything Dakota's made except for the bitter aftertaste he leaves behind.

Has Lore?

I lift my head from my hands, brushing the thought aside and focusing on another, more irking one instead. "You don't think that makes me even more upset? It almost makes me question what kind of a chef I am if it's taken me so long, and pretty boy only needed a few months."

"Iris," Lore protests. "You're beating yourself up for no reason. Who cares at the end of the day? You got an invitation just like he did, and *hello*, you've been doing these competitions way longer than he has. You have the edge!"

Lore makes a good point. Dakota is new to this game—I should call him level one. I've been playing my whole life, mastered each level, and am ready to take on the ultimate final challenge.

Now, I'm the one reaching for my glass of water on the table, wishing it was vodka, tequila, or anything to make the thought of Dakota erase my mind. That, or at least make him more bearable—if that's even a possibility.

"Wait. How exactly did you find out that Dakota got the other invite?" Lore furrows her brows in interest, flashing me a look.

"The website." I choose to withhold my encounter with him at the mailbox earlier. One, because I don't even want to think about it again. Two, well, does there even need to be another point?

Lore accepts my lie for truth as she nods, changing the subject after a brief stint of silence. "When do we leave?" she asks.

"Two weeks," I tell her, my enthusiasm finding its way back. "But don't worry, I've already got a full plan ready!"

A smirk falls over Lore's round cheeks. "Why am I not surprised?"

"So, here it is." I waste no time jumping straight into it. "I'm going to have Auston take charge in the kitchen, and Melody will take the lead on the front end—supervising Travis, of course. We'll prepare as much as we can before we go, and I'm proposing

A Recipe for Disaster

we have a later opening the week we're gone."

Lore seems amused by the plan. "I'm sure everyone will be delighted to know that they don't have to work at Hammond speed," she jokes, even though deep down, I know that her statement is true. Not everyone can work at my pace, but if you want to stay with The Sweet Red, somewhere along the way, you learn how to.

"Har, har." I reach for my phone to pull out the more detailed notes I'd composed to share with her. "Next thing. We'll need to arrive at the airport at least three hours before the flight—I know it's not international, but we cannot, and I repeat, *we cannot* miss this flight. Oh, and you know what? Let's book our taxi there in advance. Lord knows how difficult it can be to get one on the spur of the moment. Also, we'll have to double-check that we've packed our—"

"Iris," Lore interjects. "Take a breath! I'm sure everything is going to be okay. We're only going to be gone for less than a week."

I lock my phone screen, remembering that keyword of "trust" I promised Melody, even though I've already forwarded my notes to Lore's inbox. "You're right." I settle back into my seat. "Everything will work out the way it is supposed to. You're right."

With a nod Lore accepts my answer and reaches for her phone. "Now, tell me this. Do I need to book a hotel for us?" She asks. "I heard that there are some really nice resorts in Miami! I need a shiatsu massage more than anything."

"Not this time," I tell her. Lore has always been the one to secure our reservations. "The event has everyone staying at a resort that connects with the convention space. Apparently, they've already reserved all of the competitor's rooms—plus, I heard that the rooms are nice! So, you bet your ass you're getting a massage. Make that two. We'll do a couples massage together—we're expecting, after all!" I can't help but joke, playfully placing my hands on my stomach in hopes of mimicking her.

Lore lets out a boisterous laugh. "Oh, my goodness, this is going to be…" She stops, holding her hand up to her mouth, before pulling it back. "This will be…." She attempts once more, only to follow up her words with a repeat of the same action.

That laugh triggered something inside of her.

Quite literally, something.

"Are you…" I assume she's about to throw up.

"I'll be right back. "She rushes out of the booth and towards the bathroom.

As she falls out of sight, I sink further into my seat, opening back up my notes app to make a note to pack some anti-nausea for the trip. Yet, as I type, the troubling question of how is Lore going to be able to cook when the bun she's cooking in the oven is impeding her from doing just that?

I drop the thought in my mind. Lore is reliable. She always turns up and is always there when I need her to be.

She will be there.

I know she will.

Seven

IRIS

"I can't be there."

Four words that come out of Lore's mouth leave me completely shell-shocked.

"What?" is all I manage to spit out as I stand in the terminal, bags in either hand. I'd been pacing back and forth for the past hour, waiting to board the plane, wondering where in the world she was. She'd missed the taxi ride and hadn't responded to a single one of my messages. "What do you mean? Why not?"

"Iris, I'm so sorry," Lore croaks through the phone. "My nausea is so bad right now." She sounds as if she's gagging as we speak. "I'm not going to be able to come."

Reality weighs down on me, unlike anything I've ever felt. For the first time in my life, I feel gravity. The gravity tells me that not only am I about to compete alone—a task that, throughout the years of consistent competitions, I've never had to do once—but I'll be doing it in the biggest competition of my life.

"But…" I still can't seem to comprehend the truth, despite how hard it's smacking me in the face. "How can I compete without you? Lore, you're my right hand! I've never competed without you there. Never."

"I know, I know, and I'm so sorry." She pauses, a rustling coming through the line as she seemingly moves the phone away from her ear, leaving me with a less-than-pleasant sound to hear in return.

Gosh, I'm a terrible friend.

I shouldn't make Lore feel bad about something completely out of her control. Her health triumphs flying on an airplane to spend a few days focused on food when she can barely hold any down herself.

"How about I get Auston to come?" Lore returns to the line, proposing an idea I'm immediately closed off to.

"No, no," I say quickly. "Don't send Auston. Really, don't."

"But he'll be able to help you! Besides…" She pauses. "Auston knows how to operate the kitchen."

The fact is, I could list off a multitude of reasons why I don't want Auston to come. More than the list I gave him before I left for the airport, and he gave me an awkward peck on the lips.

Reason number one: I've spent the last two weeks training him on how to run and operate The Sweet Red in my absence. If he's gone, then there is no one else I can turn to or trust to ensure that things are going the way I've *strictly* outlined.

Reason number two: I'm not trying to lead him on any more than I already have. Auston and I have had a good, no-commitment thing going for us over the past few months. But in the latter portion of that time, I've realized that mixing business with pleasure is a catastrophe waiting to happen.

After the last time Auston and I hooked up, I swore that that would be the end. Besides, he's not my type…well, personality-

A Recipe for Disaster

wise, anyway.

Trust me when I say he's a great guy to get behind a closed door with—but, when it comes to carrying on a conversation, sometimes I'd rather sit and watch paint dry. So, although having Auston stay with me this entire week is awfully tempting, given his ability to release an abundance of my stress, it's got to be a hard pass.

"I'll be okay." I try to convince Lore as I try to convince myself. "Just focus on feeling better, okay? All I want is for you to be alright. But, with that being said, is there any way you can do me one favor?"

"Anything," she responds without skipping a beat.

"If you feel up to it, please check in at the restaurant. Make sure nothing crazy is happening and that things are going smoothly."

This will be the longest that I've ever left the restaurant in the hands of someone else. Typically, when Lore and I compete, we don't stay anywhere longer than 48 hours—and even then, I'm always on speed dial to answer any calls.

This time, I want The Art of Cooking competition to be my sole focus. After all, I have a task to accomplish and a grand prize to take home.

"I'm on it," she says without hesitation. "You can trust me."

"I know I can," I tell her.

"*Now boarding for flight 401 to Miami, Florida. If you are in section A, please come to the front now,*" a voice echoes over the PA system, announcing the departure of my flight.

"I've got to go," I tell her. "I'll text you when I land, okay?"

"You're going to do amazing, Iris," Lore attempts to motivate me. "You've got this."

"Thanks, Lore," I tell her. "Now go get some rest."

I end the call and move my way through the queue.

Oh boy. I can't help but think. *How am I going to do this?*

DAKOTA

"Welcome to The Lotus Inn," I hear a female voice call out as I stride my way through the pleasantly air-conditioned hotel lobby where an immediate sense of relief washes over my scorched skin.

I'm no stranger to warm climates. If anything, working in a kitchen acclimates you really quickly. You're constantly surrounded by ovens, steam, *flames*, dare I say. But Miami has proven a new level of heat-induced pain.

I shift my attention to the front desk, taken aback by the youthfulness of the receptionist, only to read on her name tag that it says "in-training".

"Can I get you checked in?" She joyfully asks.

I reach the counter, dropping my bags. "That would be great, actually."

She playfully runs her hands through her messy blonde hair, pulling a pen behind her ear. "My name's Isabella. But you can call me Izzy. What's your name?" Her voice goes up an octave.

I'm left confused yet slightly unsurprised by her informal introduction. This girl can't be more than 15 years old—a teenager, for crying out loud, working at a five-star hotel's front desk?

I'm not sure which to question first, the integrity of this establishment or the labor laws of Florida. Is she even old enough to work?

"Dakota Foster," she reads my name out loud once I've handed her my ID. "Are you here on vacation or something?"

"I'm checking in for The Art of Cooking Competition," I respond. "I'm here a bit before check-in since I took an earlier flight, but I called in advance and spoke to reception."

"Oh my gosh. That was me," she eagerly responds with a wide grin. "You spoke to me! I remember our conversation."

"Oh." I pretend to remotely understand her disturbing enthusiasm. "Well, lucky you." I can't hold back from the sarcasm. "You'll remember our conversation, then."

"Absolutely." Her eyes drift towards the computer screen in front of her. She fiddles with the keyboard, smacking the screen several times when it seems to lag on her end. "Piece of shit, boomer technology." She huffs out in frustration, chewing on a piece of gum ever so loudly.

Yep, teenagers.

I have nothing against them personally, but I know what I was like from the ages of 13 to 19, and needless to say, I wouldn't have trusted myself behind the desk of a premium resort.

"Aren't you a little young to work here?" I can't help but question with a judgmental brow.

"Young?" She retorts, visibly offended. "I'll have you know, I'm old. I'm sixteen, for crying out loud."

I scoff. "Sixteen? I have shoes older than you. You're not old, trust me," I reassure her. "If you are, then I'm prehistoric."

"Well, working here makes me feel like I am," she groans, continually smacking the monitor with her palm. "I just started here last month, and do you wanna know what they've already had me do?"

"Not really," I tell her without an ounce of sympathy. She's seemingly forgotten that she's supposed to check me in, not fill me in on her life's story. She doesn't seem to care and proceeds anyway.

"They put *me* in charge of reserving all the rooms for The Art of Cooking Competition. Do you know how much work that is?" Like a lot! She huffs, and I'm hopeful that signifies that she's finished.

"I hate to burst your bubble," I confess, even though bursting people's bubbles is totally my thing. "But isn't that the whole point of a job? To you know, *work*?"

She pulls a face. "I mean, yeah, I guess. But Sarah Atkins doesn't have a job—she gets everything handed to her, and yet here I am, wasting my weekend away at this stupid hotel." She places her hands on her cheeks, resting her elbows against the counter, waiting for me to respond.

Here's the thing. I'm no stranger to ladies' gossip—I grew up with two very vocal older sisters, after all. But there's a reason why I invested in earbuds as a child and a pair of wireless headphones as an adult. It's so I don't have to listen to people talk to me or rant about things I couldn't care less about.

I've just spent the last few hours on a plane, and the only thing I want to listen to right now is the sound of the waves as I lie my

A Recipe for Disaster

ass on the beach.

"Listen, Lizzy." I can hardly remember her name or her friends. "I couldn't care less about Sandra. The sooner you check me in, the sooner you can stop working. It's a win-win for both of us."

She purses her lips, reaching for a keycard to her left. "You're kind of a jerk, you know that?"

I roll my eyes. "So, I've been told." I respond as she swipes a key card through the machine and extends it out to me. "But, for what it's worth." I reach to accept it. "Sandra is probably a spoiled brat. At least you're making your own money—there's power in that."

My comment propels a smile to her lips. It's as if I can see her ego inflate. "Oh, she totally is!" She perks back up, pulling the key card back from my grasp.

So close.

"Thank God, someone finally said it!"

I've officially decided I cannot say another word to this girl. Somehow, my lack of interest in her and her gossip has made her even more interested in me.

For a moment, she surveys me up and down before she peers behind her suspectingly. "You know what?" She tosses the key card into the garbage when she sees that no one is watching.

"Hey!" I cry out. "No, I don't 'know what.'"

"Shh," she scolds me as she briskly types into the computer and re-swipes the new card through the machine. "You made my day with that comment, Dakota. So, because of that, enjoy the *deluxe suite.*" She smacks the new keycard back onto the counter.

"And good luck with The Sweet Cook!"

"Deluxe suite? That's amazing, this is…wait…did you say The Sweet Cook?" I hone in on what she just referred to my restaurant as when someone calls out her name from behind.

"Isabella?" The person who guides themselves to the check-in desk appears to be a manager. "Is everything okay over here?"

"All is good, sir," Isabella responds cheerfully. "I was just checking in the first competitor for The Art of Cooking Competition. He said I was doing a *really* great job and that he'd write a review about it online. Isn't that right, *Mr. Foster?*" Her eyes narrow in on me.

Fucking teenagers.

The manager peers up as I reluctantly nod my head. "That is so great to hear. Keep up the good work, Isabella!" He beams from ear to ear before his attention falls back onto me. "We hope you enjoy your stay at The Lotus Inn, Mr. Foster."

I nod, slowly taking the key card from the counter as Isabella calls out for the next guest. "I better see that review, Dakota!" She shouts as I step away from the desk. "Five stars and all."

"Oh, you'll see one," I tell her, heading towards the elevator. "You'll see one, alright."

A Recipe for Disaster

Eight

IRIS

The Miami sun beats down on me as I leave the airport terminal and step into a taxi cab.

I've only been to Florida once before—during spring break of my junior year at college. Needless to say, on that trip that it didn't take long for the red of my hair to match the color of my skin. Thus, the birthplace of my college nickname, "red."

At the time, the nickname in and of itself made me want to scream. Not because of its association with that painful memory, but at the lack of creativity people have when it comes to nicknames.

But with all that aside, over time, I've learned to embrace it. Red has become a part of my branding. Red is strong, red is passionate, red is fierce, and red has been the perfect name for my restaurant all these years.

The "sweet" part was an add-on brought to you by my dad, who always called me his "sweet girl." Little did he know of the shenanigans I used to get up to behind closed doors—the ones that I would carefully cover up before he or my stepmom Susanna could ever find out.

Poor Travis was the subject to many of my *brilliant* ideas that

I had as a kid. My favorite might've been when I convinced him that if he ate a worm, he would become the newest and most powerful superhero of all time—*worm man.*

It wasn't quite like his favorite comic book character at the time, but needless to say, it was a treat to see his face when he actually bit the bullet and ate the worm—not to mention the icing on the cake when he was scolded, and I diligently agreed with my dad and Susanna that "eating worms is not a good idea."

I suppose when I think back to that moment, I can't help but feel a tad bit remorseful. I'm certain that Travis is the only person who knows who the real Iris Hammond is, and that my restaurant should be called "The Sneaky Red" instead.

But what can I say? I've always been one to know how to play my cards. I pride myself in knowing exactly what to say and how to act—or at least, I think I do.

"We're here." The taxi driver pulls up in front of the resort, which is connected to a massive convention center where this week's competition will be held. "I'll grab your bags for you," he tells me graciously, opening my door and extending his hand out to help me step outside of the car.

"Thank you so much," I tell him as he lifts my suitcases out of the trunk. "You're the best!"

He smiles, lining them up one by one as I notice another cab pull up a few spots behind me—where an unexpected yet drop-dead gorgeous face steps out.

Sean Dellan.

Sean Dellan: he's a total veteran when it comes to The Art of Cooking Competition. He's won the grand prize more times than

A Recipe for Disaster

I can count. The best part is that if what I read on the website about the event this year is true, he's going to be one of three judges on the panel.

I guess they decided it's no fun when the same person continues to win, so instead, let's give the reigning champ the liberty of crowning the new up-and-coming chef in America. In other words, *me*. The rookie that's practically tripped over her two left feet because she's so caught up looking at Sean Dellan.

His long blonde hair, chiseled jaw, broad chest, and un-tamely, bushy eyebrows—ones that I'd typically despise—work for him. Hell, everything works for him.

"Have a great trip!" The taxi driver hands me my last suitcase, breaking my gaze from Sean, who steps towards the hotel doorway.

I nod, thank the driver again and hand him a sizable tip before quickly making my way up the entryway steps, only mere meters behind Sean.

Although I've seen him at practically every event I've attended this year, we've never formally met. But this is the trip of new beginnings, and there's no greater time than the present. So, when you see a hunk of a man standing waiting by an elevator, you shoot your shot.

Honestly, I'd always thought that an elevator was the perfect spot to introduce yourself to someone. When the doors close, you're stuck in that six-by-six-foot space for a solid 15 to 20 seconds—and let me tell you, I can do a lot in that timeframe.

"Would you mind holding the elevator?" I call out as the doors start to close, prompting me to pick up my pace as I shuffle my way through the hotel lobby.

"Checking in?" I'm interrupted by the concierge desk, halting me in place and whisking both Sean and my devious plan to try and win some "pre-competition brownie points" away.

I let out a pained sigh. "Yes...yes, I am."

"Perfect." He doesn't pick up on my hesitation. "Well, welcome to The Lotus Inn! I'll help you out over here." He gestures for me to come over. "Do you have a piece of ID?" He asks as I reach the quartz countertop.

I dig through my purse, pull out my driver's license and hand it over to him.

He smiles, taking the card and typing my information onto his computer. Shortly after, his pleasant expression shifts, and now he's staring intently at the screen.

"Is everything alright?" I can't help but grow worried as crow's feet form on either side of his wrinkled eyes.

"Yes, sorry," he apologizes as he looks down at the screen and reaches for his glasses. "It just seems like somebody has already checked in for you."

"Checked in for me?" My voice inflates with surprise. "That's impossible. I'm here by myself. I'm here for The Art of Cooking Competition."

He types vigorously against the keyboard. "There must've been some sort of glitch in the system." He leans down and takes a room key card, briskly typing in a code before swiping it through the machine. "I'm sorry about that." He hands it over to me. "You're all set to go."

While I want to question what exactly just happened, I accept the key card, feeling far too tired to debate.

"You're on the sixth floor in room 617. Let us know if you need anything, okay?" His expression is back to being friendly and personable. "Oh, and we've got a full selection of cookies and drinks available just in the foyer to welcome you! Feel free to help yourself."

"Will do." I smile, surveying the table before coming to the stark conclusion that the cookies are in fact *peanut butter*. I haven't had an allergic reaction to peanuts since I was a kid, and under no circumstance do I intend for that to change now. I divert my path and make a bee-line into the elevator, moving as far away from the table as possible. Even the scent is enough to trigger my fight or flight.

As I make my ascent up, I pull out my phone to text Lore that I've arrived safely.

> I'm here, wishing you were with me.

She replies almost immediately.

> Me too! It's going to be so hard waiting to know what happens until you get back :(

Not only is it torture that I'm here alone, but when you agree to be a contestant in The Art of Cooking Competition, you must sign a non-disclosure agreement, given that the competition is set to be broadcasted on various streaming platforms in a few weeks' time. That means that Lore and the rest of my family back home will have no idea what is about to transpire.

I tuck my phone back into my pocket as the elevator doors reach the sixth floor and re-open.

Following the signage, I go down the corridor, carefully reading the numbers as they pass by.

614.

615.

616.

617.

I stop in front of the door and tap the key card. The light immediately turns green as I twist the handle, revealing one of the grandest rooms I've ever stayed in.

Is this what all the competitors got?

"Wow," I breathe, wasting no time rushing over to the balcony that overlooks the ocean—taking in the view of the shoreline and how the sun has started to set along the horizon.

It's stunning, and all I can think is, y*ou did it, Iris. You made it. Your dreams are about to come true.*

For once, my innermost thoughts prompt a stupidly radiant smile on my lips as I fall back onto one of two queen beds.

"Iris, don't be jumping on the bed with your dirty clothes on!" My dad's voice propels through my mind. Dad always had a strict rule about separating daytime clothes from nighttime clothes, especially when it came to hotels.

But, if I'm being honest, I couldn't give two shits about that right now. I'm twenty-six years old, and if I want to lie on my bed, dirty clothes and all, hell, I will.

I close my eyes momentarily, but amidst the momentary peace, my eyes shoot back open at the sound of a man's voice that's singing a song, accompanied by the sound of running water.

As reality creeps in I take a second to scan the room around me where I soon realize that someone else's suitcase and clothes are already visibly sprawled throughout.

What the hell?

"Hello?" I call out anxiously. My heart rate intensifying with each passing second without an answer. "Is someone there?" I shout louder, questioning if the sound is actually coming from my room, or if the walls of this hotel are paper-thin. The answer to my question reveals itself soon enough.

"Hello?" A confused voice responds.

Shit.

Nine

DAKOTA

The sound of a door slamming shut forces my body to halt in place as I stand in the shower.

What was that?

No, the better question is, was that just my door?

I take a moment to listen intently, but as I do, I hear nothing—I must be losing it. Instead, I resort back to singing, a subtle pastime of mine. Dallas always told me that just because I could sing, it didn't mean I had to. I always brushed aside his comments. I'm no pop star, but I like to sing; what can I say? Am I good at it? Absolutely not. But do I care? Hell no. I'm on vacation.

Taking the earlier flight out to Miami couldn't have worked out any better. Not only have I had a chance to scope out the convention space ahead of tomorrow's competition, but I've also taken some much-needed time for some TLC—tenderness, love and curaçao.

It's five o'clock somewhere, am I right?

God, I love Miami.

I've only been here a few hours, but this won't be my last visit. I'm confident that nothing can rain on my parade—

"Hello?" I hear a soft, panic-stricken voice murmur. "Is

someone there?"

I waste no time turning off the shower.

Someone's in my room.

"Hello?" I reluctantly call back out, unexpectedly met with the sound of someone shuffling outside of my door in response.

What. The. Fuck.

I quickly I grab a towel from the rack and step out of the shower.

I wrap the towel around my waist loosely while grabbing another and pressing it firmly against my face to dry off before swinging open the bathroom door and returning to the bedroom.

"Oh my gosh!" The voice shrieks. "What the hell?!"

My eyes widen as I lock eyes with the unruliest person in front of me.

Iris.

There she is, standing in a yellow sundress, with her long hair cascading along either side of her shoulders. As I stare at her, I have to remind myself yet again why not acting on the urges of Iris Hammond will aid me.

Yet, she continues to make everything difficult. She looks ridiculously perfect, even now as she pulls off one of her shoes and hovers it over her head, ready to swing in my direction.

Violence has never looked so hot.

"Dakota?" The look on her face tells me that she's just as confused as I am right now. No, scratch that—I'm way more confused. Why is she in my room? And why do I get the sense that I'm about to get in trouble for it?

"Is there a reason why you're in my room?" I skip the

formalities of a hello.

"Your room?" She scowls. "The front desk gave *me* this key card. They said that this is *my* room!"

I'm in disbelief. Absolute disbelief. "Your room?" I protest. "How the hell can it be your room if I was in here first?"

I take a subtle step towards her, only prompting her to raise her shoe higher above her head, ready to swing.

"What are you going to do with that, huh?" I can't help but smirk at her attempt to defend herself. "Bonk me on the head with that child-sized shoe?"

"Child-sized shoe?" she repeats back to me, annoyance ridden in her voice. "I'll have you know, Dakota, that I'm a size seven! Which, for the record, is just below average!"

She lowers her arm back down and slides her shoe back onto her "just below average" foot, stomping like a child with her arms folded across her chest.

"Yeah, yeah." I continue to go about my business, rummaging through my clothes in my suitcase. As I do, I'm overwhelmed by the feeling of her gaze fixated upon me.

"Now, if we're done here, *princess*. Can you get out of my room?"

Regardless of the complexity and sheer obscurity of this situation, the fact is, I'm still sopping wet over here. I need to get changed. And, if I'm being frank, I don't care if she refuses to leave, because if Iris's not gone in the next 60 seconds, this towel is coming off, and she's about to see a whole new side of Dakota Foster.

Literally.

A Recipe for Disaster

IRIS

akota is always four things: clean, cut, pristine, and polished—well, except for his personality. His personality has always been a piece of work. But at this moment, he's the complete opposite. He's a version of himself I never thought I'd see—and worse, *like* the look of.

The curvature of his chest. How messy his hair is as it rests atop of his forehead. How his eyes appear devilishly dark as he stands in front of me, slowly loosening the fabric around his waist. I would've thought that that visual alone would've repulsed me and sent me running for the hills. But here I am, fixating on the masterpiece he is—it's absolutely and utterly sinful.

As the deep V of his lower half comes into view, finally, it registers in my mind that he's seconds away from removing his towel, prompting me to snap back into reality. "Stop!" I scream out, eliciting him to do just that. "I'm going! I'm going!" I cover my eyes, blindly reaching for my suitcases and racing out of the room—questioning if my first stop should be the hotel's emergency eyewash station to rinse the image of Dakota from my cornea. Instead, I find myself racing back to the front desk.

"Sorry!" I nudge my way through the substantial check in line that has since formed. "Excuse me!" I abruptly reach the concierge clerk who helped me earlier, butting into his conversation with an elderly couple. "I don't mean to interrupt." *Even though I really do.* "But my room has a major problem!"

He turns away from the pair, looking at me with a deep-rooted sense of panic. "'Major problem?'"

"Yes!" I nod frantically. "Major!"

He seems to weigh up what to do for a moment till he says, "I'll just be a moment," to an elderly couple as he guides me over to the side of the counter. "What's wrong? What is this 'major problem'?" He softens his voice, evidently trying to save face in front of the other guests.

I don't care and do the complete opposite. "The major problem is you gave me a key card to the room of an idiot!"

My outburst causes a few heads to turn, followed by an eerie of silence in the lobby.

"An *idiot?*" he finally speaks as the chatter picks back up. His face tells me that he's even more confused than before.

"Yes, an idiot!" I try to explain, sucking in a deep breath. "A totally annoying, frustrating and ridiculously consuming...*okay*, that's beside the point." I stop myself mid-rant. "The point is this. You gave me this key card, and it was for someone else's room."

He takes the card from my hand, scanning it carefully within his grasp before he types back into the computer. "You said your name is Iris Hammond, right?" He looks up at me in question.

"Yes," I confirm. "That's my name. I'm with The Sweet Red in New York."

He reaches for his computer mouse yet again. "New York, New York, New York," he repeats under his breath as the tapping continues.

"Is there a problem?" I watch as the concern grows on his face by the second.

"Well…yes." He gives me a brief yet terrifying answer. "One of our staff members must've incorrectly booked the rooms."

A Recipe for Disaster

"'Incorrectly booked the rooms'?" I repeat in utter disbelief. "What's that supposed to mean?"

"It means I can only see two rooms reserved for New York. One for Tavern House and one for The Sweet Cook."

"'The Sweet Cook'?" I seem to only be repeating his words back to him, considering I can't possibly fathom how exactly this has happened. "No, no, that's incorrect. You must've combined mine and…"

How do I refer to Dakota? A Friend? *No.* Acquaintance? *Hardly.* Archnemesis? *Yes, but not appropriate.* "The other person's restaurant together," my brain spits out.

"Yes." He sighs, continuing to type onto the keyboard, perhaps not entirely understanding how urgent this situation really is. "It appears to be that way."

"*Appears?*" The irritation I've done a terrible job at suppressing comes pooling out. "It *is* that way! Are you going to give me another room or what?"

The man flashes me a pained frown. "I'm sorry, ma'am, but there are no other rooms. The entire hotel is booked up for the competition."

I place a hand on my forehead. "There's got to be something, surely. You're telling me that every single room here is occupied?"

"I'm sorry, but yes," he says clearly and directly. "We're completely booked."

I rest my head on top of the counter in defeat. All hope is lost until a voice speaks up.

"You can stay with us, darling." The old couple whose conversation I'd abruptly interrupted smiles over at me. Well, the lady does. The old man is blatantly staring at my ass as I lean against the counter.

"Sure, thing, *sweet cheeks*." He averts his gaze into mine.

Nope, this is not happening.

"Wow, that's…" I try to find the right words to decline their offer without coming across as totally ungrateful, when suddenly I see Sean Dellan step out of the elevator. He lifts his head up from his phone and peers in my direction, flashing a faint smile.

I need to calm down.

There's no way he can see me like this.

I look back over at the elderly couple, forcing out a fake smile. "You know, that's really…generous, truly," I speak through clenched teeth. "But I'll sort it out." I watch Sean and a group of what appear to be his buddies head towards the bar.

"Is everything okay over here?" A manager finally reaches us at the front desk.

"Oh yeah, everything is just fine." I distort my real emotions. "Totally smooth sailing over here."

"Are you sure?" the concierge probes. "As I can check you out if you'd—"

"It's fine." I grab the original key card back from the counter and race towards the elevator before anyone can so much as utter another word.

I have a plan to fix this—one I know Dakota will not appreciate.

Ten

DAKOTA

"Are you dressed?" Iris covers her eyes as I swing open the door. "You better be dressed! If I see a penis, I'm going to freak out!"

"Why would I answer the door with my penis out?" I respond matter-of-factly as her hands still cover her face, clearly unwilling to take any chances. "What do you think I am? A nudist?"

She hesitantly peels her fingertips away from her eyes, staring up at me. For a moment, we both pause. She's clearly measuring up what insult she's about to throw my way, while I'm trying to understand why she's back here.

"You're something, alright," she sarcastically remarks. "Something for sure."

I pretend to take offense, even though her words have never had any affect on me. If anything, they nourish this fire between us. Help to keep me on track.

"Is there a reason why you're here? *Again?*" I so diligently remind her. "Miss me already?"

"In your dreams, Foster." She rolls her eyes, arms folded across her chest as she stands her whole five-foot-six ground. "I'm here to tell you that you need to leave."

"Leave?" I repeat, brushing my hand through my still-damp hair. Her eyes follow and hone in on my movements.

"Yes, leave." She pulls her eyes away, shaking herself out of it. "The hotel made a mistake."

"A mistake? What kind of mistake?"

She lets out a prolonged sigh. "Well, they accidentally booked for us to stay in the same room. So, the gentlemanly thing for you to do is to go and stay somewhere else."

Was that what Isabella had meant when she said "The Sweet Cook" at check-in? Had she combined mine and Iris's restaurant together?

Couldn't she have messed up someone else's reservation? It had to be the last person I could handle sharing a room with.

I purse my lips, weighing her stubborn frame up and down. This might be the most we've ever spoken to each other in one day. Let's see how quickly I can ruin it.

"You know what?" I tell her. "You're right. That does seem like the right thing to do, doesn't it?"

Iris's eyes light up in delight. It's like she can't believe what she's hearing. "Really? You think?"

"Yeah, no." I close the door, hearing her repeatedly mutter "bastard," under her breath as I stay put on the other side.

"Dakota!" She pounds on the door yet again. "Open this door right now! I'm not joking. I have a key and I'm not afraid to use it!"

I allow another second to pass by but eventually I re-open the door, yet as I do, I notice that Iris's attention has since shifted towards an elderly couple making their way down the hallway.

A Recipe for Disaster

"Oh honey, look! There she is." They seem to recognize her as they stop. "Remember, sweetie. You can stay with us if you need to. We don't mind the company. Do we, Marvin?" The older woman nudges her husband softly in the ribs.

The elderly man shoots Iris a suggestive wink that makes me want to throw up. "Oh, definitely not."

Are these two swingers or serial killers? I can't tell. All I know is that this is priceless.

As the amusement grows on my face, misery festers on hers, and just when it seems as though Iris is at her breaking point, I do a terrible job suppressing a laugh.

"Move," she groans, pushing past me and planting herself onto my bed.

It's a sight I never thought I'd see.

"Aw, that wasn't very nice." I brush the minuscule thought to the side as I close the door behind me, leaving Granny and Grandpa in the dust as I lean against the dresser.

"You're not very nice!" She fires back, pulling her phone out from her bag as she types rigorously onto the screen.

"Why are you upset?" I continue to tease. "Granny and Grandpa sound great! I'm sure they would love having another grandchild. Or, by the looks of it, a sugar baby. What was Grandpa's name again? Marvin? Maybe he wants to *get it on*." I wiggle my eyebrows suggestively.

"Can you just be quiet?" She ignores my ingenious comment. "I'm staying here until I find somewhere else to stay. I can't risk running into them again."

"*Again?*"

"Shush." She raises a finger in front of me. "I'm on the phone. *Oh, hi there.*" Iris puts on a tone of voice that I know is entirely out of octave for her as someone comes to the line. "I'm just calling to see if you have any rooms available for tonight. Oh, you don't? Well, could you just double check? Yeah...mhm... okay, well, thank you."

I can't help but shake my head as she looks up at me. "What?" she asks in frustration.

"What in the world was that?" I question, folding my arms across my chest.

"What was what?" She taps onto her phone again, barely giving me the time of day.

"That voice," I explain. "*Oh, hi there. I'm just calling to see...* You don't sound like that at all."

Her brows crease in unison. "You know what you sound like, Dakota? A deafening, piercing, completely irritating, annoying piece of...*Hi, can you check if you have any hotel rooms available?*" Her voice shifts yet again. "*Okay, sure, I can hold.*"

"My point exactly." I reach for my tan jacket resting on my bed, only a few inches away from her side. "You should try voice acting," I remark. "Or maybe one of those sex phone workers. I bet Marvin would give you a call."

"Leave me alone!" She whips a pillow in my direction just as the person who put her on hold seems to return to the line. "No, not you! I wasn't talking to—"

When they hang up she pulls the phone away from her ear, letting out a faint scream as she falls back onto the bed, her hair spread across the sheets as her eyes shut in defeat.

"Enjoy your calls," I backhandedly remark, taking this as precisely my cue to leave the room.

As I close the door firmly behind me, I'm overwhelmed. Not just because of the situation, but because the image of Iris on my bed has strangely electrified every cluster of emotions inside of me.

I rub my wrist.

Stop it, Dakota. I have to remind myself.

Keep your head in the game.

IRIS

I've spent the last hour calling every hotel in the area, desperate to track down a room. The words that everyone keeps telling me are "sorry," and "we're totally booked." I'm panicked, stressed, and every other tortuous emotion in between.

How did the hotel manage to mess this up? Worse of all, pair me with Dakota, of all people?

This is a nightmare—a complete and utter nightmare.

"We're booked," the last hotel on my search engine tells me, and I'm just about ready to pull this phone away from my ear and throw it across the room. Yet, right before I do, the voice speaks back up. "But, if you'd like, I'd be happy to put you on a cancellation list," she proposes. "How does that sound?"

A cancellation list?

Despite my internal defeat, her words allow me to exhale a sigh of relief. "Please," I tell her in desperation. "Yes, please. That would be great."

I end the call and fall back onto the bed. Lingering question now lives rent-free in my mind as I start to wonder: *what will I do if I don't get a room tonight?*

I groan out in annoyance. The sun is almost set, and within a matter of hours, I'll have nowhere to stay, nowhere to sleep and will have already kicked off a terrible start to this once-in-a-lifetime trip.

I sit back up at the sound of the door unlocking, followed by Dakota's reappearance in the room. "You're still here?" He asks, tucking his hands into his pockets.

"No." I waste no time standing up from the bed and grabbing my suitcase. "I was just leaving." I shuffle towards the door.

"You found somewhere else to stay?" He inquiries, his broad frame standing in the doorway, blocking my way out.

"No." I have to choke down the lump in my throat. "I didn't, and I'm pretty sure if I hear the words 'we're booked' ever again, I might seriously lose it!"

Dakota shakes his head and moves away from the door. "This is you before you've lost it?" He walks across the room.

I should leave, but somehow his comment makes me turn back around. "This is me mildly irritated," I say exasperatingly, unsure why I'm even entertaining this conversation.

"*Mildly*?" He prompts me to go on as one of his hands reaches alongside his jawline, rubbing slowly as he grazes over the top of his stubbled face.

"Yes, *mildly*." I pull my eyes away from his intricate movements that send me into a trance. "Plus, I have every right to be right now. This is total bullshit!"

A Recipe for Disaster

"*Bullshit?*"

"Can you stop doing that?" I announce. "You're driving me insane."

"Stop doing what?" Dakota plays dumb, even though I'm certain that everything he does is carefully calculated. "What am I doing?"

"You're repeating every God-damn thing I'm saying to you!" I shake my head. "What's wrong with you? Don't you know how to comfort someone when they're feeling upset?"

A silence falls over the room as he looks up in thought. "You know, one time I read a book that said repeating keywords makes people feel more validated in their feelings."

I'm not sure which to throw in his face first. That he knows how to read, or the fact that he actually knows what a book is.

"I'm just trying to be nice, Iris." He beats me to a comeback. "Considering earlier, you said I wasn't." There's a false sense of hurt in his voice.

I huff. "I don't need you to validate my feelings. And news flash Dakota, you're *not* nice."

He rolls his eyes as he reaches for his suitcase, pulling out a watch and strapping it around his wrist—right over the top of that same tattoo that, since the first day we met, I've been trying to make out.

What is that thing?

A bee?

A ladybug?

A flipping praying mantis?

Why can't I tell?

I stare away from his wrist, standing up straighter as he plants himself onto the bed. "So, riddle me this. You don't get upset? You're just Mr. Funny Guy all the time?"

Dakota torturously runs his hand along his lower lip. "So, you think I'm funny?"

I sigh in distress. I set myself up for that one.

"Funny looking, that's for sure." I try and deflect, even though there is nothing funny about how he places both of his arms back onto the bed and leans into them—staring up at me confidently. Why does he always seem so proud whenever we have an exchange like this?

"So, you mean to tell me that you don't get upset? Angry? Frustrated?" I fold my arms across my chest in comfort, listing off the adjectives. "This is just how you are all the time?"

His brown eyes soften. "You wouldn't want to see me upset, Iris," he responds somberly, and for a second, I start to question why. Why don't I want to see him upset? Has he been through something that's made him resort to sadism?

No.

No sympathy.

Dakota's a jerk.

A total jerk.

"If I'm being honest, I don't really want to see you at all," I bark out the comeback I tried holding back from, "tried" being a generous word.

Dakota sits up—his posture tall, commanding my attention. "So, let me get this right, *Iris*." He taunts me with the way he says my name. "You say I'm not nice, I'm funny-looking, and that you hardly want to be around me." He counts each point on his fingers. "Yet, here you are. Still in *my* room. It's strange, don't you think?"

I suck in a breath. He's got a point. I hate that he's got a point. Why the hell am I still here?

"You know something?" He purses his lips, standing up straight. "I was going to say, 'fine, you can stay,' but after all this bullying I'm enduring, I've decided to reconsider the offer."

Did the words "you can stay" just fall out of Dakota Foster's mouth and land in my direction? I become a snickering mess before him as I process his words.

"And you're laughing because?" He asks, clearly unamused.

"I'm laughing because you're so full of shit," I scoff. "*As if* you would just offer me to stay with you."

"*As if* you're really going to turn it down when you have nowhere else to go," he quickly retorts. "Oh wait, you do have somewhere else you can go. You can go to Granny and Grandpa's room. I spoke to them in the lobby. Truly and Marvin—a lovely couple, actually. I think they'd make you quite comfortable. How about I go and get them?" He trudges his way over to the door, leading me to race in front of him to stop him in place and pull on his forearm.

We both pause until finally I speak up. "Fine," I cut him off with a single syllable before I have to think anymore about those two.

His eyes land on the fact that I'm still holding onto him before he looks down at me. "Fine, what?"

I shake him away and take a step back. "Fine, I'll stay with you." I can't believe the words as they come out of my mouth.

Dakota subtly bites down on his lower lip. "Well, that's too bad," he taunts. "The offer expired, and if you want it back, you'll just have to ask me *nicely*."

My eyes narrow in on his devious face. I would never beg Dakota for anything other than to stop being such a pain in my ass. But as much as I want to tell him to stick his so-called "offer" where the sun doesn't shine, I'm left with no other option—unless this other hotel takes me off the cancellation list. Which, even then so, would be miles away.

So, as much as setting this bridge ablaze between Dakota and I entices me beyond belief, I need all the options I can get.

"*Dakota*," I say his name through clenched teeth as he peers down at me expectantly. "Can I stay here until I find somewhere else?" I ask him monotonically.

He raises an eyebrow, a subtle smirk on his lips. "*Nicely*, now," he requests. "I know you know how."

I'm about ready to snap, but I take a second to remember that this is only temporary. Dakota will get his payback in the competition tomorrow. I'm certain of it.

"Dakota," I attempt once more, much slower. "Can I stay here until I find somewhere else? *Please?*" I forcibly have to choke out the word.

A full-on smirk now forms on his lips. He loves this just as much as I hate him more and more by the second.

"*No.*"

The single word pushes me entirely over the edge.

This is the start to my villain origin story.

A Recipe for Disaster

"You're such an asshole!" I shout, sick of his games. "I'm leaving!"

"I'm just kidding," Dakota retorts before I can push past him, halting me in place. "Fine. You can stay here."

I refuse to thank him, especially after the torture he's just put me through. "Alright," I agree. "But just so you know, if I find somewhere else, I'll be gone faster than lightning. Then, the only place you'll see me is on top of the winner's podium."

"I think you're getting confused about where you'll be seeing me," he remarks.

I ignore his comment, watching him make short steps towards the door. "Where are you going?" I can't help but wonder.

"The bar," he answers my question point-blank.

"'The bar'? Why? What's at the bar?"

"There's a party for all the contestants ahead of tomorrow's competition, and considering you're going to be the so-called *winner*…you should probably go," he mocks, holding the door open, waiting for me to follow.

"We'll see," I tell him. He seemingly accepts the uncertainty of my answer and closes the door behind him.

Once he's gone, I let out a sigh of relief, not just because I now have somewhere to sleep tonight, but because now that Dakota is gone, the tension that filled the room is gone too.

What's at the bar that would even remotely interest me? I wonder, rubbing my face in stress until an idea comes to mind.

Iris, you're a genius.

I'm going to the bar. Not because Dakota will be there, but because earlier, I caught a glimpse of someone I know for certain is.

There may be another room I can stay in after all.

A Recipe for Disaster

Eleven

IRIS

I've never prided myself in being one to dress up. Typically, you'll find me in one of two outfits. My tried-and-true yellow sundress or my last-ditch effort to make a chef's jacket "fashionable". Which ultimately means, pairing it with some skinny jeans. As you can imagine, I'm not quite a trendsetter when it comes to fashion.

Yet, going into this competition with the knowledge that I'd be staying at a five-star resort for a week, my wardrobe needed some major rehab—a shopping spree doing just that.

Although my bank account didn't thank me, the looks I attract as I walk into the bar make it worthwhile.

I can honestly say I've never felt better.

The curves of my hips are hugged by a sleek dark purple dress and my bust is practically built for a lingerie commercial with how my cleavage protrudes in the most modest yet sexy way possible.

My presence consumes each person as I walk by. Typically, I don't love attention. But this? This I don't mind—in fact, *this*, I could get used to.

You see, everything I do is a total tactic. Don't you think I know a thing or two about the art of distraction?

My goal is simple: get into the heads of others while I can perfectly focus in mine. Check and mate.

As I shuffle my way through the bar, I recognize some familiar faces, many of whom I've competed against over the years. Not all are enemies like Dakota.

"Hey, Iris," a girl from South Carolina calls out my name. I wave to her in response until my body collides with a brick wall.

With arms.

With legs.

With...a big ole' annoying face.

"Watch it!" I hear Dakota say as he pulls back.

Of course, he's the first person I'd run into... *literally*.

"You know, you act as if you're royalty with the way you walk into the room, waving to people like that." He raises his hand, mimicking my motion in mockery.

"Well, unlike you, I actually have friends." I trudge away from him and towards the bar, ordering a drink.

"Oh yeah?" He plants himself in a chair beside me.

"Yeah." I attempt to look away but can't stop fixating on the fact that I can feel his burning gaze in my peripheral vision. It's one I'm equally as desperate to shake as I am to question.

"Is there a reason why you're talking to me?" I opt for the latter. "How about you stop worrying about how many friends I have and go and make some for yourself."

I slip the bartender some cash as he hands me my drink, wasting no time reaching for the pineapple that rims the glass of my cocktail—sinking it straight between my teeth.

A Recipe for Disaster

Dakota swallows hard as he looks down at the fruit between my lips. "Fitting," he speaks before a loud laugh echoes throughout the bar, forcing our stares to break as we mutually seek out who it belonged to.

Sean.

There he is. The reason why I came. He's sitting across the bar, chatting, smiling, and looking downright tasty. For a second, I get lost just staring at him, so much so that I'm unsure if Dakota is still talking to me or if someone is running their nails along a chalkboard. I can never quite tell the difference.

What I can tell, though, is that Sean has strategically left the top three buttons of his shirt undone, allowing his chest to poke through. Just like me, I think he knows what he's doing.

As much as Sean has a reputation for being an extremely talented chef, he's also known as a massive player. Even though he's not competing this time around, I suppose, as the saying goes, "old habits die hard," and boy, does the look of him make me want to start digging my own grave.

"Who are you looking at like that?" Dakota's voice can no longer be ignored when he snaps me out of my trance with an unamused expression.

"Like what?" I gaze at Sean, unwilling to let Dakota ruin this moment.

"Like you're undressing someone with your eyes," he bluntly speaks. "You look like a stalker."

God dammit.

I finally look back at Dakota, a sight that wouldn't be half as bad if his mouth didn't move so much. "I was not, and I am not a stalker!" I huff, trying to lower my voice. "Can you be quiet?"

"*Oh, I'm Iris, and I really like you, so much so that I can't stop staring into your soul,*" he puts on a high-pitched voice, doing what I can only assume to be a terrible impersonation of me.

"Are you done?" I ask, completely fed up with his shenanigans.

"*Will I go over and talk to you? Probably not. I'll just keep standing here for the rest of my life until you disappear, and I regret everything.*"

I place my drink back onto the table, the glass making a much louder clink than I'd expected when it hits the bar top. "What is wrong with you?" I lightly slap against his bicep. "Do you want him to hear?"

"Hey!" He raises both hands up in defense. "Don't make me revoke my hospitality, or worse, report you to the judging panel. I'm pretty sure acts of aggression toward your competition are grounds for automatic expulsion. You wouldn't want that, now, would you?"

I glare at him, biting down on my lower lip. I want to lose my cool so badly right now, but I can only wonder what Sean would think.

I shift my focus away from Dakota and back towards Sean, who continues to laugh incredibly loud as he downs a shot with some buddies around him.

"*Him?*" Dakota follows my gaze, his voice full of disgust. "What's so enticing about him?"

"*Him* has a name." I take a final swig of my drink, hopeful that the alcohol in my system will make Dakota more bearable. At this rate, I'm going to have to be drunk this whole trip. "And considering you're so caught up in this logic of *'I'm going to win*

A Recipe for Disaster

without a doubt, 'cause I'm the best chef in all of New York,'" I imitate his deep voice in return. "You oughta' learn it."

Dakota breathes as he stares back at Sean, squinting his eyes as he assesses his frame. He seems irritated by the fact that I know something he doesn't. Oh, how I love this feeling.

"Now, who's the stalker?" I tilt my head downwards tauntingly.

Dakota impatiently taps his fingers against the counter. "So, who is he then?" I can tell that he's desperate to know.

"I'm not telling." I turn away, devoting my time to catching the bartender's attention, already ready for my next drink.

"Suit yourself." Dakota stands up, and immediately, I don't like the tone in his voice.

I shift my head in his direction. "What are you doing?" I ask, halting him in place.

"Oh me?" He places a hand on his chest. "I'm just going to the culinary committee to start that incident report. I'm sure that that act of aggression was caught on camera. There are cameras in here, right?" He looks up, scanning the ceiling.

I survey the seriousness of his threat. Is he pulling my leg, or does he hate me so much that he'd jump on the opportunity to get me disqualified at any chance he can? I'm unwilling to take any chances. "It's Sean!"

"Sean?" he questions, sitting right back down. "Sean who?"

"Sean Dellan," I reluctantly tell him. "He's won this competition several times before. I guess this year, he was asked to be a judge instead." I pull out my phone to show an internet search of him, handing it over to Dakota to see for himself.

"S-E-A-N?" He spells out.

"Wow," I remark. "You do know how to spell. I'm impressed."

He ignores my jab as his eyes scan the screen. "I already didn't like him, but there's something about people named Sean that spell it like that. That just pisses me off."

I snatch my phone back and tuck it into my purse. "Everything seems to piss you off. Is there anything you actually like?"

Dakota runs his fingertips along the rim of his whiskey glass as he stares over at me. I take no notice. Instead, I follow his movements over to his hands, which are visibly that of a chef.

He's got scars, cuts, and burn marks scattered throughout—some new, some old. They're hands that show experience and hard work, and at the end of the day, as much as I wish it weren't true, they clearly know what they're doing.

My eyes trail away from his hands and back onto his left wrist, desperate to see that tattoo again. He tugs down on his sleeve and reaches towards my hand before I can get a good look.

"What are you doing?" I ask, internally questioning why I'm not immediately resistant to his touch.

"You know, your comment got me thinking. There *is* something I like…" Dakota stands up, prompting me to do the same. "*First impressions.*"

"Dakota!" I struggle to keep up with his long strides as he marches toward Sean. Now, a flush complexion washes over my cheeks as Sean visibly gets within range.

"Hey, *Seen.*" Dakota releases my hand, purposely mispronouncing Sean's name.

"Oh… hey…" Sean looks over at him. "It's actually pronounced *Sean,*" he corrects him.

"Oh." Dakota puts on an apologetic frown. If I didn't know just how much of an asshole he is, I might actually believe it. "My bad, bro. I didn't realize."

"That's alright." Sean stifles an awkward laugh. "Do I…uh…know you?"

"Me? No." Dakota shakes his head. "But this…" Dakota gestures toward me as I refuse to approach the table. "This is Iris. I'd say she's my friend, but I'd be lying."

What an introduction.

Sean doesn't seem to mind, though, as he diverts his attention away from Dakota and surveys me up and down. "You know, *Seen*," Dakota continuously mispronounces his name. "Iris here told me she thinks you're mad hot. In fact, she even just told me how you might be the most attractive guy she's ever seen—"

"Ha ha." I place my hand over Dakota's mouth, feeling how his facial hair tickles against my palm. "You'll have to excuse dummy…oh, sorry, I meant *Dakota* here. He's such a jokester." I stomp on his foot underneath the table as he lets out a wince.

Let's see if the cameras picked that one up.

As I pull my hand back, all I can see is Dakota's conniving smirk, leaving me to wonder, how is this the same guy who just offered…well, extended the invite, took it back, then made me beg…but still agreed for me to stay in his room? What happened to the nice part of him? Is he only allowed to do one nice thing a day?

I'm too embarrassed to look at Sean's face as I mutter, "I'm going to go get another drink."

As I rush my way back to the bar I'm certain that the next

drink on my agenda will be a double shot. Scratch that, *triple*.

"Let me join you," I hear Sean's voice from afar as I turn my head back in surprise.

"What?" I speak. "Really?"

"Yeah." Sean nods. "Thanks for the introduction." He pats Dakota on the shoulder, sliding his way out of the booth and to my side. "I really appreciate it."

I smile, pretending to itch my cheek with just my middle finger, conveniently aligning it so that it's right in Dakota's direction. Frustration and defeat washes all over his face—as I bask in whatever mini-victory that was.

"You'll hold onto this for me, right?" I toss my purse in Dakota's direction; his large hands catch it easily.

He glares at me as I flash him an evil grin, mouthing "that backfired," before turning my back on Dakota and facing Sean.

Second first impressions are a thing, right?

A Recipe for Disaster

Twelve

DAKOTA

This has been the most unusual day ever. I'm sure Iris brings chaos wherever she goes. She's like a tornado, spinning through my mind at a million miles an hour, and worse, making me spit things out of my mouth that should've never, *ever*, been said.

"You can stay here."

What was I thinking?

Why on earth would I offer for her to do that? It goes against every nerve ending that reminds me that keeping Iris at arm's length is the only plausible way to keep this plan in action—not having her sleep beside me.

Iris Hammond is a danger. A threat to my very livelihood, my dreams. I've only made it this far because I've made things work, and now I'm too far into the game to back out.

I let out a huff of exhaustion. This day is exhausting. She is exhausting. I should go, leave. Head back into the room and steer clear of her the best that I can until competition day tomorrow. But I can't. My eyes are glued to the sight of Iris flaunting herself in front of another guy. What makes all of this worse? It's a guy that could give anyone a run for their money.

Sean Dellan is a goon. I know this because I'm a man—we have a goon radar. But despite that prognosis, that doesn't mean Sean's not one of the best-looking guys in this bar. You don't have to be into guys to know when you see one worthy of attention.

But from what I can see, it's evident that Sean doesn't want to get to know Iris. He just wants to get to know what's underneath that dress. Something I'd be lying if I said I hadn't thought about once or twice tonight, but that's beside the point.

Iris is complicated. She has layers. She has a wit, a fire that not everyone can understand. She's the only girl I've ever met that can dish back to me exactly what I serve to her. That's why she's so much of a challenge.

I couldn't help but hope that this trip would ease some tension between us—turn us into frenemies, not only to make my life easier but allow me to stop working so God-damn hard at taking her on. But after a few hours, it's done the complete opposite. I'm confident that this girl hates me even more than I hate that I can't stop staring at the way she's looking at Sean.

Maybe I'm the goon.

The goon that she's left her purse with—one that hasn't stopped vibrating for the past few minutes as it rests in my lap.

Who is calling her non-stop?

Fed-up, I pull her phone out of the side pocket of her purse, where I can see four missed called from The Palm Beach Hotel.

She said she was on a waitlist, didn't she?

This might be my ticket to get her out of my room and focus right back on the TLC I signed up for.

"Hello?" I'm quick to answer the next call as I turn my body away from Iris's line of view, optimistic to even think that she'd peel her eyes away from Sean long enough to look over at me.

"Hi, is Iris Hammond there?" A female voice speaks.

I turn back to see her smiling at Sean. It makes me sick. "She's uh...busy at the moment. Can I take a message?"

"My name's Cindy. I'm calling from The Palm Beach Hotel in Fort Lauderdale. We just had a cancellation, and a room become available. Would you mind letting her know?"

Immediately. there's a sense of relief. My problems are resolving themselves before my very eyes. "Yeah, sure," I quickly agree. "I'll let her…wait…" Cindy's words finally seem to register. "Where did you say you were located again?"

"Fort Lauderdale," she clarifies.

Fort Lauderdale? I don't need to be an expert in geography to know that that's almost an hour away. It doesn't sound like much, but the traffic in and out of Miami is horrendous.

Suddenly, a conflicting pang strikes my stomach. The first is that if Iris does stay in Fort Lauderdale, then she'll have to be up extremely early every morning just to get here in time for check-in, prep and kick-off. If that's the case, then maybe that'll give me the edge. Is this the answer to my problems? Reduce her to total exhaustion while I emerge victorious?

But then there's the other side of the pang. The one that tells me that winning this way is not close to what I'd imagined.

It has to be fair.

"Is everything okay?" Cindy breaks the silence. "Are you still there?"

The sentence that falls out of my mouth surprises not only

me, but the receptionist too. "She's no longer interested. Please take her off the cancellation list."

I end the call and push Iris's phone back into the bag, and almost immediately an internal conflict begins.

Did I really just decide that having a roommate would be the answer to making this fair?

Yes. I did.

Why do I care? Iris is a pain. I should let her figure this out for herself.

But why should she have-to suffer for the hotel's mistake?

I turn off the voice in my mind.

It's settled.

Iris is staying with me, no questions asked. A few days won't hurt, right? Maybe, this won't be so bad after all.

IRIS

"I'm so sorry about that." I lean only a few inches away from Sean as he smiles down at me a face of perfection. "Dakota can be…" *Annoying. Frustrating. Make you want to rip your hair out…* "Difficult at times." I settle on.

"There's no need to apologize," Sean says with assurance. "So, what can I get you to drink?"

I shrug, if I'm being honest, what would be better than this delicious taste of payback on my lips as a result of Dakota's failed plan to embarrass me.

"Surprise me." I smirk.

Sean shoots me a playful wink before he mumbles an order

to the bartender and settles back into his chair. "So, you're competing this week, right?" he asks.

"I am." I nod enthusiastically. "In fact, this is my first time competing in The Art of Cooking competition."

"Well, congratulations are in order then," Sean remarks as the bartender hands us our drinks, prompting him to raise his glass to make a toast. "It's not easy to get here, so you must be very talented."

In more ways than one.

"I really appreciate you saying that, thank you." I connect my glass with his and take a subtle sip.

"So…" Sean leans in closer. "What restaurant do you work for?"

"Well…" I forcibly choke out after swallowing whatever that horrendous drink was. "I own, operate, and am head chef at The Sweet Red in Brooklyn, New York My colleague and business partner Lore Lloyd was supposed to join me, but she just found out that she's pregnant, so needless to say, she's been pretty sick and wasn't up for making the trip out here."

"That's understandable." Sean nods. "But it seems like you know exactly what you're doing. I've actually seen you compete before."

"Really?" I question, a sense of giddiness unleashing inside of me. I keep it together. "Where have you seen me compete?"

As Sean taps on the side of his drink, looking up in thought, one of his rings connects with the glass. It's like a sexy hand scene in a movie. "I believe it was in Philadelphia." He snaps me out of it. "You won first place, if I'm not mistaken?"

"You're not," I respond as a wave of confidence rushes over me. If there was any competition that I kicked butt in last season, it was the one in Philadelphia. "But that must've been what? Five months ago? How do you remember me?"

Sean brings his drink up to his immaculately shaped lips. Someone took their time making him. "You've got a face that's hard to forget." I watch him take a slow sip as I try to process if this is the alcohol talking or if Sean Dellan is really telling me that he also thinks I'm hot too.

'Cause if that's the case then let's just get the hell out of here. I'm not the type to go through all the formalities when it comes to hooking up. It's as simple as do you wanna get a room? You do? Great. Let's find one. In this case, yours, while I wait for this hotel to let me know if I'm off the cancellation list.

Wait, where's my phone?

Shoot.

I'm reminded that I left my phone with Dakota across the bar for some ridiculous reason, and now rather than focusing on Sean, I'm searching for Dakota instead.

"If it isn't the judge himself!" A stocky man brushes past me and pats Sean on the back. "How's it going, bud? They're some people I want you to meet." The man gestures towards a table at the back of the bar.

"I...uh..." Sean appears to be measuring up whether or not to stay or go. "Well..." His one word confirms his decision. "It was nice meeting you, Iris—"

"Hammond," I clarify as a pang of sadness rushes through my stomach. "Iris Hammond."

A Recipe for Disaster

"Right. Well, good luck again tomorrow." He smiles, grazing my arm. "I hope you liked your drink. It's one of my signatures."

"Liked" is a generous word. I didn't even remotely enjoy the drink.

At the same time as Sean disappears from my line of view, Dakota makes his way back into it—mimicking my exact motion, one that I hadn't realized I was even doing. He's got one hand resting on his cheek and the other fanning himself obnoxiously.

I pull my hands away from my face, stand up and march over to him with Sean's "signature cocktail," in my hand.

"So how was *Seen*?" Dakota sneers.

"Why?" I raise a brow. "Do you want him to buy you a drink too?"

Dakota stares down at the glass that has a green, almost brown tinge to it before he pulls a face. "That looks disgusting," he remarks. "Did he seriously order that for you?"

Do I really want to give him the satisfaction of this right now? Knowing all too well that if I openly tell him that this drink is terrible, he'll just spend the next five minutes going on about it.

"What are you talking about. It's good," I lie, sliding it in his direction. "You should try it."

"Hard pass." Dakota slides it back over to me.

"You call yourself a chef but refuse to try something?" I mock. "Now, that's just sad."

My words strike a chord because, without wasting a second, now Dakota reaches across the table and takes a massive gulp of the drink, proving to me that he was capable of much more than just a taste.

Immediately, his face goes red, flustered—it's as if I can see the flavor smacking against the back of his taste buds. I let out a genuine laugh. There's no greater sight than what I'm witnessing.

"That was the…" Dakota looks like he's going to be sick but swallows to stop it. "The most disgusting drink I've ever tasted in my life!"

"He said it was his signature," I barely choke out as he dabs his mouth with a napkin, his cheeks fading into a rosy shade of pink.

"You said he's won this competition how many times?" Dakota questions, shaking his head in disgust.

"More than we have." My laughter subsides as I push the drink aside while Dakota stands up from the table. "Where are you going?" I question.

"To get you a real drink." He walks back over to the bar.

At this point, I'm not even going to argue. So far, I've been at the bar for 30 minutes and I've only had to pay for one drink. So, as much as I dislike Dakota for reasons, I can only scratch the surface on—*free is free.*

While he orders by the bar, I notice my bag that I threw at him earlier resting on the back of his chair. Quickly I pull it into my lap and reach for my phone to check my notifications.

None.

Shit.

I should call the hotel. See if they forgot to contact me. Yet, as I go to click re-dial, I notice a 30-second incoming call in my call history, which clearly happened while I was talking to Sean.

Dakota.

"There was an incoming call on my phone? Was it the hotel? Did you answer it?" I bombard Dakota with my questions the second he walks back over to the table with two bright red drinks in his hand.

"Too many questions." He slides a drink in my direction, but it doesn't appease my death stare one bit.

"The hotel?" I repeat point-blank. "Did they call me?"

"No." Dakota sips on his drink. "It was just a scam call. Don't worry, I dealt with it. Now here." He lifts a straw in my direction. "Try this instead."

For a moment I'm hesitant. Can I put it past Dakota to try and poison me and knock me out of this competition? Is he really the spawn of Satan that my imagination makes him out to be?

Dakota sighs and pulls the straw out of his drink and into mine, taking a big ole' sip before he hands it back to me. "No poison." He shakes his head, reading my mind. "Now, are you going to try it or not, *chef*?"

It's frustrating how he uses my words against me, but more so when I take a sip of the drink and actually enjoy it, so much so it's taking everything in me to hold back an "mhm," but I can already tell that my eyes give it all away.

"That's *my* signature." Dakota smirks as his tongue gently caresses his bottom lip, taking another sip.

I try to distract my mind from the way I'm watching his mouth move and, worse, liking it, by bringing up another topic that's not so pleasurable.

"So, I guess since the hotel didn't call, I'll be staying with you then." I hate that it's come down to these words leaving my mouth. "But only under one condition."

"And, what's that?" Dakota asks, pulling back from his drink.

"That I get the bed closest to the bathroom."

"Done." Dakota chugs the rest of his drink and slams it down on the table.

"That's it?" I ask, caught off guard by his willingness.

"Yep," he responds. "Unless you have any more conditions?"

"Do you snore?" I think out loud.

He smirks. "I guess you'll just have to find out."

Thirteen

IRIS

Dakota fucking snores.

It's been 45 minutes since he decided that it was "lights out"—sounding like some summer camp leader as he said it, and since then, the only sound that fills the room is that of a wildebeest roar…aka Dakota's airway.

I'm getting triggering flashbacks to when my dad and stepmom would take Travis and I on vacation. Most nights we'd lie awake staring at each other, wondering how in the world we were going to get any sleep over my dad's snoring.

"You married that thing?" I remember asking Susanna one morning when I was eight years old. It was a remark that she thought was the funniest thing she'd ever heard, and the beginning of what she believes is my ability to "roast" people into oblivion.

I'll admit, I have a good tendency to dish it out—I guess that's why I'm a chef. The ability to dish things out both physically through a meal, and verbally through a comeback is second nature to me.

Yet, where it all began isn't sunshine and rainbows. The walls up, fists out, Iris Hammond started way before Susanna and Travis ever came into the picture—this version of myself is a result of my real mom leaving.

I hated that she left us. I was only five. But really, what I hated the most was that I missed her. Her leaving broke a part of me. A part that remained broken until Susanna and Travis came along.

At first, I cried, considering I'd always wanted a sister and not an annoying little brother, but Susanna and Travis were the greatest gifts for my dad and me. They allowed us to start over, give life another go, and made me believe that second chances do exist.

To this day, I hold onto a lot of resentment towards my mother, and after talking to Melody about it, she believes that's why I live my life in that "in-between".

I don't allow myself to get to the top of the rollercoaster because I'm too afraid to let it all go. It's part of the reason why I keep most people in my life at arm's length, because deep down, I'm scared.

The last time I was reliant, someone walked away. The last time I was vulnerable, I was left alone. The last time I trusted someone, I was wronged. It's aggravating, to say the least, that it's been over twenty-one years since she left, and I'm still dealing with the same bullshit.

I turn back onto my side, staring over at Dakota in the bed a meter away, wondering how I'm having this profoundly deep thought amidst his roaring.

Gosh, this guy needs to see a doctor.

We both have to be up bright and early tomorrow morning to start the first round of competition and at this point, I'm hardly going to get any sleep.

A Recipe for Disaster

"Hey, *Shrek*! Can you turn on your side or something?" I can hardly verbalize the sheer frustration I feel.

My outburst only causes him to shift slightly. The guy can't even hear me over his big fat mouth.

I reach towards one of the pillows on my right, throwing it over in hopes that it lands right on his face—putting us both out of this misery. Me for my sanity and him for his breathing problem.

"What the hell?" He stirs awake, eyes barely open as I shoot him a glare, one that I know Travis would translate to "fix-up."

"Why are you throwing a pillow at me?" Dakota's raspy voice fills the room. "Save the pillow fights for your girly sleepovers," he groans, turning onto his side and facing the other way.

"That's it!" I reach for a few pillows and a blanket, storm out of bed and march into the bathroom. I've slept in a bathtub before and I'm not afraid to do it again.

Fluffing out my pillow, I place it along the back wall of the tub and proceed to get inside, doing everything I can to force myself to sleep. It takes me a while, but eventually I do.

Dreams are my favorite thing. They're really the only reason I like to sleep. Usually, I'm a complete night owl, and honestly, I find sleeping to be a big waste of time. I know you need it to function and all, but just think about how much of your life you waste asleep.

Because of this, over the years I've made my dreams more productive. Think about it this way. Have you ever fallen asleep and, in your dream, you're thinking? Like you're planning out the next day or generating new ideas that can actually be purposeful?

Well, that's what's happening to me right now as I'm in this tub, getting one of my life's best sleeps.

Shockingly.

Mentally I'm trying to plan out what the first round of competition will look like in a mere few hours. What signature dishes should I think about making? How can I iron out a timeline if I only have two hours? Or what will happen if I only have 30 minutes?

It's essential to be prepared, and while my competition is sleeping the night away, I am too, but I'm sleeping with purpose.

After a short period, my thoughtful dream turns into an actual dream—and for some reason, I can't help but think about the last time Auston and I hooked up at the restaurant.

I know, I know, the hypocrisy of that statement, considering I yelled at Travis for doing the exact same thing. The main difference? The Sweet Red is *my* restaurant. Therefore, I can do whatever *I* want there, with whomever *I* want.

Point blank.

I brush Travis out of my mind and focus right back onto Auston. I have to admit, he's stupidly good-looking, strong, and has a beautiful array of tattoos that cascade down his bicep and into his forearm.

In this figment of my imagination, he's got me pinned up against a wall between the fridge and freezer, tempting me with his touch.

"You…you really want to do this here?" I ask in anticipation, our face's seemingly together as one.

"I want to do you everywhere," Auston whispers temptingly

into my ear, forcing a shiver to rush down my spine as he effortlessly lifts me into the air and wraps my legs around his waist.

It's as if I can feel the tingles rush through my stomach just from the thought alone. It's pathetic, really.

"Let's go in here," Auston suggests, pulling me into the fridge, the door slamming shut.

"In here?" I ask as his lips reach my neck, a tremendous rush of cold air washing over my body.

"Gosh, Iris, you make me so hard for you," a voice confesses, yet, without hesitation, I can tell that it's not Auston. Auston's voice is higher and has less vibrato. This voice is husky, strong… *familiar.*

"Auston?" I swallow, even though I know it no longer is. "What's going on?" I ask frantically.

As I look down, I take into account a pair of brown eyes. Realizing that the face that pulls away from my neck is not that of who I anticipate.

It's Dakota.

"Just admit it, Iris," Dakota hums with his sly smile and devilishly handsome face. "You've always wanted me too."

DAKOTA

"Iris!" I shout for what must be the tenth time in a row, yet it's no use. She remains sound asleep.

I allow for a long-drawn out sigh in frustration. The last thing I thought I'd wake up to this morning was an empty bed beside me. At first, I thought she was gone, only for me to find her snuggled up in my bathtub. I'll admit, she's an angelic sleeper, but I don't have the time nor the patience to be Mr. Nice Guy for a second longer. I need a shower, and by the looks of it, she needs a wake-up call.

An idea comes to mind.

Don't do it, Dakota, it's mean. The angel on my shoulder reminds me despite the sheer escalation of my thoughts.

Do it. It'll wake her up real quick. The devil's voice is louder and, if I'm honest, much funnier. I'm compelled to turn on the shower. Within a moment, Iris's eyes startle awake as she lets out an exasperatingly high-pitched scream.

I take a step back, but not before turning off the faucet and stopping the water. I can be an asshole, but I'm not a total dickhead.

"Wow, you really are a deep sleeper!" I playfully remark. It's evident that Iris finds this less than comical as she jumps out of the tub and pulls the linens out one-by-one.

"What is wrong with you?!" She discerns my expression, her voice full of conviction. "Are you crazy?! Like, have you lost your mind?"

"Says the one who was just sleeping in the bathtub," I retort, folding my arms across my chest.

She sucks in a pained breath. It's as if I can see piping hot steam coming out of her ears, just like in the movies. "I was only sleeping in there because of your snoring. God dammit, Dakota, I bet this whole floor had to sleep in the tub last night because of you!"

"That's bold considering I don't snore," I attest, even though

I know I do. I snore really badly. I'm your ultimate sleepover nightmare.

Before she can rebut, a faint shutter passes through her body, and my eyes instantly gravitate towards the goosebumps that now rise to her fair skin.

"Couldn't you have just shaken me awake? Called out my name? You know, done anything else besides turn on the water?" Iris lists of all the plausible ways I could've woken her up, but somehow opted against.

"I did," I lie, defending my honor by raising my hands. "But you were out of it, clearly stuck in a dream. So, I decided plan B was better. Besides…I need a shower."

Iris now stares at me with pure intent, and as she does, I can't help but watch as tiny beads of water roll down her neck and melt into the fabric of her now completely…translucent…shirt.

Shit.

I whip my head away as quickly as possible. I've seen more than enough to know I cannot—and I repeat, *cannot*—look back. I hadn't factored that turning on the shower would turn her white shirt virtually invisible. Nor did I think she wouldn't be wearing a bra.

Lord have mercy.

"What?" I can hear the sudden confusion in Iris's voice as she turns her head in the direction of the mirror and gasps.

"Holy shit." She throws her hands across her chest, quickly realizing the *sheer* reality beneath her. "I need to get out of this bathroom."

Her face is flooded with embarrassment as she attempts to

march past me. Only as she does, her bare feet to skid across the sopping wet tiles.

"Woah—" she cries out, milliseconds away from landing flat on her back, but instincts are quicker as I instinctively reach out and catch her. My arms securely wrap around her body as my hands stiffen around her waist.

"Careful!" I remark, which is also a friendly reminder to myself not to look down. "Are you okay?" We mutually freeze in place.

She looks up at me with startled eyes, and for a moment, I'm left wondering why despite her newfound steadiness, her arms remain wrapped up in mine, clinging onto me with all her might.

But it isn't her nails that pierce my skin that stings the most. It's the pure delicacy of having her in my arms—a concept I never thought would come to fruition.

The clearing of my throat pulls us both away after another moment. The confusion is evident between us as I help her to regain her balance and stand upright.

"I'm fine," she fires back contemptuously. I deserve it—I've been the root cause of this catastrophe of a morning and, frankly, the reason for her descent.

"Are you sure?" Remorse washes over my voice. "You're not hurt, are you—"

"I said I'm fine," she's sharp with her tone as her hands find refuge back over her chest, attempting once more to "rush" out of the bathroom, only this time she proves to be successful. "Enjoy your shower." She firmly closes the door behind her.

"Shit," I whisper, rubbing my hands alongside my face as

A Recipe for Disaster

I stand on the other side of the door, fighting the painstaking feeling of her touch being released from mine.

Fourteen

IRIS

"Welcome everyone to the 73rd annual The Art of Cooking Competition. My name is Sean Dellan, and I will be one of your judges this year!"

An uproar of cheers floods through the venue. I can't believe it. I really can't believe it. I'm here. I'm finally here. It's a dream, an absolute dream come true.

"Today, I'm joined by Colbie Carmichael, owner and head chef of Daisy Dekes, based out of Albuquerque, New Mexico."

The crowd's cheers pick up again, as do mine. Colbie has become one of my many culinary icons. She's a badass businesswoman whose restaurant has become a franchise in her home state. It makes me think that my vision for The Sweet Red isn't that far out of reach.

"I'm also joined by special guest judge Bruno Sosa," Sean continues. "Infamous pastry chef joining us all the way from Uruguay to participate in our competition this week!"

I know Lore would be screaming internally and maybe a little externally right now if she knew Bruno was here. Online, they had only released that Sean and Colbie would be the judges, so the fact that Bruno, who has been one of Lore's favorite chefs to

A Recipe for Disaster

rigorously watch online, is here is beyond exciting. If I don't get her an autograph by the end of this trip, I think she just might kill me.

"Now, here's how day one of today's competition is going to work." The noise dies down as Sean's husky voice echoes throughout the speakers. "By the end of today, we will be left with a hundred competitors."

A gasp radiates throughout the space.

"Yes, you heard that right. By the end of today's competition, fifty of you will be getting the chop," Colbie chimes back in. "This year, we're cranking the heat up!"

A slight flutter floats through my chest as I crane my neck from side to side. There is no way I've flown all the way from New York City just to be sent home during the first round—I'm making it all the way through to the end of this thing. Nothing is going to stop me.

"As always, our judging panel will rank your dishes according to the following: taste, flavor, quality, uniqueness, and creativity. By the end, you'll be assigned a number from one to a hundred—and as Colbie mentioned, those that don't rank will be eliminated from the competition. Understood?"

I nod my head, eager to digest the instructions. I cannot allow any sense of poor listening to impede me, unlike Dakota, who, across the way, is more focused on conversing with a competitor from California than the main stage.

I can only imagine he's making some sarcastic comment about Sean. Saying something like, "have you ever licked the bottom of a shoe? No, you haven't? Well, ask Sean to make you his *signature drink*, and you won't have to."

"Is everyone ready to get started today?" Sean catches me off guard as he shouts into the mic. Now I'm doing the complete thing I swore I wouldn't—not listening.

I join in on the applause as Sean lifts the microphone back up to his lips, "Well then, let The Art of Cooking Competition begin!"

As each judge walks off the main stage, I feel the presence of four eyes on me. Sean who shoots me a smirk as he walks by, looking dapper as ever, and Dakota, who, despite being across the room, seems to pick up on it. I can feel his glare as he tightens his apron around his waist.

We haven't spoken since our awkward encounter this morning. You know, where he casually saw my boobs. With full transparency, he's not the first guy to have seen them, and if I'm being honest, if there is any part of my body I'm most proud of, it's the girls.

But I know right now is not the time to dwell on that—even though I can't seem to stop the words, *"I've always wanted you, Iris. Just admit it, you've always wanted me too."* From looping through my mind.

They say dreams result from your subconscious thoughts, feelings, and emotions… but how can that be the case? None of it makes sense.

Sure, I've pictured Dakota beyond just that of a target on my dart board. I'd be lying if I said I hadn't. He's a good-looking guy. Tall stature, golden sun kissed cheeks, effortlessly perfect hair. There are many faults to Dakota, but the creation of his face and body is not one of them.

Regardless, at the end of the day, all of that doesn't surmount the sheer frustration that comes with him. Dakota is sarcastic, annoying, always in the way and now the loudest mouth breather to ever exist.

And I'm Iris—the girl determined to flush any and all thoughts of him out of her mind and focus on the task at hand.

Enemies to lovers is certainly not in the cards here.

The first round of competition commences after six hours. During that time, we were tasked with making two dishes. The first being our top selling item at our restaurant, which for me is so obviously our New York strip loin with roasted potatoes and a side of sweetened glazed red peppers. It's the dish that essentially encompasses everything that The Sweet Red stands for. And what gives it that extra kick? The peppers and steak are sweetened with pineapple juice, providing that perfect combination of acidity to balance out the meal.

I'm all about the hidden messages. So, when I explained to the judges that those extra touches were a nod to Pineapple Street, their faces lit up. Bruno even went in for a second bite, which told me that I must've done something right.

The next dish needed to be a childhood favorite. "What would you serve your ten-year-old self?" This one threw me for a curve ball because even though I'm a chef now, I was a picky eater as a kid. Bread, pasta, chicken fingers. Those were my go-to meals.

For a moment I was stumped on what to make, until I looked around to see that my competitors were prepping simplistic meals—things like macaroni, french fries, hamburgers, and that's when it hit me.

"*Go!*" *I push Travis as Susanna and my dad sit in the living room watching TV.*

"What do I say again?" Little Travis looks up at me, eyes full of hesitation as I let out a tiring huff.

"You're going to tell them that you're hungry and that you want them to order a pizza tonight—and not just any ole' pizza! Make sure you say that you want the pizza from Fabrizio's, okay?"

Reluctantly, Travis nods as I shove him into the living room. I learned early on that if I asked for take-out, Dad would say "not tonight." But, if little baby Travis asked, it would be an immediate yes.

I'm not sure if Dad is still worried about saying no to Travis since he and Susanna are still fresh in their marriage—or if it's Travis's convincing puppy dog pout that I so diligently trained him to do. Either way, I'll take what I can get.

"Um, Dex?" Travis walks into the living room as I diabolically peer around the corner.

Dad takes no notice. His eyes are fixated on the TV screen, forcing Travis to pick up his voice a bit louder this time. "Dex?" he calls out again.

Dad's attention finally shifts away from the screen and onto him. "Oh, hey, buddy, what's up?" he asks with a smile.

"Um..." Travis stutters, toying with his fingers in nervousness. I place my hand on my forehead. We'd only rehearsed this 100 times, and now he's drawing a blank?

"Um..." Travis turns around to look at me for re-assurance, but I hide

behind the wall, only peering back around again when I hear him finally articulate a sentence. "Could we....uh....get pizza tonight?"

"Not just any pizza," I mutter between clenched teeth. "Fabrizio's! Fabrizio's!"

"Pizza?" Dad tilts his head in query, looking over at Susanna for a sense of approval. Susanna is a major pushover.

"Of course," Susanna agrees. "Pizza sounds amazing. Where should we order it from?"

C'mon Travis, this is the moment we've been waiting for.

"Fab...Fabri...Fabrico's." Travis turns around yet again, sending me a toothless grin to say, "I did it."

Yet, before I can hide behind the wall, Dad follows Travis's gaze, a smirk rising to his lips.

"Sure thing, pal," Dad agrees, patting Travis on the shoulder, leaving me with ample opportunity to dart towards my bedroom, grab a book off my shelf and pretend to be as busy as can be, when a knock comes through my bedroom door.

"Who is it?" I remark, trying to be as unsuspecting as possible.

"Iris," Dad's voice is full of displeasure as he draws out my name.

"Come in," I waste no time responding, sinking my face deeper into the book I've frantically grabbed off my shelf.

"Sending your little brother to do your dirty work, eh?" I don't even need to look up to know that Dad's crossing his arms and shaking his head. It's his signature stance.

"Stepbrother," I correct him. "And I don't know what you're talking about." I flip to the next page until I realize it's upside down.

"Oh? That wasn't you watching him as he could barely pronounce Fabrizio's? Besides, do you expect me to believe that gourmet pizza is what a six-year-old really wants?"

"What can I say?" I continue to stare down at the words in front of me, flipping it the right way around. "He's got good taste."

Dad lets out a breath. "You're lucky I don't want to cook tonight, sweet girl," he remarks, and once I hear him close my door a massive smile forms on my face.

Mission accomplished.

"Did I do good, Iris?" Travis runs into my room a few minutes later, eagerly jumping onto my bed.

"You did, perfect," I tell him.

Just like the judges tell me the second they bite into my Fabrizio's inspired pizza.

"What's this on the crust?" Sean takes an extra second to stop and assess my perfect pie.

"Well, I like to glaze my crust with garlic butter and a faint layer of parmesan and parsley. It's my *signature*." I shoot him a discreet smile, tucking a stray piece of hair out of my face and behind my ear.

Sean shoots me a subtle smirk, swiping his index finger alongside the crust and placing it between his lips. "Delicious," he murmurs and I'm certain my ovaries just about explode. "Well done, Iris."

Well done indeed.

DAKOTA

After a full day's worth of competing, the only thing I've learned is that Sean Dellan is a total menace and should not

A Recipe for Disaster

be judging this competition.

The man can hardly keep his dick in his pants as he interacts with Iris, and he's not just been like that with her, he's been acting this way with almost every female competitor here. I thought he was a supposed prestige chef? Instead, he's acting like a frat boy at a college party. What Iris sees in him is beyond me.

Sure, he and the judging panel seemed to enjoy my rendition of my signature dish—rosemary chicken and parmesan encrusted brussel sprouts. Sean even shot me a thumbs up after he took a bite of my sloppy joe—the food that I'd serve my childhood self.

"This reminds me of when my dad would take me to the baseball game," Sean said as he went in for seconds.

Other chefs may have found the comment offensive, but me, I appreciated it. No one serves a better sloppy joe than the vendors for the *MLB*, so to me, not only was it a compliment, but it was a reminder of my childhood.

Growing up, my pops and I were never all that close, yet it was our mutual love of baseball that bonded the two of us together. Each year, Dallas, my dad and I would go to the home opener of the *Colorado Rockies*—my favorite team. One year I even caught a ball. Some may say it was a fluke, I say it was the best day of my life. I'd never won anything before. So, to know that the ball found its way in my direction, felt lucky… *special*.

"You a baseball fan?" I asked Sean, trying to prompt some conversation.

"Tried and true," he responded cheerfully, placing a hand over his heart. "*The Los Angeles Dodgers* are my team."

I forcibly held in a groan at his revelation, considering the

Dodgers are known to be one of the main rivals of the Rockies—was sports imitating life?

"Great team," I lied, paining my voice as I said it.

"Great dish." Sean and the other judges nodded as they made their way back over and onto the stage.

"Everyone, please join us at the in front, we will now be releasing the results of today's competition," the devil himself speaks up, as the crowd rushes to the stage, anxiously waiting for the results.

At first, they announce those that ranked in the top 25, of which I find myself—ranked my lucky number nine.

I accept the receptive taps on my arm congratulating me until the next name appears on the screen.

Iris.

Her eyes dart up before somehow finding their way to mine. I can't believe I scored higher than her, and by the look on her face, she can't either.

I don't let that surprise translate towards my body language as I let out a taunting shrug, forcing her eyes to narrow and her lips to tense as she swiftly shifts her head back towards the screen, smacking the girl behind her with her ponytail.

Without letting a second go by, Iris rigorously apologizes, especially considering the girl is crying because she clearly didn't rank in the top 100.

I feel bad. Well, as bad as I can feel. At the end of the day, it's a competition, and there can only be one winner, and after today I feel that much closer.

"Thank you, everyone, for a great first day of competing."

A Recipe for Disaster

Sean jumps back onto the microphone as the crowd begins to disperse. "Tomorrow is a rest day. We will have excursions available along the beachfront for you to participate in. Please join us then, and we will see the top 100 on Wednesday."

Iris paces herself just ahead of me as we exit the conference center, until a hand lands on her arm, stopping her in her tracks.

"Iris!" She turns around at the sound of her name.

"Sean." She smiles, as I internally groan.

"I wanted to say I'm sorry about last night." He waves to a few female contestants as they walk by, practically falling at his feet.

"It's alright." Iris looks away, giving him minimal to work with.

Good. She shouldn't. Sean is a certified douche who decided that spending time with his buddies was more important than talking to her.

Does she look like the kind of woman you shrug off?

"Let me make it up to you." Sean turns on his charm.

"Oh?" The way her eyes light up in response, makes my stomach drop. "And how are you going to do that?"

I refuse to put myself through this torture any longer, pushing my way past the two of them.

My presence somehow prompts Iris's eyes to divert from Sean and land on me. It's as equally amusing as it is confusing that I can pull her attention away at any given moment.

"Meet me by the beachfront tomorrow and find out." Iris's eyes shift back to him, and low and behold, I don't have to hear her response as I stand waiting for the elevator to know that she's just agreed to go out with him. The way she's got this love-struck smile on her face as she waits beside me gives it all away.

"You know, I would much rather drown than meet that guy at the beach tomorrow. Better yet, get eaten by a shark," I can't help but proclaim, exposing that I was just listening in on her conversation.

Her inquisitive stare turns back to a glare as the elevator doors open. "Now, Dakota," she speaks. "I think I like both of those options."

Fifteen

IRIS

It's been three days since I arrived in Miami, and I've safely come to the conclusion that my neck never has, nor never will be, as kinked as it is right now. Why? Because last night I stupidly chose to sleep in the tub again.

Realistically speaking, I could've easily slept in the room, all considering the competition didn't end 'til late, and I was so exhausted that I likely would've fallen asleep before Dakota's snoring began. But, the second the two of us got back into our hotel room, I grabbed the first few articles of clothing I could find and sought refuge in the tub. I needed to be alone.

Now, I'm paying the price as my habitual movement of craning my neck has become almost unbearable.

"Good morning, sunshine," Dakota snarls in a sarcastic tone as I emerge from the bathroom. "Or dare I say bathroom hog? Do you know how inconvenient it is to have to go to the lobby to use the bathroom in the middle of the night?"

Whoops.

I didn't even consider the fact that my occupying the bathroom meant that that space would make it completely off-limits for Dakota. I'm sleeping in a tub because of him, for crying out loud.

The least he can do is give me the whole bathroom.

I ignore his comment and make note of the fact that despite being on the sixth floor of this hotel, plastered over Dakota's face is a pair of obnoxious sunglasses. The opportunity to poke fun at him has virtually fallen into my lap, but I can't seem to find the energy to bust his balls. Instead, I seek out this time to remind him of his menacing words from yesterday. "I thought you said you'd rather drown than come to the beach."

"I would." He meets me by the door. "But lucky for me, I'm not going with *Seen*. You are."

I roll my eyes and as we both reach for the door handle simultaneously, our hands connect. It takes a second but, I end up being the first to dramatically pull my hand back as if I've just dipped it in hot lava. Dakota seems to take no notice as he swings open the door and theatrically gestures for me to go ahead.

Without hesitation, I shuffle past him, opting to take the stairs as he waits by the elevator. I can't stand being in Dakota's presence right now. Last night my dreams were the least productive they've ever been, and it's all his fault.

Rather than thinking ahead to the next round of the competition, I couldn't stop ruminating on the fact that Dakota's name was above mine on the leaderboard. Not by much, mind you—but still that was leverage. It was fuel to the fire, and I know that if I openly start a conversation with him, he's bound to bring it up again. Today, I know my limits, and right now, all I need to do is relax before the competition picks back up.

"Iris!" I hear Sean's voice call out my name as Dakota and I frustratingly reach the lobby at the same time.

A Recipe for Disaster

"Hey!" I smile at him, yet I can't seem to pull my eyes away from the front desk, where a receptionist has just called out Dakota's name and waves for him to go over. As he does, she eyes him up and down, just like Beth did that first day we met.

The girl is blonde, petite, and her mannerisms come off as way too desperate. Seriously, she needs to take a chill pill. It's downright repulsive how she's twiddling her hair between her fingers and bursting into a ridiculously fake laugh as Dakota speaks. I know it's fake because it's impossible that Dakota could say anything that funny. Besides, she's definitely not his type, and he's so not into her.

Or is he?

"So, what do you say?" Sean's voice finally registers as I peel my eyes away from Dakota and meet his enthused face. "Sound like a good idea to you?"

"What?" I ask, considering I hadn't heard a single thing that he'd just said.

"Parasailing," he proposes. "It'll be fun, don't you think?"

Is that what constitutes as fun nowadays? Being suspended in the air by a single piece of fabric? I'd rather not. But how can I possibly say no when he seems so adorably excited? Plus, I'd be lying if I said I didn't want to see him without his shirt off—which going out on the water virtually equals. We'll see how that adorability turns into sex-ability in a matter of seconds.

Despite the reluctance I feel I nod my head in agreement. "Perfect." Sean's eyes glimmer with delight. "So far, it's Colbie, Bruno, his wife, you and me but, I think we need six in order to do it."

"Well, who can we have as the sixth person?" I dare ask.

Sean stops. "Oh, I've got it," he calls out the name of a certain someone who has since pulled away from the receptionist and is headed towards the front door. "Hey, Foster!" he shouts, cupping his hands around his mouth.

Dakota stops in his tracks, turns around and tilts his head upwards, clearly just as taken back as I am when it comes to Sean's outburst.

"Care to join us parasailing?" Sean generously extends the offer I oh so wish he hadn't. "We're a person short."

Behind Sean, I shake my head profusely, even though I know I'm certain I know what Dakota's answer will be—a big ole' hell to the no. He made that abundantly clear earlier.

Time slows down for a moment as Dakota looks me in the eyes, raises an brow, before finally, he stares back over at Sean.

He better not say yes to this.

"No, it's okay." Dakota turns back, and instantly I feel a sense of relief wash over me.

"Oh, c'mon, man," Sean persists, walking towards him. "Without you, we won't be able to do it."

"I'm not interested." Dakota keeps on walking.

"What if I throw in some free drinks and dinner," Sean offers in a last-ditch attempt. "Will that change your mind?"

Dakota's shoulders relax as he turns back, tilts his sunglasses in a downward motion. "How many drinks are we talking?"

No. No. No.

"As many as you want." Sean insists as he makes his way back over to my side—placing a careful hand on the low of my back.

A Recipe for Disaster

It's an action that Dakota's eyes follow as he makes slow steps towards the two of us.

This seriously can't be happening.

For God's sakes. I'm completely fed up with him and now to make matters worse, I have to spend another whole day with Dakota, on a boat, suspended in the air.

Is this my hell or his?

"I'll meet you both at the dock in five." Sean releases me from his touch as he walks out of the hotel.

I watch as he leaves, and once he's out of earshot, I snap at Dakota. "Seriously?" I cry "Do you realize that you're a hypocrite?"

Dakota shrugs. "Sometimes plans change. Besides, I've got to stay at the top somehow."

I clench my teeth as we make our way outside. "Would've thought you were going on a date with that blonde from reception." I roll my eyes, unsure why I'm so offended by his choice of women.

She was beautiful—stunning, in fact. Why wouldn't anyone choose to spend their day with her? Dakota's single, or so I'm assuming. It's none of my business who he spends his time with, despite how much I want it to be at this moment.

He looks at me in disgust. "'A date?'" he repeats back with a scoff. "The only date that she's going on is a study date."

His words start to register. "She's a high schooler?" my voice picks up more than it should in delight.

"Yeah," he responds as I hold back a satisfied smirk. "Very much so. Skipping class to cover a shift."

I open my mouth to say something, but Sean beats me to it. "Over here, guys!" he announces, waving his arms dramatically as Dakota and I trudge along the warm sand.

Dakota groans, shaking his head. "God, I can't think of anyone more annoying."

I look up at him. "I can," I respond smugly, forcing his eyes to glare in my direction.

"Seriously Iris, don't pretend that you're not seeing what I'm seeing right now." Dakota gestures ahead. "The guy looks like he's landing a damn airplane!"

Before I can scold him, I have to choke down a laugh. "Can you try and be nice for once? I know it's hard for you, but an attempt would be something."

Dakota smirks. "Be nice? This is me being nice."

"Well, try harder," I mutter as we reach the dock.

"Here you go, guys." Sean hands us both Dakota and I a life jacket to put on. "Captain's orders."

"Aye, aye," I say, prompting Dakota to mock gag as I take it from his grasp and slip it on over top of my tank top, fastening the belt buckles in place one by one.

"Uh…" Sean's hesitation prompts me to stop and look up at him. "You're supposed to usually put it over top of your swimsuit. You are wearing one, right?" he inquires.

"Oh…I've got a swimsuit alright," I admit as I un-buckle the lifejacket and push it into Dakota's chest. Once he's got it, I waste no time pulling up on either side of my tank top to reveal the bikini I carefully chose for this trip.

It's bold, bright and beautifully compliments the fullness of my chest—leaving little for the imagination.

Tossing my tank top in Sean's direction I hardly make eye contact with Dakota as I take the life jacket back from his hands, clip it into place and make a special mental note to leave the top buckle unfastened.

The girls need to breathe somehow.

"Okay, now I'm ready," I say with confidence as Sean clears his throat, a sense of sexual tension not only evident across his face but also underneath his shorts. "Shall we go?" I peer at Dakota when no voice follows, seeing he's equally flush.

I can't help but wonder what's going through his mind right now. Is he thinking back to yesterday morning where he saw much more than what I'm offering right now? And if he is, how would Sean feel if he knew that was the case?

The thought alone sparks some unexplainable playful spirit.

"Yep, let's go." Dakota's brows furrow as he fixates on the fact that Sean's gaze on my body hasn't broken once. It's like he's a teenager who's just searched "boobies" on the internet for the first time.

"*Hello?*" Dakota attempts again, only this time with more conviction than the last. "Are we just going to stand here or what? Let's get this moving."

It takes a second but eventually Sean peels his eyes away from my chest yet remains in place.

It's incredibly awkward.

"I'll…uh…meet you two on the boat." I gesture back, pulling my hair into a ponytail as I opt to walk ahead.

"God, the rack on her." I hear Sean say to Dakota, assuming

that I'm far enough away so that I wouldn't hear.

I do. I hear everything, just like how I hear the sigh Dakota emits, telling me one simple truth: that I don't need to turn back to know that he's pissed.

Sixteen

DAKOTA

"Everyone, this is Iris and Dakota," Sean introduces us to the two infamous chefs whom Iris visibly couldn't be any more excited to be spending the day with—despite how much my agitated presence is killing the mood.

I can't help it. Since Sean's comment, I've been even more dry, blunt and unpleasant than usual. Plus, I don't think the fact that mine and Iris's thighs are practically smooched against one another in this concerningly small boat is helping either.

"It's great to formally meet you two." Bruno smiles before he gestures towards the brunette on his right. "Allow me to introduce you to my wife, Sasha."

"Hi Sasha, it's wonderful to meet you!" Iris nods eagerly before she draws her attention back over to Bruno. "Bruno," she squeals. "I've got to get your autograph! My best friend, Lore, who couldn't be here with me for the competition, loves you… like totally loves you…sorry Sasha," she jokes.

"I'm flattered." Bruno laughs as his wife reassuringly squeezes his hand. "I'll tell you what, Iris. Find me after we're done, and I'll send your friend a video message. How does that sound?"

"That sounds amazing!" Iris cheerfully responds, her attention so profusely caught up in praising Bruno that she's negating to see that across the boat, Colbie is sat in Sean's lap.

Hold on. Hold on. Let me get this straight. Sean invited Iris on this boat yet here he is secretly fawning over another girl?

What the fuck.

"Welcome!" A voice catches us all off guard as they shout loudly into a megaphone, only the volume comes out way louder than expected, as does a horrendous screech that seems to deafen and scare us all half to death.

As Iris flinches into my side, I watch as Colbie stumbles out of Sean's lap and falls closely beside him—just in time for no one to take notice.

"Whoopsie daisy." The resounding apology comes from is none other than the boat driver himself as he pulls the megaphone into his chest and fiddles with the controls.

"God," Iris whispers into my ear, flashing me the side eye. "I think that might've been worse than your snoring."

"My ears are fucking ringing," I groan out, toying with my earlobe. "Can someone please throw me in with the sharks now."

"Shush." She nudges against my thigh. "Don't tempt me."

"Sorry about that everyone." The boat driver scratches the top of his glistening bald head. "My name is Randy, and I'll be taking you on your excursion today. But, before we begin, I've just got one question for you all…" He steps towards a speaker on his left and flicks it on, prompting the opening chords of *Thunderstruck* by AC/DC to rattle throughout the boat. "Is everyone ready to PARASAIL?!"

Before anyone can respond, Randy irrationally and

unsuspectingly pulls the boat away from the dock and starts to rock his head back and forth with the music.

"That's it, we're all going to die," I announce, debating whether or not to let out a ridiculous laugh or a prayer. Sure, this might be the most comical thing I've ever seen in my life, but Randy is hardly looking where he is going.

Our lives are seriously at risk here.

"I guess your wish will come true then, won't it?" Iris acts as if everything is just dandy as she sticks out her tongue, holds up a rocker sign with her two hands and joins Randy in bobbing her head along to the music.

I place my hands on either side of my temples. I can't tell which is making me more recoiled. Iris's theatrics or Randy's presence. Maybe it's the combination?

"I like your energy, little lady!" Randy shouts as he guides the boat into the middle of the water.

"I like your energy too, Randy!" Iris cups her hands around her mouth, calling back.

I purse my lips.

Yep, it's definitely the combination.

"Alright, everyone, are you ready?" Randy turns off the boat's ignition and scoots his way down the center aisle, squeezing past us all. "Excuse me...sorry...whoops, I'll pretend as if your knee didn't just go in there," he remarks as he finally reaches the back of the boat.

"So, Randy," Colbie, whose voice I can hardly hear because the music continues to blare, shouts over. "Can you explain how all of this is going to work exactly?"

Randy turns around as he adjusts the parasailing straps. "Well, everyone is going to be going up in pairs. So, grab a partner while I set this up."

As a collective, the group looks at one another in an attempt to decide on the pairings.

"Well, we're, of course, going to go up together." Bruno gestures between himself and his wife.

Colbie holds two big thumbs up before she leans over to Sean and speaks directly into his ear, a little too flirtatiously if I do say so myself.

When she pulls back that, the pained look Sean shoots Iris tells me everything I need to know. Clearly, Colbie's just asked to go up with him, leaving me with no other choice than to go up with—

"Iris!" Colbie shouts far too proud as I shoot her a humorless glare. "Sean and I are going up together. We've got some judge things to talk about…So, you'll just have to go up with Dakota. Okay?"

I hate to say it, but I'm slightly relieved. Colbie is the last person I would've wanted to go up there with. Send me in with the sharks for all I care. But despite my utter distaste for Sean, I would've done it if it meant I wasn't going to completely ruin Iris's date.

Iris.

I look towards her, expecting to see a reaction to Colbie's revelation that reads, "I'd rather jump off this boat and swim back to shore before I have to go up in this parasail with Dakota." Instead, she's frozen, still, with anxiety evident all over her face.

A Recipe for Disaster

She swallows hard and hesitantly nods in agreement, prompting Colbie's eyes to light up.

Something is not right.

"Alright, you two." Randy breaks up the discussion, pointing towards Bruno and Sasha. "You two are up first!"

The two of them stand up, get strapped in, and within a moment, as Randy speeds up the boat, they're whisked away into the sky.

"Oh, this is terrible, this is so bad," Iris says out loud, watching them airborne. I seem to be the only one to hear it as Colbie and Sean stay engaged in conversation.

"Afraid of heights?" I peer down at her, our height difference still noticeably different despite being sat.

"Very," she says solemnly, placing her head into her hands, only lifting it back up as Sean blurts out a massive "woah" the second he and Colbie are sent next into the sky.

I've never been more tempted to cut a cord in my life.

"Get ready you two!" Randy shouts over to the two of us as Sean and Colbie make there way back down. "You're up next."

"Dakota!" Iris painstakingly says my name. "I don't know if I can do this. I'm going to freak out, have a heart attack, and then I'm going to die!"

I can't help but stifle a laugh at her melodramatics. "It'll be alright," I try to reassure her as Randy stops in front of us, beginning the run-down on what seems to be the million and one things that we're *not* supposed to do while suspended in the air.

"The rules are simple. Don't take off your life jacket, don't undo the strap, don't make too many crazy movements, don't pull on the string of the parasail and finally, and this is the most important one…"

Iris listens much more intently.

"Don't forget to have fun!"

I let out an exasperated groan. So cheesy for no reason.

"Now, come on over," Randy encourages Iris and me as he straps us up individually.

"Are you sure the straps are tight enough?" Iris questions as Randy walks back over to the front of the boat, igniting the engine.

"I guess you'll just have to see for yourself!"

IRIS

A blood-curdling scream exits my body as we're swept into the sky. Frankly, I can't feel any sense of embarrassment for my actions, considering all I can feel is complete and total terror.

"Oh my God! Holy shit! No, No, No. We're high up! There's the ocean….*yep*, we're in the sky! Crap." I lean back, unwilling to meet Dakota's eyes as I shout sheer nonsense into oblivion.

"You're okay," Dakota attempts to soothe my trembling state. "You're alright!"

His words don't ease my anxieties any less. "Talk to me… distract me!" I demand, never once believing that those words would come out of my mouth. Let alone to Dakota.

"*Hey*." He now places his hand over the top of mine as I cling onto the harness for dear life. "Iris," he says, his thumb moving in a circular motion. "Look at me," he speaks, forcing our eyes to make contact. "Relax, okay? I won't let anything happen to you."

For once, it feels like his words are genuine. There's no sarcasm or backhanded nature. Does Dakota care about me right now? The way his deep brown eyes look concerningly into mine almost makes me believe it.

"Just take a breath," his calming voice instructs. "Try and breathe."

I repeatedly do what as says until I feel the weight fall off my chest. "I'm okay," I'm compelled to say. "I'm okay now."

Dakota pauses momentarily, seemingly realizing that my words indicate that his lingering touch is no longer required. He pulls away with some hesitation, an awkward silence now passing between the two of us.

"So…nice view, huh?" Dakota's words come out awkward and choppy.

I shoot him a death glare.

Why would he say that?

"Sorry," he chokes out, stifling a laugh. "Wrong thing to say right now. Is there something you want to talk about? Something that'll help you to get your mind off things?"

I never once thought that I'd be in a situation like this. Forced to speak to Dakota because it's the only plausible way of not passing out. What do I even want to talk to him about? I mean, maybe I should ask how he suddenly came out of the blue and flipped my world upside down. That's always a fun-looming thought in my mind.

"Tell me…have you always been from New York?" I can't help but wonder. "Or are the depths of hell not called that?"

He shoots me a playful smirk. "No, I'm not originally from New York. In fact, I was born and raised in Colorado, but I moved to New York because I wanted to try something different. I wanted to see if I could make it on my own and prove to my family that I have what it takes to have one of the best restaurants in the state."

I pick up on a keyword in his statement. *Family.* I need to know more about the people who raised someone like Dakota.

"Tell me more about your family," I pry. "What are they like?"

He looks up in thought. "Well," he begins. "My parents are historians. They both work at the History Colorado Centre."

His words throw me for a curve ball. "Historians?" I tilt my head in confusion. "I didn't expect that one." I laugh. "What kind of history do they study?"

"Well, let's just say that they're big on anything and everything American history. They know everything about each of the states."

"Really?" I can't help but question as an emerging thought comes to mind. "So, is that why your name is Dakota? Are you named after those states?"

He shoots me a look that confirms that my mock statement is, in fact, true. "No…" I choke out. "Wait…do you have siblings? What are they called? Carolina? Georgia?" My laughter intensifies.

"Hey! You're named after a part of an eyeball, so don't be laughing too much, missy."

"Aw, don't get offended," I joke, seeing the playful frown on his face. "But seriously." We somehow fall into natural conversation.

A Recipe for Disaster

"Do you have any siblings?"

"Three." Dakota holds ups the fingers to match. "Two older sisters and a brother, by only five minutes." He leans back towards the sky.

My eyes grow wide as I make sense of his words.

By only five minutes?

"You're a twin?" I ask in disbelief.

He nods.

"Oh my gosh…there's two of you? What did the world do to deserve that?"

Dakota's mood shifts. "He's not like me at all," he explains. "He's—"

"Friendly, pleasant and less irritable?" I complete his sentence for him.

He gulps, and I can tell that some part of what we're talking about is striking a chord. "Precisely," Dakota says solemnly as if suppressing a sense of sadness.

"What are your siblings names?" I ask, afraid to question his visible reservations, resorting back into the discussion on what Mr. and Mrs. Foster named the rest of their kids.

"Charlotte, Savannah and Dallas," he rhymes them off one by one.

This is everything.

"So, when I tell you my parents love the USA." Dakota purses his lips. "I mean it."

"Oh, boy." I giggle, as for once, I see a genuine smile appear on his face. A look that grants me access inside his hard exterior—one I hadn't realized I would've wanted any entry into.

"You know, my parents would have a hay day with your name." He draws me out of that thought.

"Yeah, yeah. 'Eyeball,' we get it. Think of a new joke." I roll my eyes.

"No." Dakota shakes his head. "Not your first name. Your last name."

"Hammond?" I say. "Why? What's wrong with Hammond?"

"It's not what's wrong with it," he begins. "It's the fact that there are two states in the USA that have Hammond as a major city. Indiana and Louisiana," he tells me, and I'm mind-boggled how he knows this right off the top of his head. I guess being around history buffs your whole life does that to you.

"I'll stop if you want, but if my parents were here, they'd tell you all about the cities, including population, things to do, major historical events, and bodies of water surrounding the area. Shall I go on?" He smirks.

"Please don't," I beg as we're left staring at one another peacefully until I'm reminded that although this parasailing ride has been pleasant enough, that doesn't excuse the fact that I'm still up here with Dakota and not Sean. Like I wanted to be.

"Why did you agree to go on this parasail? For this boat, for that matter?" I fall back into the argumentative nature in which we only ever seem to communicate in with one another.

Dakota scoffs. "It's not like I had much of a choice, did I?"

"I mean, you did," I rebut. "You had every choice but to come on, and still you decided to."

"And what? Let that meathead spend the entire afternoon staring at you like you're some sort of..." His sentence trails off as he seems to catch onto his own words.

It doesn't matter, though, because I know exactly what he was about to say, but I don't understand why he would give a shit?

Now, there's another more awkward, drawn-out pause in the conversation before Dakota flips it back onto me. "Let's go back to what we were talking about before. How about you tell me about your parents—your family," he requests.

Immediately I fold, dropping our fight altogether. It's a first.

"There's not too much to tell you," I explain. "Dexter is my dad...well, everyone calls him Dex. He's cool. He's always been fun, lively and supportive. He's actually a Broadway performer. My mom is too...*stepmom*," I correct myself, stumbling on my words.

"Broadway?" Dakota seems just as, if not more, shocked than people usually are when I tell them that. Dad isn't a massive star by any means, but he has been on Broadway for over 20 years, typically playing more minor roles or supporting background characters. That tells you where I get that spectacle side of myself, right?

"He and Susanna—*my stepmom*," I clarify again, "met when they got cast in a show together. But with Susanna came my stepbrother Travis. Who might just be more annoying than you."

Dakota shakes his head in disapproval. "Which means he's probably not annoying at all, and that he and I would most likely get along just fine."

I roll my eyes at that thought. "Travis is annoying," I inform him. "Just close your eyes and picture a frat boy in the gym with beefy muscles and a whole lot of air in his head."

He smirks, not complying with my earnest request.

"Go on, do it," I tell him with an earnest laugh, playfully nudging against his shoulder.

"Fine, fine." He complies, closing his eyes.

As he does, I can't help but fixate for a moment on the way his eyelashes perfectly curl upwards, and just how delicate his features are when you really look at him. I've never noticed that before. The simplicity that lies beneath the complications he makes me feel.

As Dakota reopens his eyes, I swallow the lump in my throat. "Did you see it?" I choke out, now discovering that his eyes have subtle hues of amber when reflected against the sunlight.

"I saw it." I carefully watch as the response falls out of his lips.

"Okay, you two!" Randy screams through his megaphone, breaking us free from whatever serene moment we were just having. "It's time to come down!"

Already?

"See," Dakota speaks as I feel our descent begin. "I told you."

"Told me what?"

He smiles. "That I wouldn't let anything happen to you."

Seventeen

IRIS

We spend another hour out on the water before we return to shore, and it's just in time. Now, it's late in the afternoon, and if I don't get something in my stomach as soon as possible, it won't be the sunstroke that takes me out, it'll be my low blood sugar.

As we pull into the dock; I waste no time stepping off of the boat and marching towards the hotel.

Sean and I hardly spoke to one another once Dakota and I came down from the parasail. I tried to talk to him like I did most of today, yet someone else always seemed to grab his attention first.

This "rest day" certainly hasn't gone to plan. I guess that's been the theme of this whole trip so far—*chaos*.

I can't help but want to feel sorry for myself, order some room service, and perhaps lie down in bed tonight, even if it's just for a bit before Dakota's imminent snoring begins.

"Iris!" I hear Sean yell out as I step back into the air-conditioned lobby, yet I choose to ignore him and pick up my pace.

"Iris!" Sean attempts a second time, but this time he actually catches up with me and places a careful hand on my wrist. "Iris." He's out of breath.

I stop and turn around.

"I had no idea you were afraid of heights. I'm so sorry! I wouldn't have chosen parasailing had I known."

I withhold myself from rolling my eyes in displeasure—all these feelings for Sean have given me so far is whiplash. This flirtatious energy I'm putting out at him does not seem to be reciprocated—and if this is his attempt, then he has a weird way of showing it.

I flash him an empty smile as Bruno walks over and interrupts our conversation. "Here's your phone back, Iris." He hands it over to me. "I hope your friend enjoys the video."

As promised, on the ride back to shore, Bruno said he would film a quick message so that I could send it to Lore—continuing my reigning title as the best friend in the entire world.

"I know she will. Thank you so much," I tell him. He graciously nods in response as he walks ahead with Colbie, whose glaring between Sean and I for reasons I can't explain.

"Sean? Are you joining us?" Colbie asks eagerly. "We have a committee meeting in fifteen minutes!"

"I'll be there in a second," Sean responds, shifting his attention back onto me as Colbie continues to walk with Bruno.

"You shouldn't keep them waiting…" I make the first few steps towards the elevator, unwilling to meet his consistent eye contact when he stops me again.

"Iris, wait…I need to be honest with you."

I pause in place, prompting him to go on. "I think you know

that I'm attracted to you. I'm sure I've made that abundantly obvious." Sean pulls my tank top from out of his back pocket—the one I threw at him earlier. "But obviously…" He suspectingly peers over his shoulder to see if anyone's listening. "This…well, *this* is a bit of a conflict of interest, isn't it?" He gestures between the two of us.

With pursed lips, I faintly remove some tension from the towel that wraps around my cleavage, the cold air taking my breath away as much as I can see that this view is taking away Sean's.

"So…" I tempt. "What are you going to do about that, then?"

"I…uh," Sean starts to stumble, folding at my feet before he visibly snaps himself out of it. "Listen…tomorrow after the competition, we have a finalist's party for the top fifty contestants. Let's meet up after. I'll make it up to you then."

His request is triumphed by the information he just disclosed. Did he just say 50? Does that mean that another 50 people are getting eliminated tomorrow? They really aren't messing around this year.

"And how exactly do you know that I'm going to get through?" I can't help but question his optimism.

Sean takes a slow step closer to me. "Well…cook like you did yesterday." His lips graze my ear, sending shivers down my spine. "And there won't be a problem."

"Sean?" Colbie calls out a second time, prompting him to quickly pull back. "Are you coming?"

"I've got to get going," Sean tells me. "So…I'll see you tomorrow then?"

I subtly nod with a playful smile on my cheeks, one that

quickly dissipates the second Sean turns around and abruptly bumps into Dakota.

"Whoops, sorry, man," Sean apologizes, steadying himself against Dakota's chest.

Dakota brushes him off in irritation. "It's fine."

There's an awkward gap in conversation until Sean pipes back up. "Oh," he speaks, fumbling with his other back pocket. "Before I forget." He pulls out one of his room key cards and hands it to Dakota. "Here you go."

Dakota assesses it in his hand. "What's this?" he asks bluntly.

"I owe you dinner and drinks, remember?" Sean reminds him of their earlier agreement. "I'm a man of my word, so just tell the restaurant to add your bill to Room 870 under Dellan."

Clearly no longer interested, Dakota hands it back. "It's okay, don't worry about it."

"No." Sean places a firm hand on Dakota's shoulder. "Take it, I insist." He holds it in front of his face.

Seeing the two of them interact with one another gives me mixed feelings—feelings I can't quite explain, considering I can hardly understand them myself.

In response to Dakota's unwavering face, Sean looks back over at me for assurance. "You know what?" A lightbulb seems to go off in his mind. "How about you take Iris?"

"Me?" I question, placing a hand on my sternum. "No, I'm more than okay."

"Sean!" Colbie calls out like a broken record. "Seriously, let's get a move on!"

"Take it." Sean slides the card into Dakota's front pocket.

A Recipe for Disaster

"Enjoy your meal." He discreetly winks at me before he jogs out of view.

Once he's gone, I look over at Dakota. "Don't worry about taking me anywhere for dinner." I tell him. "I'm just going to pay for some room service and crash."

"Fine, but you know what?" Dakota strides towards the elevator, clicking the button. "You're not paying for room service. He is." He pulls the room card out of his pocket. "And guess what? We're getting the most expensive room service this hotel has to offer."

"What?" I laugh as the elevator doors open. "Are you being serious right now?"

"Oh, definitely." Dakota nods as the door closes, and we begin our ascent. "Not only does Sean owe me one, but he owes you one for subjecting you to that terrible drink the other night and ignoring you all day. You don't invite someone out, then spend the entire time fawning over someone else."

I'm taken aback by the latter part of his sentence. I know Sean and Colbie talked a lot today, but was he really fawning all over her? And if he was, how did I not notice?

I shake myself out of it as the doors re-open, and before I can say anything else, Dakota and I are back in our room, searching for the hotel's menu.

DAKOTA

"Shut up!" She laughs as I dodge one of the pillows that she throws in my direction. "That is so not true, Dakota!"

"It's true." I sink my teeth into another slice of pizza. "I swear on my life. On my restaurant." There's no difference between the two—they are one and the same.

"Dakota Foster, you are so full of shit." She shakes her head in disbelief. "There is no way you climbed onto your high school roof and stayed there all day without anyone noticing. There's just no way!"

I try to chew my food, but the laughter makes it impossible. Somehow between the midst of our feast, we'd opted to explore the topic of our teenage selves—most notably, our craziest high school story.

To Iris, the "worst" thing she'd ever done was skip class to wait in line at a concert, forging her dad's signature.

Because of that, I knew I had to divert my story. Climbing onto my high school's roof was nowhere near the top of the shenanigans I got up to, and she still can't believe it. Would she believe me if I said that I never wrote a single math exam throughout high school?

I mean, when you have an identical and smarter twin brother, you have to reap the benefits.

"It was a dare, and I was never one to turn down a dare. Especially when twenty dollars was on the line," I explain. "Besides, Charlotte and Savannah will tell you it's true. They were the ones I first called to help me when I figured out, I couldn't get back down. How come you don't believe me?"

Iris shakes her head with a smirk, arms folded as she sits crisscrossed on the bed. "You're just not believable," she protests. "So…I'll just have to ask them for myself." She seems as surprised by her answer as I do. She'd want to talk to my sisters…about me?

I don't have time to toy with the thought considering her next question has already fallen out of her mouth. I hadn't realized she was so inquisitive. "Did Dallas go up there with you too?" She sips on her drink.

How has she remembered everyone's name so quickly?

"Nah." I swallow, pretending to be as unphased as I really am at her mention of him, rubbing my wrist. "Dallas had some sense. He'd never do anything stupid like that."

"Maybe, you should've been more like Dallas then," she half remarks, twisting her fork in her bowl of pasta.

I wince slightly at her words, closing the pizza box that rests ahead of me as I reach to pour myself a glass of champagne. Talking about Dallas calls for alcohol.

As I pour myself a glass, I can feel her eyes burning into me. She feels bad—but she shouldn't. Her words don't sting because of some comparative twin complex imposed by my parents. They sting because her words are valid. I should've been more like Dallas. The thought haunts me every single day.

As she continues to look at me, I'm unsure whether or not to excuse my shift in demeanor or move on. I decide the latter, reaching for a shrimp and sinking it between my teeth.

We really went a little overboard with the room service. We ordered two pizzas and practically every other item on the menu, including a burger, seafood, spaghetti, steak, and pasta. Iris initially felt terrible, but then I reminded her of Sean's "signature", and all she could do was order another bottle of expensive ass wine to make up for it.

I lean back against my headboard. With the conversation stagnant, I opt to change the subject as we continue eating. "So," I speak, catching Iris's attention. "Earlier, you mentioned about your mom and brother—"

"Stepmom and stepbrother," she's quick to correct me, shooting me a glare in the process.

My brows crease in unison. "Why do you keep doing that?" I question.

"Doing what?" She spins her pasta delicately around her fork.

"Having to clarify that they're "step" every single time. From what you shared; it sounds like they've been in your life forever. So why do you feel the need to keep saying that?"

"Because it's true!" she says abruptly, her guards going straight up.

As an eerie silence passes between us, the only sound now comes from her fork making contact with the bowl.

It's clear she's withholding her real reasoning from me. I just don't know why. "Should I drop it?" I wonder out loud, hoping to ease some tension.

She nods, unwilling to further entertain this topic, yet I can't help but do the opposite.

"So, I guess asking about your real mom wouldn't be a good idea then, would it?" I assume, noting that in her family rundown, she hadn't once mentioned her mom.

"Definitely not," she tells me with total certainty. "I don't like talking about her."

It pains me to see the look of sadness that she's holding out on in her face, but it's evident in the water that builds up in her eyes.

"Alright." I direct my attention back onto the TV that hums in the background. "Noted."

Iris had demanded that once we got back into the room, we turn on some reality TV—a request that made me groan in disgust.

"I don't watch garbage on TV," I protested, flicking the channel to baseball, where the *New York Yankees* were playing against the *Colorado Rockies*.

Perfectly fitting.

"So, why do you watch the Rockies then?" she playfully fired back at me, a smirk washing over her lips as, for the first time, it was as if she could tell that one of her comments had struck me to my core. How could she insult my beloved team and look so damn perfect at the same time?

Stop that. I scold myself as Iris stands up and clears the food from her mattress. "I'm going to start getting ready for bed," she tells me, lingering by the footboard.

"Okay." I nod in return, unsure if that means she'll be in the bathroom for the rest of the night or will be joining me back in the room.

Regardless, I continue to sip on my glass, making a pitiful attempt to re-shift my focus back onto the TV as I try not to think about the fact that Iris is changing in the room next to me.

God, she looked beautiful today. Nothing pissed me off more than the way Sean looked at her as if she was nothing more than just some arm candy—especially when he made that comment.

Iris doesn't need to stand in the sunlight to light up a space. The way she's emerged from the bathroom in an oversized t-shirt, pajama pants and slippers, tells me that no matter what, she'll find a way to illuminate a room.

I can't help but hyper-fixate on her black t-shirt choice. I think she's scorned after the white t-shirt incident, a visual permanently embedded in my mind.

As she stares intently into the mirror, she runs some cool aloe across a faint layer of redness that cascades along the bridge of her nose and cheeks.

"Do you want some?" She gestures in my direction, squeezing some into her hand.

I take another sip of champagne. "Why? Do I need some?" I probe.

Stop.

She walks towards me, taking a subtle seat on the edge of my bed. "Hmm." She inspects my face. "Maybe along your nose?" she suggests.

I gulp down the liquid that I'd let sit in my mouth as her hand inches toward my face. "May I?" I'm taken aback by her offer.

No, no, you can't.

"Yeah…sure." I faintly nod.

Dakota.

As her fingertips brush along the bridge of my nose—I'm confident that the heat radiating from my skin isn't from the sunburn. If only aloe could be applied within.

Pull away.

"Your forehead is burnt too." She frowns, brushing a few stray strands of hair to the side as she gently applies the aloe.

This is bad news…she's bad news.

Looking her in the eyes, being this close to her, all I want is to pull her in and—

"You're all good." She pulls back, breaking me out of my thoughts.

I clear my throat. "Thanks," I murmur so softly that I can hardly hear myself say it.

She nods, closing the lid to the tube and planting herself back onto the bed adjacent to me as she stares at the TV.

So, she *is* staying?

"You know," she speaks up, breaking our silence. "I dated a guy who once played on the New York Yankees."

"You did?" I can't help but ask with inflection, desperate to know everything and anything about this guy. "Who?"

"Relax over there." Her eyes shift back to the screen as she bites down on her lip. "It was nothing."

Fuck.

I settle my agitated body back into the mattress, realizing that somehow, her comment not only managed to strike a chord, but worse, she noticed it.

"I think he was a field player or something. Nothing that important." She shrugs nonchalantly.

"Field player?" I dispute. "You mean, outfielder?"

"Something like that." She refuses to entertain my continual stare. "He was hot." Her words guide me towards the edge. "Definitely knew how to use his hands, that's for sure."

And I'm over.

IRIS

*E*very word that leaves my mouth frustrates him increasingly, even though everything I'm saying is a total lie. The truth is that was a test. I wanted to see if it was just Sean, who Dakota had a problem with, or if it was my interactions with any guy he didn't like. Clearly, it's the latter. But why, though? Is it that Dakota doesn't like me, so anyone I like gets mutually shunned? I don't understand his logic.

"What were you talking to Dellan about earlier?" Dakota, who's visibly uncomfortable, changes the subject matter.

Yet, his remark confirms that he was in fact, watching our interaction in the lobby after all—I had a hunch he was.

"Tomorrow," I answer bluntly, giving him minimal to work with.

He raises an inquisitive eyebrow. "Tomorrow?" he repeats. "Why? What's happening tomorrow?"

Did what Sean shared with me give me an edge? Or am I now just worried about how likely I am to make it to the top 50, even though I was top ten yesterday? The odds are in my favor, and so is one of the judges, but for some reason, something about this whole thing isn't sitting right with me.

Dakota continues to stare, impatiently waiting for my response. "Another 50 people are getting eliminated tomorrow," I admit, caving at the desperation on his face. "Can you believe it?"

"What?" he stumbles with the truth. "In only the second round of the competition? Are you being serious?"

"Yep." I tuck myself underneath the blankets, letting out an exhausted sigh. It feels slightly better to know that I'm not the only one now with this looming thought ahead of tomorrow. "Maybe they're trying to put more emphasis on the finals?" I shrug.

Dakota shakes his head, turning off the TV. "Are you nervous?" he asks as he pulls back the sheets and sinks into the bed.

"No," I lie, unwilling to give Dakota any inkling of my real emotions—complete and total anxiety.

"Good." He surprises me with his, for once, supportive comment. "Because you have nothing to worry about." He looks over softly as he turns onto his side, resting on his arm.

I allow him to stare for a few extra moments before questioning the gesture. "Is there a reason why you're looking at me like that?" I debate. "You know, you need to close your eyes to fall asleep."

He smirks. "That's why I'm keeping them open. I'm waiting till you fall asleep first. That way, I can go to bed."

"What? Why?" I stutter, blowing some hair out of my face.

"Well…" He rolls onto his back. "You said I snore, which I don't believe is true," he playfully remarks. "But I'll take your word for it."

"Wait." His words finally start to register. "Are you really saying you'll stay awake until you know I'm asleep?" I explicitly repeat what he'd just said to me.

"Yeah." He shrugs as both arms come up from behind his head, and that same contentious tattoo hardly comes into view.

What is that thing?

A bee?

An ant?

A beetle?

Why am I still guessing when he's right here for me to ask?

Ask him.

"Dakota," I say his name in a way that, for the first time, feels like it's not followed by undeniable frustration or a sly comment.

"Mhm?" He turns his head back to me, running his tongue along his lower lip.

I swallow. "Um…what's your tattoo?" I ask in curiosity. "You know…the one on your wrist."

He pulls his arm back, looking down slightly as a vague sense of sadness washes over his eyes, and for some reason, the look on his face pangs me with a strong sense of remorse.

Maybe I shouldn't have asked.

"We should get some sleep." He confirms my thought. "Goodnight, Iris." He flicks off the lamp and turns to face the other direction.

Eighteen

IRIS

"Iris," a voice calls out to me. "Iris, dinner is ready!"

"Coming, mom." I race down the hallway, my red curls flowing down my back. Today is Sunday, meaning tonight's roasted chicken and mashed potatoes. Mom's go-to end-of-weekend meal is my favorite dish in the whole world.

"Dex!" she calls out. "Dexter, come join us at the table."

Dad walks into the kitchen, planting a kiss on my forehead as he takes a seat beside me.

"Here you go." Mom places Dad's dinner in front of him. She's always been good that way, making sure we're served and happy before she takes a seat.

"Thanks, hon." He looks up at her in sheer adoration. We all do.

Mom is beautiful. She's the most beautiful woman in the world. I love that we both have red hair. Mom tells me that red is the color of love. A love that she feels for me deeply, a love that she says she's always felt from the moment she first met my dad.

Mom and Dad met in college, where they fell pregnant shortly after graduation—it wasn't the most idealistic plan since Mom had big dreams of exploring life outside of New York City. But nonetheless, the universe had another plan—me.

Mom told me that she wanted to name me after a flower from the moment she found out she was pregnant. Therefore, when she saw Iris flowers growing outside the hospital where I was born, she knew it was perfect. Mom said she'd always envisioned me as a delicate little girl—but I'm far from it. I'm strong, resourceful, powerful, and very independent. So much so that I don't like to be served my dinner. I want to serve myself.

Mom sits beside Dad, her fork planting straight into her mashed potatoes because she always eats carbs before protein. Dad and I are the opposite.

I scoop my food onto my plate, taking extra-long, considering a five-year-old only has so much talent with silverware.

"Iris, don't forget your vegetables," Dad remarks as I walk back to the table. He didn't even need to look up to know that my plate had no carrots and peas.

Mom's head stays down as I walk back to the oven and throw a few veggies on—just enough to satisfy Dad. He knows how picky of an eater I am.

Throughout dinner, we laugh, joke, and thank Mom for another amazing meal. I love my family. I'm certain I was given the best parents, life, and city in the world to be raised in. I truly couldn't have asked for anything more.

After we're finished eating, Mom collects our dinner plates and places them in the sink. "Wanna watch a movie?" Dad looks at me from across the table, gesturing to the living room.

"Yes!" I eagerly stand up from my chair. "Can we watch a superhero movie, Dad? Please?"

"Sure thing, my sweet girl." He smiles, tucking in his chair and heading into the living room. "Let's go!"

As I trail closely behind him, Mom calls out by the dishwasher. "Wait, Iris."

A Recipe for Disaster

I stop in place, turning around with a toothless grin. "Yes, Mommy?"

"I..." She stutters, her mood solemn, just like it was throughout dinner. "I just want you to know that I love you. I will always love you. You know that, right?"

I rush over to pull her into a warm hug, oblivious to the wary look on her face. "I know, Mommy. I love you too."

She hugs me back, but not the way she usually does. This hug feels distant. Cold. For some reason, she's not acting herself. Why isn't she acting herself?

"Iris, get your butt in here!" Dad cheers from the couch. "The movie is about to start!"

Before I can question Mom's less-than-reciprocating touch, she releases me from her embrace. "Go." She takes a subtle step backwards. "Go, watch your movie with your dad."

I nod with some reluctance.

"And Iris," she calls out as I finally look up to meet her heavy eyes. "Just always remember what I said, okay?"

"Okay, Mom...I will." I run into the living room, planting myself beside Dad, who wraps a comforting arm around me as the movie starts.

After washing the dishes, Mom turns off the kitchen light and heads upstairs. Usually, she'll come to join us when we watch a movie, but again... tonight is different.

As usual, Dad has fallen asleep after the first 25 minutes of any movie we watch, and here I am left watching all by myself.

The movie is almost finished when I hear a rustling by the staircase. I promptly shift my head over my shoulder, catching a glimpse of Mom wearing her jacket and hat. It's mid-January in New York, meaning it's freezing outside and covered with snow.

Next to Mom is a suitcase. A purple suitcase. One that we took with us on our family trip last summer. Why does she have it…and why is she walking towards the door with it?

She's unsuspecting of my curious stare until her hand connects with the front door handle and she momentarily peers in my direction.

"Mom?" her name comes out as a question. "Where are you going?"

"Iris, I," she hesitates, her breathing untamed before she confidently opens the front door. "I'm sorry…" is all she mouths before she closes the door behind her.

"Mom!" I frantically stand up from the couch, forcing my dad to stir awake.

"Iris?" Dad sits up. "What's wrong?"

"Mom!" I disregard his question, rushing after her.

"Iris, stop!" Dad's now a few steps behind me as we see the taillights of Mom's car pull out of the driveway.

"Mommy!" I scream again, chasing her down the street with no shoes, no jacket, no hat…nothing. Just sheer hope that what I think is happening isn't actually happening.

But it's no use. She doesn't stop. Her car continues to race down the street until she's out of view…out of sight.

"Iris!" Dad finally catches up to me, my teeth chattering as he guides me back into the house.

"Where did she go?" I desperately ask him, tears pooling out of my eyes. "Where did she go?"

He tries to speak, but nothing comes out—he has no words. He doesn't know either. "Iris I…I…"

I escape his grasp, rushing upstairs and into my parents' bedroom.

Reality finally finds its way to weigh me down the second I swing open the door.

All of her things are gone.
She's gone.
She left me.
She left us.

"Iris!" Firm hands shake me awake. "Iris?" The voice repeats the same actions as finally, I come to my senses.

My breathing is erratic as a cold sweat beads down my forehead.

"Hey, hey." The voice drops an octave. "It's just me. It's just me." I realize it's Dakota as my frightened eyes meet his troubled ones.

I pause momentarily, assessing his frame as he hovers over my bed. His fists are bunched between the sheets as he leans in endearingly, lips parched as he waits for me to speak. I don't speak, and before I know it, my arms are wrapped around him, my face nestled into his broad frame.

He hardly allows a second to pass as he releases the sheets from his grasp and encapsulates me into a hug.

"You're okay," he whispers into my hair, his voice humming through my body as he pulls me tighter. "You're alright."

The comfort Dakota's touch grants my body is nowhere near that of my mind—a place I only wish I could escape from as the reminder of my dream plays on a never-ending loop. I haven't had that dream—that nightmare—in years. *Years.*

Why now? For what reason?

Dakota gently pulls back, guiding his thumb toward my face as he brushes away a few strands of hair that have managed to escape from my ponytail. "You're awake now."

I nod faintly, peering up at him for a moment until I realize that I'm still clung to his chest. "I'm sorry," I force the words out, shifting back into my pillow and squeezing it instead. "I didn't mean to wake you up."

"It's okay." Dakota's softened face displays not a single ounce of annoyance. Still, even amidst the faint moonlight that fills the room, I can see the worry in his eyes. "Was it just a bad dream?" he inquires.

My hands fall over my face as my repressed emotions somehow manage to well up in my eyes. "I guess you could say that."

"Hey, hey, hey." Dakota brushes a series of tears from my cheek. "Don't cry. You're awake now. You're safe. I promise."

"Am I, though?" I refute. "It's been 21 years, and I still can't get over it. She left us. She left us without a single explanation why! Our life was perfect. Were we not enough? Was I not enough? How can this still haunt me?"

A deafening silence falls between us as now, the concern on Dakota's face turns into confusion. "Iris," he murmurs, peering down at me. "Sometimes, no measure of time is enough to heal the pain from our past. Sometimes, we just have to do our best to live through it. You know?"

I glance up at him, trying to analyze his words. His now shirtless body rests in front of me—his muscular chest, his vascular arms, his hands that carefully rest a top of his wrist, covering yet again, the one thing I'm desperate to see.

His tattoo.

"Iris." The sorrow fills his eyes. "You're not the only one whose past comes back to haunt them."

"What?" I sit up slightly. "What do you mean?"

Dakota's left hand rubs over the top of his wrist before he finally pulls it away, and for the first time, I can actually make out what the tattoo is.

My pitiful attempts at guessing every insect in the book were wrong. So wrong. Dakota's tattoo isn't an insect at all. It's pretty simple, really. It's two D's, interlaced with one another. Yet, what sets them apart and has left me guessing for months is that one of the D's has a wing. A wing of an angel—leaving me with a spiral of questions.

"The tattoo." I speak in a whisper. "What does your tattoo mean?"

Dakota slumps into the bed, turning his wrist upright so it's clear as day. "Can I?" He goes to reach for my hand.

I gulp, yet willingly lend him my touch, as he delicately guides my fingertips over the tattoo. I can tell is still relatively new.

"It represents Dallas and me."

"How so?" I wonder.

"Let me explain." He lingers my touch over the first initial, guiding me ever so slowly. "This D is for me—Dakota. And the other D…" He places my hand over the top of the initial with an angel wing, "is for Dallas."

Before I can even ask the daunting question, Dakota carries on. "You've said it yourself; frankly, you've always been right. I'm not a good person, unlike Dallas. He's good. He's calm. He..." His voice starts to break. "He *was* the better man of the two of us."

I make a note of his use of *was*.

I swallow the dryness in my throat. "You're a good man, Dakota," I attempt to reassure him. Sure, he pisses me off, unlike anyone else I've ever been around, but Dakota's not all bad all the time. There's good in him. Good, I've seen more today than ever before.

"I'm not, though," he disagrees. "I've made mistakes that I won't ever be able to move on from."

My eyes scan over to the clock—it's just after three o'clock in the morning. My body is exhausted, but I know one thing to be true. Unless Dakota tells me everything I can see him suppressing, I won't be able to go back to sleep.

"What kind of mistakes?" I stutter. "What happened?"

Dakota exhales deeply, rubbing along his face before he parts his lips. "It's a long story, Iris." He shakes his head and attempts to stand up from the bed. "We should go back to sleep. We've got to be up early."

"Tell me," I plead, pulling him back down. He meets me with regret as I mutter the single request. *"Please."*

Dakota caves, easing himself back into the mattress and settling onto his side as we lie face to face. Somehow my panicked breathing seems to subside as I look into his eyes—an effect I hardly have time to assess before Dakota speaks back up.

"It's an awful story," he admits, timidly looking away. "It's not the kind of story you'd want to hear before you go to sleep."

A Recipe for Disaster

I remain silent. It's almost as if Dakota's trying to talk himself through this rather than out of it. I don't care how awful this story is. Right now, I know that it's the only thing I need to hear.

"Where do I begin?" He looks up in thought, brushing his hand through his hair. "I guess some context might help."

I subtly nod and as I settle my frame back, my body naturally gravitating into the warmth of his.

"Well," he begins. "What's important to know is that Dallas and I did everything together. Everything…except when I was stupid. Dallas always had a good head on his shoulders. I'm certain he got all those academic traits in the womb. I was the troubled one who trailed behind everything he did."

"Did that frustrate you?" I can't help but pry. I'm finding a sense of comfort in diving into Dakota's past as a way to combat my own.

"That's the thing," Dakota's hand caresses my arm in a soothing motion. "I was never jealous of Dallas. He was my big brother. I loved him. I worshiped the ground he walked on. When I was in trouble, Dallas would take the blame. When I was sad, Dallas would pick me up. When I was doing poorly in class, Dallas made sure I passed. So eventually, to lessen his load of taking care of the burden that was me, it became easier to just do everything the way Dallas would. This lasted up until college."

"You went to college?" My eyes widen with inquiry.

Dakota smirks, finding some playfulness in our conversation. "That surprises you?"

I bite down on my bottom lip. His revelation doesn't surprise me at all. I can just see Dakota in some sort of fraternity house or as the judgy roommate on a college campus. If anything, that role was made for him. But I can't visualize Dakota being in a classroom at all. He's too independent, strong-willed, and too talented at cooking to be cooped up in four walls that aren't a kitchen.

"Partially." I have to admit. "Where did you go?"

He stares down at me softly before continuing. "Dallas and I went to the University of Colorado. Dallas had applied for a business program there, so naturally, I, too, applied for the business program. We both got accepted and ended up living on campus together for the first year. But after that, we lived off-site with a few of our buddies, where I became the mother hen of the bunch."

"'Mother hen?'" I can't help but giggle as I envision Dakota in a robe and slippers, flipping pancakes in a kitchen. "What in the world does that mean?"

He smiles. "It means that I used to cook for everyone. You wanna know the worst part about it?" He raises an eyebrow.

"What?" I speak, interest all over my face.

"The worst part is...*I liked it*. Can you believe it?" He jokingly shakes his head in disbelief. "I actually liked cooking for those assholes."

I smile. Truly. It's a special thing when you discover a passion, and boy, does a passion for cooking have its way of coming out, as much as you try to suppress it.

Dad had always wanted me to go to college, but I always knew culinary was my path. We found a compromise when he sent me to culinary school. Once I graduated, I willingly partook in an entrepreneurship-based course just so that I could equip myself for the journey of restaurant ownership. As always, I needed to be prepared.

"So...what happened next?" I'm desperate to hear more. "Did you stay home and cook all the time, *mother hen*?" I mock.

I fixate on the dimples in his cheeks, ones I hadn't noticed he had until I really looked. "Essentially, yes," he admits. "But the problem was, I was skipping class because I couldn't get out of the kitchen. I became obsessed with trying new recipes, meals, food combinations, everything. Cooking took over my life."

The way his eyes light up tells me just how much Dakota genuinely loves what he does. Is this the first thing we can mutually feel excited about together? Can Dakota and I find common ground in a passion that dominates our lives?

"Dallas was frustrated that I wasn't focusing, though." His cheery expression shifts as his face falls flat. "At this point, we were seniors and weeks away from finishing our degree. I knew, I had to stop slacking off to please him. I finished my degree, and within the first few months that followed graduation, the two of us fell into this cookie-cutter lifestyle where we both worked nine-to-five, wore dress shirts daily and sat behind desks in an office with no windows. To others, that might've been okay, but to me, it was hell. Torture, even."

I frown. "And Dallas? Did he like it?"

"He loved it. Within the first year at our marketing firm, Dallas got promoted to management. He was living his dream."

"*Year?*" I pull out a keyword in his response, leaving him to nod. "Dakota." I blink slowly. "How long did you end up working there?"

He sighs again, rubbing the stubble along his face. "Years." He leaves me surprised by his answer.

"Years?" I repeat. "As in more than one?"

Dakota purses his lips, clearly ashamed of his truth.

"How come you didn't quit?" I throw the question out there, wondering how he lasted in something he hated for so long.

"Oh, I did," Dakota scoffs. "Many times. But Dallas was stubborn." He raises his hands in defeat. "Each time I tried to quit, he'd talk me back into staying or rip up my resignation letter. It's definitely tough when your boss is also your brother."

"But what about cooking?" I remind him. "Were you still doing that?"

His smile comes back. "From the second I got home from work until the second I went to bed. At first, I only cooked for Dallas, but then he got a girlfriend, and they moved out together. One night, I invited him and Heidi over for a meal, and that was when Dallas mentioned that a cooking competition was coming to Denver. I'd only really cooked for family, friends, maybe the occasional girlfriend from time to time, but I'd never cooked competitively before…ever."

I can't help but grind my teeth at his mention of the word "girlfriend." How many girlfriends has he had? What were they like? Why didn't it work out? Does he still talk to them? More importantly, why are these questions blazing through my mind?

He takes no notice of my furrowed brow and carries on.

"I was nervous, but Dallas really encouraged me to compete, so I did. And low and behold, I won." His face lights up amidst the dark room. "For the first time in years, I was genuinely happy. From that day onwards, I decided that I needed to be honest with myself. Cooking was my passion, and opening up my own restaurant was what I wanted to do."

I can feel a looming shift in the story, prompting me to readjust myself. "What did Dallas think about everything?"

Dakota looks away before he re-meets my eyes. "Dallas was always supportive. He came to every competition and event and he even helped me at one point. Let's just say he was no chef." He chuckles, brushing my hair behind my ear. It's a mindless motion that leaves me to swallow a since-formed lump in my throat.

"But once Dallas started to enter my world, he finally saw just how badly I'd been struggling in his. After a few months, I'd finally hit rock bottom. Every night after work, I'd end up at the same bar, where he'd imminently find me and take me home. It's an awful feeling, feeling as though you're destined for something else but too scared to do it. Dallas was my crutch."

A final drawn-out period of silence fills our hotel room as I muster up the courage to ask the question that still remains unsolved.

"Why is Dallas the angel, Dakota? What happened?"

Nineteen

DAKOTA

Eighteen Months Earlier

*I*t's early December, and as usual, I make the only plausible choice to leave our annual holiday work party and go to the bar. I couldn't stand to be there any longer, surrounded by the achingly painful business executives I already have to deal with five days a week. People who love the environment I so adamantly hate.

Dallas didn't see me escape the party early. In fact, it wasn't until he got a call from the bartender, who frequently calls him to pick me up, that he even realized that I was gone.

Unlike the other hundred times where Dallas has come to rescue me, tonight is different. Tonight, I'm wasted. So completely wasted. I am no longer Dakota Foster. I'm just a pool of alcohol and a bottomless pit of sadness.

The bar is empty, and as I lay with my head against the counter, I hear the front door chime throughout the room.

"I've had enough of this, Dakota!" Dallas shouts, forcing me to jolt my head up in surprise. "This can't keep happening. It can't!"

"Dallas." I stand up from the bar stool, stumbling my way over to his irritated frame. I hate this disapproving look in his eyes. I hate it more than anything. That's why I always conform to him. That's why I've let my dreams slip away so Dallas can achieve his.

A Recipe for Disaster

"Look at you!" Dallas grabs hold of either side of my arms, shaking me angrily. "Just look at you!"

I don't need to. Dallas and I are identical. I can only imagine what I look like. I'm him, only more disgruntled and full of whiskey.

"I'm sorry, Dallas," I groan, hoping it's enough for him to forgive me. "I had to leave. I couldn't stay any longer."

We stare at one another for a minute before he releases me from his grasp and pushes me into a booth. "God dammit, Dakota." He lets out a pained sigh, planting himself across from me. "I'm not mad at you," he admits. "I'm mad at myself."

His words surprise me. "What? What the hell are you talking about?"

"This is my fault." He closes his eyes and pinches the bridge of his nose. It's silent for another moment before he speaks up. "I should have realized this sooner. I'm mad that I haven't been a good brother to you."

"Dallas…" I start but can't seem to find the words to finish my sentence. I don't have to, though. As always, Dallas knows precisely what to say.

"Tell me." He tilts his chin up. "What makes you happy?"

"'Happy?'" I repeat back to him. "I don't know." I shrug. "Nothing makes me happy."

"Stop lying, Dakota." He huffs in annoyance. "Who are you trying to convince here? Me or you?"

I stay silent. There's nothing more to be said.

Dallas softens his mood. I think he realizes that starting a fight is not how we're going to have a productive conversation. "Listen." He releases a breath. "Is cooking what you love, Kotes?"

Kotes.

He called me Kotes. He hasn't called me that in years, and hearing it fall out of his mouth right now only makes me sadder. Where has the time gone?

How are we already halfway through our twenties? It felt like just yesterday we were kids. Yet here we are, me drunk in a bar, and him, coming to save me. This isn't what I wanted adulthood to be like.

He prompts me once more. "Is it?"

Reluctantly, I nod. Of course, cooking is what I love. It's the only thing that seems to keep me sane. That and a bottle of Jack Daniels.

"Then you need to do what you love," *he tells me with absolution.* "And I can't stand in the way of that. I want you to be happy, okay?"

I slump my shoulders but he carries on. "You know, Dakota, you're so closed off all the time. I should call you the Closed Cook."

I'm struck by the gravity of his words, left repeating them back to him. "The Closed Cook?"

He disregards my inquiry and carries on. "Let's just talk in theory for a moment." *Dallas waves to the waitress for two glasses of water.* "If you could restart everything, what would you do differently?"

I don't even need to think about it. I've asked and answered this same question on repeat for years.

"I'd open up my own restaurant and have it be a major success. Nothing would make me happier."

Dallas folds his arms across his chest, as a smile rises to his lips. "Oh yeah? And where would this majorly successful restaurant be located, huh?"

That I think about for a moment. "New York City."

"New York City?" *He jokingly scoffs.* "Why New York City?"

"It's the city of dreams." *I raise my arms. theatrically* "Plus, it would be a fresh start. A new beginning."

Dallas opens his mouth to speak when our waitress reaches our table, placing down two glasses of water. "You boys should get going soon." *She lingers as I gulp down the first glass.* "They're calling for a big snowstorm tonight."

"Is that right?" Dallas sits up straight, concern plastered along his face. "Well then, we'll get the bill." He hands her his credit card.

"No." I pull his arm back, but he remains unbothered.

"The bill." His eyes stay firm on the waitress as she takes his card and disappears behind the bar.

"Get ready." Dallas tosses me my jacket while pushing the other glass of water in front of me. "I'm taking you home. I just need to call Heidi first."

Standing up, I place my arms into my jacket, doing exactly what I'm told as Dallas disappears from the table. "Here's your brother's card back." The waitress returns.

"Thanks." I frown, tucking it into my pocket as I chug down the next glass of water.

"You know, I hope I don't see you again for a while, Dakota," the waitress admits, toying with her thumbs.

I cock an eyebrow. What's that supposed to mean? I'm her best customer.

"Why do you say that?" I gulp down the liquid in my mouth.

"Because." She places her hands on her dainty hips. "I've seen you cook, you know."

"Oh yeah?" I smirk. "Where?"

"Last weekend," she reveals. "In Aspen."

"You were there?" I recall the last competition I competed in. "How come?"

"My brother was competing." She shrugs nonchalantly. "I thought I recognized you. It's clear as day that you love cooking, and after what I saw, you seem to be quite good at it."

An arrogant sense of confidence rushes through me before she squashes it by saying, "too bad you're wasting your gift."

"Dakota!" Dallas interrupts our conversation before I can mutter out another word. "Let's go," he instructs, placing his arm over my shoulder as we exit the bar and walk towards the car.

The snow has already started to fall, and frost covers every square inch of Dallas's windshield. As we start to drive, not only does the snow intensify, but so do the road conditions.

"Maybe we should pull over." I suggest, seeing how the slick ice glistens off the tarmac. "Wait 'til it passes?"

"It's fine," Dallas protests. "I want to get you home. We're nearly at your place, anyway."

"Alright." I try not to debate with him, although it's clear that the conditions are no longer safe.

"Hey, Dakota?" Dallas says softly after a few minutes of silence.

"Yeah?" I keep my dazed eyes glued to the road.

"You know that all I want is for you to be happy, right?"

I look at him in disbelief. "Of course," I respond wholeheartedly. "Why would you even ask me that?"

He scoffs. "Fine, let me ask you this instead. You want to make me happy, right?"

I answer with certainty. "Always."

"Well, alright then." His eyes peel away from the road for a split second. "You're fired."

My eyes widen.

"Fired?" I question, shooting the word right back at him.

"Yep, you're fired," he responds dryly. "Sayonara!"

I do a terrible job of suppressing a smile, which only prompts Dallas to laugh. "You might be the only person happy to get fired, you know that?" He shakes his head with a grin. "You're a total dork."

A Recipe for Disaster

"I know," I tell him with a smile, knowing what this means. Dallas firing me means that Dallas is letting me go. Maybe he's clung to me all along as much as I've clung to him. Does this mean that for once in our lives, we're actually going to go our seperate ways?

"I love you, Kotes." He looks over at me. "You're going to do amazing things in New York, and I want to be your first honorary customer. Promise me that."

"I promise," I tell him as our eyes meet. "I love you...DALLAS!" I scream out as headlights come racing towards our car. In a flash, I try to reach out for him, my seatbelt digging into my shoulder as I try to cover his body with one arm and grab the steering wheel with the other. For the split second that my eyes meet his, I'm met with the sight of the car lights illuminating his face in terror until all at once, everything turns dark.

The road, my mind, my whole world.

I spent Christmas in the hospital that year. The tractor-trailer that hit black ice and came racing towards Dallas's car had left me in a coma for three weeks.

I broke my neck. Bruised the fuck out of every single part of my face and woke up with a total loss of my short-term memory.

But the worst injury of all? When my sisters and parents tell me that Dallas didn't make it. Instantly, I knew that no amount of medicine, bandages, treatment, anything, would ever heal the pain in my heart.

For weeks on end, despite the progress I made my body was utterly numb. I had no emotion, no feelings, nothing. Nothing except a gaping hole in my heart—one I feared would last me a lifetime. People came to visit me daily, trying to brighten my spirits the best they could. Amongst those guests was Heidi—Dallas's long-term partner.

It was hell seeing her. I could hardly look at her. I mean, how could I? I was the reason Dallas had been driving that night. I was the reason they were no longer together.

I'm surprised that when I do finally make eye contact with her, there isn't overwhelming anger on her face like I'd anticipated. It's just sadness as she pulls me in for a hug.

"I'm so sorry, Heidi," I repeat over and over again, squeezing my eyes shut so tight that I'm seeing stars. "I'm so, so sorry."

"Dakota, stop." She soothes me as I cry into her shoulder. "It's okay," she whispers shakily. "It's okay."

"It's not okay." I look at her with blurred eyes. She knows it's not okay. Nothing about what had happened was okay, and it never would be again. Dallas was gone. My brother. My best friend. Gone.

For a while, Heidi and I sit together. Sometimes in silence, sometimes talking about things that make no sense in the grand scheme of all the trauma. But grief doesn't make sense. Nothing about it is linear. Everything is confusing.

"You know, Dallas called me right before you guys got on the road," Heidi speaks up.

I try to re-jog the memory, even though I was drunk as hell and the impact of the accident has left my mind spotty.

"What did he say?" I can't help but ask.

Heidi flashes me a faint smile. "You really want to know?"

"More than anything."

As she reaches for her side, she pulls an envelope from her bag and hands it to me.

"What's this?" I stall, toying with the paper.

"Open it," she prompts me. "C'mon, open it."

Reluctantly, I lift the flaps on either side of the envelope, pulling out what appears to be an open-ended one-way plane ticket to New York City. As my eyes scan the words, the memory of mine and Dallas's conversation comes flooding back to me.

"He told you?"

Heidi plants herself onto my hospital bed. "I don't know exactly what you two talked about, but I do know it meant something to him." She brushes some hair behind her ear. "He asked if I could book a one-way ticket to New York City, right then and there. I didn't dare question it. I knew it must've been for you." A few tears slip from her eyes as she smiles and wipes them away with the palm of her hand.

My head falls back onto the pillow. I have no words. No words, except for, what did I do to deserve him as a brother, and why did the universe decide to take him and not me? He was the angel. He was the good out of the two of us. So why am I the one that's still here?

"You need to go." Heidi places her gentle hand on my shoulder. "You need to do this for him."

"I can't." I start to tear up again as I shake my head profusely. "I'm not ready."

"You've always been ready, Dakota." She reaches to rub along my cheek. "Dallas believed in you. Please, go make him proud."

"Go make him proud." I finish saying the exact same four words to Iris, whose blue eyes are riddled with sadness and heartbreak as she looks up at me.

It's the type of sadness that makes me believe that she's also been struck by the loss of someone she loves. It's a grief like no other—and as much as I hate the feeling, at this moment, I can't help but want to take it away from her. I would do that. I would.

"Dakota," she says my name, and it's refreshing to finally

hear her voice, considering all I've listened to is my own for the past hour.

"So, that's the tattoo." I cut her off, placing her whole palm over the top of it. I never realized just how warm her touch was, and it causes a lump in my throat that I have to forcefully swallow down. "Now you know. Dallas is always with me. We're on this journey *together*."

Her glazed eyes peer up at me once more. I've never been this close to her for so long, and truthfully, I don't know how to comprehend the fact that she's allowed me to.

Her face gives me no indication of where we go from here—what sharing all of this meant. Instead, she remains silent for a brief moment before leaning up and planting a slow, tender kiss on my cheek.

I swear I stop breathing. Her touch lingers for a final moment, and before I can even rationalize her action, she pulls back.

"Thank you for telling me." Her words follow a trail of unaccounted-for emotions. "For trusting me. Dallas would be really proud." Her voice is as soft as her eyes sweet as she looks up at me. Her words bring a soft smile to my own lips as I nod, finding it difficult to look away from her. "We should probably get some sleep," she suggests faintly.

I nod in response, still overwhelmed by the sheer impact of her lips—a part of her body I never thought I'd feel the touch of. "Sure," I speak softly, unable to formulate anything else. "Good night, Iris."

"Good night, Dakota," she repeats, turning onto her side as her hair flows down her back.

A Recipe for Disaster

Momentarily I stare at her, watching her body rise and fall with each breath in and out. There's no oxygen left in this room. All I can breathe in is her.

I stir, knowing that I can't stay here any longer. Shifting my legs, I sit up from the bed and trek back into my own.

"Stay." I hear her voice whisper, her hand wrapping around my wrist. "You…you can stay."

Even in the face of complete uncertainty, I don't debate the thought. In fact, I say nothing except hum out a faint sound that I'm not even sure constitutes as a response.

There's no way I can go back to sleep with this conflicting emotion that's taken over every sense of my being.

It's an emotion that unveils a harsh truth. The truth is that my plan not to fall for Iris Hammond was doomed from the start.

Why?

Because you can't fall for someone you've been down for the whole time.

Oh, Dakota, what a mess you've gotten yourself into.

Twenty

IRIS

I wake up alone in bed, with no sign of Dakota in the room. It's just after seven o'clock in the morning, and the next round of competition is set to start in an hour.

Thankfully, after the events that transpired last night, I managed to get a bit of extra sleep. But as I run my hands through my soapy hair in the shower, all I can think about is Dakota and how wrong I've been about him this whole time.

Despite my prior judgment, Dakota has a heart. A damaged one, but it's there, and it beats, and boy, did it beat when I kissed him on the cheek last night. It's an action that I can't seem to rationalize as much as I can't seem to make sense of. That, and the fact that I asked him to stay.

Stay.

The word felt foreign, strange, yet fitting.

But that's our theme, isn't it? Not many things between us seem to make sense. But last night, our conversation, the *kiss*… that did, and above all else, I don't regret it. I don't regret it one bit.

I push the complication that is him to the side, thinking back to the one regret that kept me stirring. The fact that in opening up, I came to realize that my actions towards Susanna and Travis may have potentially hurt them over the years. Perhaps the reason why I've been so insistent on using the word "step" before I refer to both of them, is because removing it makes it all too real.

Calling Susanna my mom means I'm accepting that she *has* been for most of my life. Calling Travis my brother means that our families are actually blended. All the while, it feels like I'm letting go of the fact that there's still a piece of me longing for my mom to return. Even though it's been 21 years, I can't deny that there is still hope.

I turn off the shower, reach for a towel on the rack, and wipe down my body before staring into the mirror. I want to let out a boisterous scream. I really do. Maybe a scream will release all the stress in my mind, this newfound version of Dakota I've come to learn, and the anxiety of today's competition. But then I have to remember, I'm in a hotel room and not the streets of New York City.

Instead, I decide that it's crunch time. No more distractions, and no more thinking about the past when I have a future to work for. I came here for a reason.

After I thrown on my chef's coat, I walk out to the balcony for a breath of fresh air. And as I scan along the beach, that's where I see Dakota, running, shirtless with sweat beading down his forehead and glistening off his chest.

Seriously?

He really had to do that the second I decided no more distractions. I swiftly close the curtains shut, rush to the door, and head straight down to the competition.

Right now, avoidance sounds like the best plausible plan.

DAKOTA

I'd love for someone to explain why my first thought this morning was to go on a run. I never run. I hate running and any form of physical exercise that doesn't involve a woman and a bed.

But as I looked down at her asleep by my side, there was nothing else I could think of than to run off whatever emotion I've been desperately holding out on. I'm really on my last straw here.

If Dallas could see me right now, he'd be laughing his ass off. Saying something like, "you're really whipped for this girl, aren't you?" I mean, he wouldn't be wrong—I rub my wrist at the thought.

Before last night, I'd never told anyone entirely about what happened with him, especially not to that level of detail. It had always been too painful, too triggering, but last night I couldn't help myself. Iris brings out that side of me. A side that makes me want to push her away as much as I want to pull her in.

Are things changing? Was I wrong to leave her this morning? I can't decide. All I can do is continue to run. I've run so long that I can't remember when I started.

I look down at my watch, seeing that it's only an hour until the competition starts. "Crap," I mutter, picking up my pace before rushing back to the hotel lobby and into the room.

Will she still be here? Will she want to bring up last night? Or

A Recipe for Disaster

are we just forgetting that anything ever happened? I've never felt so flustered...so confused in my life.

I stride my way into the bedroom, and immediately I know that I don't need to call out her name to figure out that she's not here. She's not. For her presence within any room is always known. I can always tell when she's not around from the absence that fills me when she's gone.

"Snap out of it, Dakota," I find myself in the bathroom, instructing my reflection in the mirror. "You're here for a reason, and don't fuck it up."

"Is this thing on?" Bruno repeatedly taps into the mic, forcing the echoing sound of his touch to radiate throughout the speakers.

"It's on!" Someone shouts from the crowd as a smile forms on his lips.

"Well then." He secures the microphone between his hands. "Hello, everyone. Are you excited to kick off the next round of the competition?"

An abundance of cheers erupts throughout the space as everyone's attention turns to the stage, yet I can't stop my eyes from scanning the crowd, hoping to find Iris.

It only takes me a few minutes of searching until I catch a glimpse of her red hair. Of course, she's right up at the front of the stage, listening as intently as ever. There's no doubt in my mind that she will make it to the finals. No doubt. The doubt, however, starts to creep in on whether or not I have what it takes to be up there with her. Hell, can I even make it to the top 50 today?

"You might be wondering why you aren't starting today's competition at a designated workstation," Bruno announces. "The reason is that today's competition comes with a twist. Before you arrived, the judges and I equipped each workstation with a unique culinary tool that you will be randomly assigned to use. You will each draw a number individually, indicating which workstation you will work from. Make sense?"

A few heads nod in agreement, along with some panicked looks. I've never been that great at trying out new tools, but I've always been one for problem-solving and I'm certain that whatever gets thrown my way, I'll be able to figure it out.

"Please form a single file line. Once you select your number, you must walk to your designated workstation and wait for the next steps."

The crowd does as told and it takes a few minutes of waiting before I can even reach the front.

When I do, Colbie dips her hand inside a bowl full of small, folded pieces of paper and displays the number seven.

"You're just over to the left, Foster." She points. "And it looks like your friend is too."

I glance over to the station beside mine, where not only do I see Iris, but we exchange stares for the first time since last night. The encounter is awkward—I think we're both unsure of what's going on between us, but one thing is for sure, Sean's picked up on our interaction and doesn't seem to like it.

"Is everything okay?" He pats me on the back a little too firmly as I snap my head in his direction.

"Of course." I brush him off, my heart pounding out of my chest. "Everything's good," I lie before heading to the station beside Iris's.

"Hey," I say casually as I tuck myself in, debating what else can be said right about now. We'd exhausted everything last night.

"Hi," she mumbles back to me, just as clumsily. I've never seen her unsure before. She's always a ray of confidence, yet now she seems almost avoidant. We must be the only two people in the world to have a heart-to-heart that only pushes us further away than pulling us both in.

"What are the odds, huh?" I can't help but speak, the silence deafening me as I fasten my apron around my waist.

"I'm not surprised." She nervously toys with her hands behind her back. "Not surprised one bit."

I purse my lips. "And why's that?" I wonder.

She finally turns to look at me, making direct eye contact. "We can't seem to escape one another." She releases a breath, biting her lower lip. "Can we, Dakota?"

"I guess we can't." My voice fades into nothing as the microphone turns back on.

"Competitors!" Sean announces, breaking us free from one another. "Here's today's instructions. In front of you, you will find a basket. Inside that basket is a unique culinary tool you will need to use in some way, shape or form to create a harvest-inspired dish of your choosing. You'll have two hours to create your dish and prepare it for presentation along with a taste test from the judging panel. Does everyone understand?"

The crowd nods their heads, as do Iris and I, as we momentarily glance at one another for what appears to be reassurance.

"You good?" I say to her.

She nods. "You good?" she mouths back to me.

"Of course," I admit, prompting a half smile on her end before I divert my attention back onto the stage.

Sean.

He's staring right at the two of us, this time as intent as can be. Even from 50 yards away, I can see a sense of jealousy wash over his eyes.

Jealous over what, that I'm not entirely sure. But what I do know is that I know a jealous man when I see one. I've been one all week when it comes to him and Iris, as much as I hate to admit it.

"Well then…" Sean clenches his jaw, his voice turning serious. "Let the competition begin, shall we?" He looks directly at me as he says it.

I shoot him a confident stare as the buzzer goes off, signifying that the competition has begun.

If I'm being honest, I couldn't care less if Sean is jealous. He's dug his own grave when it comes to Iris, and frankly, I don't mind sealing the coffin shut. My only concern now becomes how will his jealousy translate into his scoring. Lord knows Sean thinks with his downstairs Dellan when it comes to women and probably his heart when it comes to anyone who hurts his fragile feelings. This better not come back to bite me in the ass when nothing has even happened between me and Iris.

A Recipe for Disaster

I reach for the box in front of me, pulling out what appears to be an immersion blender tool. It's an item that immediately prompts a memory to come to mind as I'm transported back to my youth.

"*How much longer till we get there?*" *I complain as the four of us are cramped into the backseat of Grandpa's pick-up truck.*

"*Dakota, can you stop complaining?*" *Savannah flicks my ear in annoyance.* "*You're so whiny all the time.*"

"*Hey!*" *Dallas's voice inflicts with conviction.* "*Don't talk to my brother that way!*"

"*He's our brother too,*" *Charlotte remarks, sticking her tongue out.*

"*Yeah, but he's my twin brother, which makes him more of a brother to me than to you,*" *he protests, looking her up and down.*

"*We're here!*" *Grandma announces, perfectly timed, as we pull into an unpaved local family farm parking lot. The car bounces through the uneven ground as we all shift together in laughter—already forgetting about our fight.*

"*Get out slowly,*" *Grandpa instructs. We do the opposite, rushing out of the car and straight into the pumpkin patch.*

Charlotte's 13. Savannah's 11, and Dallas and I are nine. Mom and Dad wanted us all to be close in age so that we were friends, but considering it was two girls, then two boys, all it's done is pin us up against one another.

"*I bet I can beat you in a race to that pumpkin,*" *Dallas challenges me, and before we know it, we've run to the other side of the patch. Dallas beats me, of course. He's always been the faster of the two of us, but I'm taller, so technically, I win because that gives me something to tease him about.*

"*Boys, come back over here!*" *Grandpa shouts.* "*You each need to choose your own pumpkin.*"

"*Hmmm…*" *Charlotte reaches for a pumpkin filled with warts and* dents. "I want this one!"

Dallas and I shoot a look of disgust at one another. "That's the ugliest pumpkin I've ever seen!" Dallas torments her as I start to snicker. I'm always the instigator.

Charlotte gives us the middle finger causing us both to act like she's just committed a federal crime. The worst part, Grandma and Grandpa don't even see, and Dallas and I both know better than to tattle when there's no proof.

"Beauty is in imperfection," Charlotte tells us as Grandpa lifts her questionable pumpkin into the wheelbarrow. We both shake our head's considering Charlotte is in her "I'm an alternative teen," phase.

"Savannah?" Grandma calls out. "Which one are you choosing, honey?"

"I like this one." Savannah chooses the pumpkin I had my eye on.

"No, Savannah!" I snatch it from her hands. "That's the one I wanted!"

"Well, I saw it first!" She yanks it back. "So, that means it's mine!"

"No, it's mine!" We fight back and forth as Grandma reaches in to separate the two of us.

"Okay, okay, you two." She kneels down. "Dakota, Savannah found it first, okay? You can find another one."

"But I wanted that one!" I frown, my emotions all over the place. "It's the best pumpkin in the entire world."

Grandma sighs as she looks over to Savannah, whose already proudly loaded the pumpkin into the wheelbarrow, while Grandpa helps Dallas choose his.

"How about this," Grandma proposes, taking my hand. "You and me, we can go and choose something from inside the shop. I have to pick up some things anyway. Hm? What do you say?"

The frown immediately dissipates from my face as I interlace my hand with Grandma's. Getting an item from the shop is way better, all considering

A Recipe for Disaster

Dallas will let me carve his pumpkin with him anyway.

"Okay then." Grandma kisses my forehead, announcing to Grandpa that we're heading into the shop.

"Hey! That's not fair!" Savannah and Charlotte pout as Dallas finds contentment atop Grandpa's shoulders.

"Uh-uh," Grandma scolds them. "You girls can pick something else out from the patch. That's the deal."

Grandma's always been a good mediator between us four. "C'mon, Dakota." She guides me into the shop as I mumble, "stop being so whiny," to the girls as I pass by.

The shop has a grocery section, which Grandma gravitates towards, selecting a mixture of items, one of which is an oblong-shaped vegetable.

"What is that?" I ask her, intrigued.

She smiles, raising it out of her basket. "Oh, this? It's butternut squash. It's cool looking, right?"

I nod enthusiastically.

"I'm going to make a soup out of it tonight," she tells me. "It'll be delicious."

"A soup?" I question. "Out of that? Really?"

"Mhm." She nods. "So…" She appears, ready to head to the checkout. "Decided what you want yet?"

I think for a moment before I rush back and across the store, re-emerging with a butternut squash of my own.

"A squash as well?" she laughs with a hand on either hip. "Is that really what you want?"

"I want to make the soup with you, too," I tell her. "Can I? Please."

"Darling boy." She takes it from my hands, kissing me on the forehead. "Of course, you can."

That night, while everyone has a game night with Grandpa, I follow Grandma's every move as she prepares the soup. She starts by roasting the butternut squash with some shallots on a baking sheet before pulling it out of the oven.

"What now?" I ask as she reaches into one of her cabinets, pulling out a tool I've never seen before.

Grandma is full of surprises.

"It's called an immersion blender," she explains. "It's to puree the roasted squash. Here." She hands it over to me. "You take the lead. I'll just make sure it stays put." She places her hand over top of mine as I blend the squash into a bowl, followed by completing every other step involved in making Grandma's infamous soup.

"This is amazing!" Grandpa gleams with delight at the dinner table.

"I have to admit, it's super yummy!" Charlotte chimes in, prompting Savannah and Dallas to agree.

"Thanks." Grandma smiles, playfully nudging my shoulder. "It's mine and Dakota's secret recipe. Isn't that right?"

I nod proudly. "That's right."

"So, figured out what you're making yet?" Bruno pulls me out of my flashback as he and the other judges guide their way over to my workstation.

"That I have." I nod in assurance. All but Sean are receptive to my response and move along, leaving him and I to face one another briefly.

"Like what you see?" I mock, unsure why he's intricately surveying me up and down.

"What's going on with you and Iris?" He bypasses the comment, wasting no time jumping straight into a confrontation.

A Recipe for Disaster

"Me and Iris?" I say quietly, considering she's only a few feet away. "I'm not sure what you're talking about."

"Is that right?" He stares blankly at me, unbelieving of my words. "You do know that Iris likes me, and I like her, right?" He straightens his spine, tilting his chin up.

"Really?" I don't back down at his pitiful attempt to tower over me. "Well, it didn't seem that way yesterday."

Sean cocks a brow. "Excuse me?"

"You don't need to pretend." I fold my arms across my chest. "I saw the way you had your eyes all over Colbie, not to mention the way she *so conveniently.*" I put the words into air quotes. "Fell into your lap. It's clear something is going on between two of you."

Before Sean can respond, Bruno calls out his name, instructing him to join them as they make their rounds.

"I'll be there in a second," Sean responds before he looks back at me. It's visible that my words just irked him. "You know, Dakota," he pauses. "You wouldn't want to make any accusations now, would you?" He tilts his head and tucks his hand into his pocket. "After all, I'd hate for you not to make it far in this competition."

I grind my teeth together as he mockingly frowns.

Fuck this guy.

"Let's just say if you know what's good for you, then you won't throw a wrench into Iris and me." He takes a few steps ahead before stopping a final time. "Good luck, Dakota," he slyly remarks. "'Cause you're sure as hell going to need it."

Twenty-One

IRIS

This couldn't have turned out any worse. A pasta maker? Really? I pride myself in being able to use a plethora of kitchen tools, but a pasta maker, I can't seem to figure out for the life of me.

I was first introduced to the dreaded tool when my culinary class and I embarked on a tour of Italy. I'd never been to Europe before. Rather than learning how to cook, I was more hyper-fixated on the sites around me—one of which was our culinary instructor in Venice—Giovanni Romano, whose job was to teach our class how to make the perfect pasta from scratch.

Unfortunately, around this time, I was in my boy-obsessed phase and spent the duration of the class learning the way around Giovanni and not the tool itself. My love-hate relationship with the device fizzled out once we returned home, and since then, I've never once had to use it until now.

"Dammit," I mutter under my breath as the memory fades into the distance.

What did everyone else get? I peer across the room to see tools such as a food processor, air fryer, and blender. The list of simplistic appliances goes on until I look over my shoulder, only to see that Dakota has pulled an immersion blender out of his basket.

I let out a pained sigh. I could do so many things with that tool instead, but low and behold, here I am. Trying to come to the stark reality that if this is what fate has selected for me, then this is what I've got to work with.

I should've listened to Giovanni Romano.

On the bright side, making homemade pasta is simple—flour, eggs, oil, and salt. Easy. The hard part becomes making this dish harvest inspired.

I briefly place a hand on my forehead, rubbing it in thought, until my attention is diverted to the judges that work their way towards my booth, following what appeared to be their brief encounter with Dakota.

"Iris!" Bruno smiles cheerfully, rubbing his hands together. "Oh! It looks like you've got the pasta maker. You do know how to use one, right?" he gestures. "Every great chef does."

Oh well, that's just splendid.

"But of course, Bruno." I smile enthusiastically through the pain, lying through my teeth. *Fake it till you make it.* Bruno accepts my truth as Sean is the last to join in on our conversation.

"Of course, she'd know how to use it, Bruno," Sean sings my praises. "We've got to watch out for this one you know. She might be the top one here." Sean points at me, shooting me a wink before diverting his attention to the judging panel.

The redness rushes to my cheeks at his flattery. Flattery that Colbie doesn't seem to take lightly, as an apparent glare forms on her face—a glare that only shifts once she realizes that I'm staring directly right at her.

"Ha ha." She fakes a laugh. "Girl power!" She raises her fist into the air, clearly trying to mitigate the look.

I nod reluctantly, going along with this mixed-emotion conversation until I catch a glimpse of a bracelet on her wrist. It's subtle, dainty and is encompassed with daisies all throughout.

"Hey, Colbie," I speak before she braces herself away from my station. "I really like your bracelet," I compliment, hopeful to get on her good side.

She places her hand directly on top of it. "Oh, this?" She twists it around as I analyze the pearls that make up each delicate petal. "Thanks so much. It was a gift. It reminds me of my restaurant—Daisy Dekes."

I nod, catching the reference. "Well, it's beautiful," I manage to say before she walks over to the next station and leaves Sean trailing behind.

"Good luck," he reassuringly whispers to me. "You'll do great."

I force out a smile until Sean too falls out of sight, and I sink my head back down in confusion.

What am I going to do?

"C'mon." I twist the handle yet again, but the pasta dough refuses to make its way through. Instead, the handle falls off entirely.

Heat now rises to my cheeks as stress overwhelms my body.

A Recipe for Disaster

Only 30 minutes remain on the clock, and although my mind has been in complete and total chaos, I've at least managed to figure out that I'm making a pumpkin and cheese stuffed ravioli for my harvest dish.

The filling and sauce were simple enough to make, and thankfully, fresh pasta only takes a few minutes to get to al-dente once it's been added to the boiling water. But to even get to that stage, one massive hurdle still stands in my way. I need to thinly roll out this dough.

Ugh. Life would be so much simpler if I could just use a rolling pin and have done with it, but no, this pasta maker continues to torment me with every attempt.

"You stupid piece of crap!" I smack it as I try to reconnect the handle. "Get on!"

"You alright over there?" I look up at Dakota's concerned voice. He's stirring what appears to be a soup on his stovetop, with a fresh batch of biscuits rising in the oven to his right.

"No!" I huff in frustration. "Things are not alright. This machine is a nightmare. It's not working!"

"Well, do you know how to use it?" Dakota blatantly responds, dipping a plastic spoon into his soup to taste it before he tosses it into the garbage.

I debate whether or not to tell him the truth. But as I look over to see that the judges, Sean included, are out of sight and out of earshot, I decide to continue this theme of forthcoming we have between us.

"No," I groan quietly. "I don't, and don't you dare tease me about it, okay? I'm stressed out enough right now."

Dakota's eyes soften as he scans the room, reducing his stove top to a simmer as he reaches across his workstation to take the pasta maker out of my hands and place it into his own.

"Dakota!" I say far too loudly. "What are you doing?"

"Shh," he instructs me with glaring eyes, placing a single finger on his lips. "I'm just trying to help." He fiddles with the handle. "Let me fix it."

"No, stop," I scold him. "We're going to get in trouble, and I don't want to get disqualified—"

The handle snaps back into place as Dakota peers up at me with amusement. "Told you I could fix it."

"Oh, thank gosh," I mutter, quickly taking back the machine. "But…with one problem solved," I sigh. "I'm still left with another."

He leans in. "Which is?"

"That I don't know how to use it!"

"Well, for starters," Dakota's voice commands my attention. "You've got it on too thin of a setting. You've got to start a bit wider so that the dough can go through, then you go smaller as it gets thinner. Twist the knob."

I place my hand over the top of the knob he's referring to. "This one?"

"That's right." He nods, rushing back to his stove top to stir his soup again. "See how the slot gets bigger and smaller when you twist it?"

I fiddle with the feature as it does just that, twisting it open so that the dough can securely fit inside as I crank the handle.

"Looks like you've got it," Dakota says as the dough goes

through seamlessly.

"Thank you," I say to him, only as I do, he looks away. The judging panel are now making their rounds yet again.

"It's looking good over here." Sean smiles as Colbie and Bruno walk ahead. "And I'm not just talking about the food."

I'm taken aback by his sudden forwardness. Why is Sean acting like this? He did say yesterday after parasailing that he'd make it up to me but, is this his way of doing that?

In my peripherals, I can see Dakota following our exchange before he looks away and heads back towards his oven, pulling out his biscuits and placing them on the cooling rack.

"Don't make my head get too big now," I joke, smiling back up at Sean as I try to play along with his comment.

He smirks. "Are we still on for tonight?" he asks, a bit too loudly, as I glare at him.

Wasn't this supposed to be on the down low?

Sean doesn't seem to care, though, and carries on anyway. "Does nine work for you?" he suggests.

I gulp at the thought yet somehow manage to nod simultaneously. "Nine is good."

Sean winks before he glances back at Dakota. "Can't wait."

"Everyone, thank you for another wonderful day of competition," Colbie announces into the microphone. "After tasting your dishes and judging them as per today's challenge requirements, the judges and I have made some decisions."

I nervously toy with the cuff of my sleeve as I stand in the crowd, anxiously waiting for the results to appear on the screen. Today was one of the most challenging competition days I've had. Not only did it leave me with an abundance of stress, but it also left me with an overhaul of questions, all of which surround why Sean is acting so off—so different.

As I peer to my right, Dakota stands out in the crowd. Without him, today would've been a disaster, and for the first time, I can't help but feel some ounce of gratitude for his involvement. Yet on the flip side, I need to win this competition all by myself. No handouts. No free passes. Just me, myself and I.

"On screen, you will see the names of the top fifty contestants going through to tomorrow's three-part finale, where we will crown the winner of The Art of Cooking competition," Bruno cheers, as does the crowd before the moment of truth is revealed.

I can't believe my eyes. Once the results appear, I scan the screen, subconsciously searching for Dakota's name before my own. It takes me a second to find it, but when I do, I'm gob smacked.

Forty-ninth.

What?

I dart my head in his direction before I look for my name, an action he seems to mimic just the same.

As I analyze his face, the look I see isn't of defeat. It's that of frustration as he shoots Sean a scowl before storming out of the venue.

For some reason, I feel compelled to go after him but decide otherwise. Now, Sean's found me in the crowd and is mouthing "good job."

I remember that I still haven't checked the screen.

10th place: Iris Hammond—The Sweet Red.

How is this possible?

There's not enough time to process the thought, Sean's voice pulls me back in. "To our top fifty, congratulations! You are amongst some of the most prestigious chefs in America, and tonight, we'd like to celebrate that. So, join us tonight for drinks and food on behalf of The Culinary Committee of the United States, and get prepared. Tomorrow, your future awaits!"

Twenty-Two

DAKOTA

I hate him.

He sees Iris, and I exchange some *meaningless* glances, and he gives me forty-ninth place? Are you kidding? He's sending me a message, and boy, is it loud and clear. I can't imagine what he would've done had he known Iris and I slept together last night. Well, not like that…but you know what I mean.

Not only was the shock was all over my own face, but it was plastered across Iris' when they announced it on the screen.

Was my dish that bad? It was a family recipe, the perfect culmination of the tool given to me and the theme of the challenge.

No.

The dish wasn't that bad. Sean's just a total dickhead who's had his ego rocked. He's trying to make his intentions clear, his comment about how he's meeting up with Iris tonight that he proudly announced so that I could hear confirms it.

I'm mad.

Frustrated.

I've made it through to the finals, but that doesn't appease me one bit. I still have a lot of work to get to the top of this thing, and with one of the judges out of my favor, should I already start counting myself out?

I have to cleanse my mind of the stupidity that that thought possesses. I'm being irrational—idiotic. My judgment is swayed, twisted, delusional and I'm folding, just like I feared the second I let Iris in. I can no longer think about the competition right now. It's impossible to think about the competition when all I can think about is just how perfect Iris looked earlier as she stood in front of the mirror and applied a crap-ton of makeup products to her face—products that I don't need to know the names of to know that she doesn't need. Iris Hammond is perfect. Even bare faced at three AM, crying in the middle of the night, she's beautiful.

Sean hasn't seen her like that, and I can't help but wonder how many people have. Yet, she doesn't know it. Iris doesn't know quite how impactful she is on every single person around her. That's why it pisses me off so much when she asks, "do I look alright?" As we exit the room and enter the elevator.

"Yeah," I say bluntly. Our conversations have remained minimal since the competition. She, likely too stressed to talk about last night or my score, and me, knowing that if I do speak, all I'll be able to do is completely word vomit that Iris is the most perfect woman I've ever seen.

If I thought I loved that purple dress she wore the night we arrived, then I'm obsessed with the one she's wearing right now. It's red, a color that has become my favorite somewhere along the way. It draws out the depth of her hair and the blue in her eyes. It's a show-stopping piece, and she knows it, but why she needs my approval is beyond me.

"Do you think Sean will like it?" She asks me through one of the mirrors that surrounds the elevator.

I glare over at her, refusing to entertain this conversation. I think Iris knows what she's doing and how I feel about Sean.

How would she feel if she knew Sean threatened to eliminate me from the competition if I spilled the beans about my accusation of him and Colbie? I'd never seen someone get so agitated by a comment, especially if the said comment wasn't true. The truth about Sean will come out. I'm certain of it. I just don't want Iris to be a part of the collateral damage.

She notices my shift in expression as she takes in my less-than-approving gaze and reaches to her side. "Shit," she mutters as we reach the lobby.

"What?" I can't help but ask. "What's wrong?"

"My bag," she huffs, clicking six yet again on the elevator panel. "I left it in the room."

"I'll get it," I tell her, holding the elevator door open.

"Are you sure?" She doesn't seem to rebut the thought, one that earlier in the week, I know she very well would've.

Oh, how things have changed.

Sure, we're not fighting like we used to, but this tension between us has only gotten worse.

"Yeah." I nod. "Besides, I left my jacket in the room." I'm lying, but Iris doesn't pick up on it. "I'll get it for you, don't worry."

She pauses momentarily, analyzing my face as if she wants to speak when someone outside the elevator calls out her name.

"Go." I tilt my chin upwards, signaling for her to exit. "I'll grab it, okay?"

She faintly nods before she scurries out, leaving the doors to close immediately as I ascend.

Once the elevator reaches the sixth floor, I walk down the hallway toward the room. For a second, I run into Granny and Grandpa, the two swingers who were adamant about having Iris stay with them earlier on the trip.

Frankly, I'm surprised that they haven't knocked on our door to invite us both over. Of course, that would never happen, but the look on Iris's face if it did? *Priceless.*

As I reach into my back pocket for my key card, I catch a glimpse of Sean walking out of a room down the hallway. I thought he was on the eighth floor? At least that's where Iris and I billed the room service to last night.

"Oh, don't be such a prude!" A mop of blonde hair and long legs follow him outside the room. "Just one more, please?"

"Fine." Sean leans in to kiss her lips. "But I've got to go, okay, I'm already late—"

The kiss escalates as her hands cascade along his blazer, prompting Sean to pin the woman up against the door, his hands trailing up her skirt. And that's when I see it.

It's *Colbie.*

Colbie Carmichael.

Are you fucking kidding me?

I knew it.

For a moment I debate my options. Do I act as if I saw nothing and blackmail Sean in return? Or do I end this and rush to tell Iris immediately—despite the repercussions?

My heart decides the latter before my brain can even process the best feasible option as I abruptly clear my throat.

Without skipping a beat, Sean releases Colbie from his embrace and with wide eyes, his face drops when he realizes who he's looking at.

Me.

"Oh...hey Foster." Sean awkwardly adjusts the collar of his shirt as Colbie shies her face away so that it's out of view, but it's too late. The damage is done. I've seen enough. More than enough.

What did these two think was going to happen? They're kissing in the hallway of the hotel where all the contestants are staying. Did they really not think anyone would see?

Sean is a downright idiot, so that was likely his thinking. And as much as I respect Colbie for her expertise in the culinary world, I can't respect her choice of men or decision-making at this moment, just like how I can't let Iris be the next one to fall into his trap.

I ignore Sean's continual stare and lift my key card against the lock, pushing through the door as I search for Iris's bag. There's no way I'm letting her be around that guy tonight. No way.

IRIS

It's been over half an hour, and Dakota still hasn't come down with my purse, and although I'm surrounded by the celebrations of making it to the finals, I can't help but worry if he's okay, but at the same time, question if that's even my place to wonder.

A Recipe for Disaster

I know I probably shouldn't have mentioned anything about Sean to Dakota in the elevator. The subject is touchy enough, considering I know Dakota knows I'm waiting for Sean tonight at the bar. He's terrible at eavesdropping and even worse at hiding his emotions.

Thinking of Sean only as a tangent to Dakota reminds me that he, too, is late. He said he would meet me at nine. It's almost ten. Did he really stand me up?

"Iris!" Sean calls out my name, spotting me by the bar and parading his way over. "Hey!" He leans in to kiss my cheek, reviving the hope that was just lost.

"Hey…" I'm taken aback by his affectionate touch.

"You look beautiful tonight." He plants himself beside me, slightly out of breath as he scans the space around him.

"Thanks." I blush. "But are you alright? You seem a bit flustered. Did you run down here?"

"Yeah." Sean waves to call down the bartender. "I did, actually. I knew I was late and didn't want to keep you waiting any longer. Besides, the elevator was occupied."

I half nod, accepting his answer as he orders a drink for the two of us, one that I'm praying isn't like the swamp water from last time.

"The competition was fun today, don't you think?" Sean remarks.

I try not to roll my eyes. "Sure, I guess *fun* is an acceptable word." Even though nothing about nearly crying over pasta is remotely fun.

"You did amazing," Sean praises me as the bartender delivers our drinks. "Cheers to the finals!" He raises his glass as we connect them together.

"Cheers," I take a sip. This time, the drink is digestible. "But forty-ninth for Dakota?" I can't help but feel irked about his score from earlier. "What was that about? Surely his dish wasn't that bad."

Sean's expression shifts at my mention of him. His eyes narrowed; his posture taller. "Must've just been an off day…" He connects his glass to his lips. "Hopefully tomorrow will be better."

I awkwardly sip on my drink, nodding in agreement despite knowing that today definitely wasn't an off day for Dakota. Not only did he prepare what seemed to be a top-tier dish, but he helped me out in the process.

Despite feeling unsatisfied by Sean's justification, his mention of tomorrow prompts further questions. "Speaking of which, any chance you can give me insight on what to expect tomorrow?" I pry. "I'm kind of on the edge of my seat waiting here."

Sean smirks. "Ansty now, aren't we?"

"I suppose you could say that." I try to feed into the sexually suggestive nature that seems to be going on between us.

"Well…" Sean leans in closer. "I'm sure I can tell you a few things. But some may require a bit of persuasion if you know what I'm talking about."

"I think I'm picking up what you're putting down—"

"Iris!" I hear Dakota call out my name right in time to interrupt my conversation with Sean—a very leading conversation, might I add.

I jolt my head away from Sean, locking eyes with Dakota,

who makes his way through the crowd—determination plastered all over his face. "I need to talk to you," he demands once he finally reaches me. "Now!"

I look over at Sean, who refuses to make eye contact with Dakota for reasons I can't explain.

"Can we talk later?" I grind my teeth. "I'm kind of in the middle of something."

"No," Dakota insists, swallowing deeply. "I need to speak to you now. It can't wait."

I can see the strain in his eyes, forcing a pit to form in my stomach. The pit tells me that whatever he needs to talk to me about is important.

"I'll be back." I place a hand on Sean's wrist. "Okay?"

Sean hardly nods, finally making eye contact with Dakota, who shoots him a daunting glare as he wastes no time pulling on my wrist to drag me as far away from Sean as possible.

"Slow down!" I tell him as we work our way through the crowd and out of the bar. "Dakota!" I snatch my arm away from his grasp as we reach the front lobby. "What are you doing? What is going on?"

"Don't you dare go anywhere with him," he frantically speaks. "Do you hear me?"

"Excuse me?" I retaliate, frustrated that he thinks he has any right to tell me what I can and can't do.

"Iris," he stutters, running his hand through his messy hair. "I know you think you like Sean for reasons I can't explain. But he's not a good guy. He isn't."

I can't rationalize his words. Instead, I can only remember

him saying the same thing last night.

"Didn't you tell me *you* weren't a good guy?" I throw his words back in his face and immediately regret it as I see the sting in his eyes.

"Sean and I are nothing alike. Absolutely nothing. I'm a better guy than him," Dakota snaps.

"Oh, yeah? How? Enlighten me. How are you such a good guy?" I place my hands on my hips. "Up until yesterday, you've always been an ass."

Dakota sucks in a breath. "If I were such a bad guy, I wouldn't have helped you today!"

I suck in a breath at his reminder—a part of me knew he'd use it against me. Now, as appreciative as I am, I'm angry.

"Plus, I'm not a two-timing scumbag!"

I tilt my head to the side, taken aback by his words. "What?" My voice is full of disbelief. "What in the world are you talking about?"

"Colbie," he reminds me. "Sean's seeing Colbie."

I cross my arms. "This again? You have no proof, Dakota. You saw a couple meaningless glances and are reading too much into it!"

"They were kissing!" he protests, placing a hand on my arm. "I saw them kissing in the hallway when I went back to grab your bag."

I look down at his careful touch, a flutter overwhelming my stomach, scaring me as much as it entices me, prompting me to pull away again.

I calm my breathing. "Listen," I speak. "I know you don't like

Sean. Trust me, you've made that abundantly clear. But lying and making this up?" I say in disbelief. "That's a new low, Dakota."

He takes a step back more. "Why would I lie? Why would I make this up? For what reason? What do I stand to gain from this?"

"Maybe because you don't like that Sean likes me, and I like him back."

He rolls his eyes at my remark, making me go for a low blow instead. "Or maybe," I'm reminded of his earlier comment. "You're jealous."

"'Jealous?'" he repeats back to me. "Jealous of what?"

"Jealous that I scored higher than you today! That's why you're reminding me that you helped me, isn't it? Don't you think I can do things on my own?"

His face falls flat as an eerie silence falls between a once loud lobby. "You know that's not true, Iris," Dakota's voice drops. "Don't be so ridiculous. Why would I be jealous?"

I shake my head. I refuse to entertain this conversation any longer. "Listen, I know we had a moment last night, but that doesn't mean we're suddenly best-friends. Do you understand?"

My hurtful words burn the tip of my tongue as I watch Dakota reluctantly look away.

That was harsh. Too harsh. Why did I say that knowing it was nothing but a lie? How could it not be? Last night held something special…something I refuse to believe as much as I refuse to think about a second longer.

"I was just trying to look out for you," his voice drops like a hurt puppy dog, narrowing in his stare. "Just like I have been doing the entire time we've been here."

I'm left confused by the latter portion of his sentence, but respond anyway. "Well, that was your first mistake," I argue. "I don't need you to look out for me. Just like I didn't need your help today. I would've been just fine without you. I do things on my own. I don't rely on others!"

Dakota takes a step back, pursing his lips. "You know what?" He raises his hands in defeat, revealing the purse I hadn't realized was in his grasp the entire time.

He did actually go and get it.

"You're right," he tells me. "You do whatever you want, Iris. After all, we hate each other, right?" I can hear the betrayal in his voice, and before I can mutter so much as another word, he tosses me my purse. "Let's go back to that."

"Dakota, I—" He pushes past me and towards the staircase and immediately I feel every ounce of suppressed remorse completely take over my body.

Before I can process my next thought, Sean makes his presence known by pulling up beside me and placing his hand on my lower back. "Is everything okay?" he asks in concern.

I nod, even though nothing about what just happened between Dakota and me is okay. I feel awful, regretful, and, for the first time, like I need to go and apologize. I need to make this right.

"Well, in that case…" Sean's touch inches down my spine, while one hand turns my chin, so that we're face to face. "Wanna go upstairs?" he whispers seductively into my ear, planting a wet kiss along my neck. And before I know it, somehow, I'm in the elevator, on my way up to his bedroom.

A Recipe for Disaster

Twenty-Three

DAKOTA

Lying? Why the hell would I lie? What motive would I have to make up everything about Sean? It makes zero sense. But in the same breath, I ask myself, why not just tell Iris the truth—the truth about it all?

The truth about my hotel waitlist interference.

The truth about what Sean really said to me.

It's like I'm clinging on to these easier truths only to help mask the hardest truth of all.

The truth about how she makes me feel.

I'm a fool to think she'd ever want anything more than to hate me. Our heart-to-heart last night meant nothing. That kiss on my cheek was nothing—a simple pity peck, even though the palpitations in my chest told me otherwise.

The reality is, I'm nothing more to Iris than a pain in her ass. That's all I've ever been, and all I ever will be, and frankly, I'm tired.

I'm tired of keeping up with this lifestyle. I thought I was playing her game, but all along I've been the pawn. The reality is it was never the battle between us that exhausted me day by day. It's been the battle that's been going on internally as I deny every nerve ending that dotes on Iris Hammond.

She wins.

I fold.

I can't take this any longer.

Leave. Go. The voice tells me in my mind, despite the fact that the tattoo on my wrist reminds me of the exact reason why I need to stay. I divert my line of vision. I don't care anymore. I can't stay in this hotel a second longer. Nothing can overshadow the torture of knowing that she's two floors above me with him.

Not the prize.

Not the title.

And not my promise to Dallas.

I can no longer play this game.

Now, it's game over.

IRIS

I've hooked up with five guys out of a relationship.

Two in my sophomore year of college, only as a post-break-up rebound.

One in my senior year of college, at a graduation party, where we both got way too drunk off jelly shots and cheap tequila.

Some guy I matched with on a dating app after I realized he wasn't an axe murderer or serial killer—just an accountant that worked off Wall Street.

Auston.

And now, Sean who wastes no time letting me know exactly the reason why he wants to take me upstairs. The second the elevator doors close, he hoists me up against the wall and begins planting firm kisses along my lips and down my neck.

"The elevator," I prompt him, having difficulty falling into a rhythm. "You…you didn't click a number."

He carries me over to the wall where the buttons are. Smacking his hand against the number eight before that same hand caresses my hair.

"I've been waiting for you all week." His touch intensifies as he pulls down on the straps of my dress.

"Mhm," is all I manage to mutter out, trying to pace his oh-so-eager touch as I kiss along his neck to slow things down.

Kissing Sean is nothing like what I imagined it to be. There's no passion, no spark, *nothing*. Nothing about him excites me like I thought it would. Hell, it's been over a month since I've had sex, and I could pass on the opportunity at this moment.

That's bad, right? To want to stay celibate despite having a hot-ass man practically tearing your clothes off.

As the elevator doors re-open Sean pulls away, reaches for my hand and leads me down the hallway.

"After you." He unlocks his room, swinging open the door.

I'm hesitant to step inside when I see just how messy it is. He knew he was going to bring me upstairs and didn't even bother to clean? His God-damn underwear and socks are flung throughout. He's nothing like Dakota, whose kept our room so pristine, even housekeeping has hardly had to come in. But as I stand in Sean's room, I'm left questioning if we're still in a five-star resort or a pig sty.

But before I can debate the thought any further, I'm back in the air as Sean pushes his suitcase and other miscellaneous items off his dresser and places me on top. Immediately he drops to the floor as his mouth trails up my leg.

I swallow hard as he tenderly grazes my core, yet all I can focus on and think about right now is Dakota—even through the frustration, he overwhelms my mind, and it's not just because of our fight. It's every single memory with him that's haunting me. Even those I hadn't realized were as important until now.

The moment we met. How I accidentally "hit" his car. The way his eyes widened when he first saw me in his hotel room—mine too, but from the complete and total shock in response to his half-naked body. The dream. The way his hands felt when they first wrapped around my waist. How he comforted me on the parasail. The laughs we shared as we pigged out on the bed. The vulnerability we showed as we talked about the past. The way he looked out for me today—despite how much I'm internally still trying to come to terms with it.

Everything.

Every moment.

It's him.

Him.

Him shirtless on the bed.

Him styling his stupidly perfect hair in the morning.

Him running on the beach.

Him tying his apron.

Him laughing.

Him smiling.

Him joking—

A Recipe for Disaster

"Dakota..." I moan out so faintly that even I have difficulty hearing his name fall out of my mouth.

Oh my God...did I really just do that?

"Yeah, say my name, baby," Sean muffles beneath my dress as I'm reminded that it's him that I'm with, not Dakota.

I stiffen beneath his touch at the reminder, my head falling to the side as I re-open my eyes. Only when I do I notice a single item that Sean hadn't managed to push off his dresser.

It's a bracelet.

A woman's bracelet.

With daisies.

"I really like your bracelet."

"Thanks so much. It was a gift, actually. Reminds me of my restaurant—Daisy Dekes."

Colbie.

What the fuck?

"Is everything okay?" Sean pulls back as I close my legs shut.

I rush to my feet, stumbling off the dresser. "No," I say almost too quickly. "No, everything is not okay."

"What?" Sean backs away in confusion. "Why? What's wrong?"

I refuse to look at him, my eyes remaining fixated on the bracelet. He draws follows my gaze as he snatches the bracelet off the table and tosses it into his back pocket.

"Colbie?" I finally look at him with conviction. "You've been seeing Colbie this whole time, haven't you?"

Dakota was right.

He was telling the truth.

I feel so stupid.

"It's not what it looks like," Sean protests. "I swear, we were only meeting in my room."

"I'm sure you were," I scoff, reaching for my bag.

"It was competition-related, Iris." He can hardly look me in the eyes as he says it. "Nothing happened, I swear to you."

The room falls silent. I refuse to entertain his lies any longer. "I'm leaving." I shake my head. "I'm going."

"No." Sean tries to stop me, but I brush him off.

"Listen," I say to him pleadingly as I pause and meet his eyes. "Can we just forget that this ever happened...*please*?"

Sean stays still for a moment, assessing me with his hands in either pocket. "Sure." He nods faintly as I waste no time rushing out of his hotel room, embarrassed beyond belief and hopeful that no one saw us.

I can't believe I thought that this was a good idea. I've lost sight of the whole plot. This trip was supposed to be about cooking... fulfilling a dream.

My dream.

The Sweet Red.

Not about some ridiculous hook-up with Sean and certainly not fantasizing about Dakota Foster.

I trudge my way down the hallway and towards the elevator, clicking the sixth floor, yet as the doors re-open, the person staring back at me, with bags in either hand, leaves me speechless.

Dakota.

"Iris?" he questions, face full of confusion.

"Dakota," I respond, stepping out of the elevator as the two of us now stand face-to-face in the hallway. "What are you doing?" I gesture to the bags in his hands. "Where are you going?"

He lets his bags fall to either side of his body. "I could ask you the same thing." His brows crease. "Done so soon? Would've thought Mr. Big Shot would have lasted longer than a few strokes."

I ignore his spiteful comment. I deserve it. The words I said to him earlier weren't fair. They were far from it.

Rather than retaliating, I remain silent, turning my back on him and storming down the hallway towards our room. I can feel his presence trailing behind me, and for a moment, I'm scared. What else is he going to say? Is there anything left to be said? And where was he just going?

My mind spins as I step in through the door, only to hear him close it from behind. Things were a whole lot simpler when we barely spoke to one another. Let's go back to that.

"What are you doing back?" Dakota plants himself in front of me, giving me his undivided attention—the last thing I want him to do.

I slam my bag against the dresser and kick off my shoes. "Just leave me alone." I place my hands on top of my head. "I don't want to speak to you. I don't want to hear your voice, and I especially don't want to look at you!"

"Me?" He seems offended. "What the hell did I do?"

"*What the hell did you do?*" I ask rhetorically. "The better question is, what *don't* you do, Dakota?" I shout as he sits on the edge of the bed while I pace back and forth. "Ever since I met you, all you have done is completely infuriate me, drive me insane and bring nothing but an unwavering sense of frustration. You challenge me like no one has ever challenged me before. You make me work ten times harder than I already am…"

He appears as if he wants to jump in, but I don't allow him. Instead, I can't stop my mouth from uttering these words.

"You consume me. You consume every single one of my thoughts, day and night. Night and day. I can't get your stupid face and snarky attitude out of my mind. Fuck Dakota…I couldn't even have sex with some guy who likes me all because I couldn't stop thinking about you!"

Dakota stands up, working his way over to me, gently caressing my arm.

"No." I pull away, my voice barely above a whisper, knowing how powerful his touch is. "Just go," I instruct—despite how badly I want him to stay. "I mean, that's what you were doing, wasn't it? Leaving? Everyone always does."

"Everyone" is an easy scapegoat to avoid saying my mom. But the reality is, she's been the only one to have ever walked out of my life, and as a result, I've become the one that pushes people away.

I refuse to get close. I refuse to attach. Why? Because of this exact moment right here.

It's easy to tell someone to go because it was your choice, than watch them leave on their own merit.

I need to keep pushing him away. I need to keep fighting. Because I know if I let him in, it's only going to hurt that much more when he eventually leaves.

"Stop," Dakota demands. "Stop that right now. It's not like that, Iris. It's never been like that." He lets out a breath, forcing me to look into his eyes. "Do you think that this has been easy for me? Do you really think that seeing you this past week, being around you nonstop and sharing a fucking room together has been easy? Do you?"

I don't know what to say, and for once, I decide silence is the best answer.

"I'm certain, Iris, that you were put on this earth to equally enrage, sway, and torment me. So don't pretend that this is all about you. Don't you dare do that. This hasn't been easy for me either."

He sucks in a breath before his face meets mine, only inches away, and without a doubt, there it is.

The spark.

The spark that I was missing. It's here. It's always been here. It's always been with Dakota.

"*Fuck*," he murmurs, daringly close to my lips. "I need to hate you, but I want you so badly. So badly, Iris. I always have."

I shake my head in refusal yet make no attempt to move away from him. "This can't happen," I speak. "You can't happen."

Dakota runs his hand through my hair and behind my ear. "Then go," he tells me. "Go back to Sean, go. Go be with the guy you're so clearly pretending to like."

I swallow hard. "I do like him!" I protest, lying through my teeth. "I like him a lot." The lie intensifies, considering Dakota was right—Sean is a two-timer, but I can't give him that satisfaction right now.

"You wanna know what you like, Iris?" he fires back. "You like the way the two of you together makes me feel."

I'm taken aback by his truth, a truth that keeps on going.

"Tell me, do you really like the way his touch makes you feel?"

No.

"Does he ignite that fire inside you instead of putting it out?"

No.

"Do you think he could ever *fuck you* the way I could?" He runs a single finger down my arm, radiating chills throughout my spine.

No.

"If you answered yes to any of these questions Iris, tell me, because if that's the case, I'll go. I'll leave the competition. I don't care anymore because, truthfully, I can't stand seeing you near him for another second, nor can I hold back on how I feel about you any longer."

"Dakota," I try to protest before he lights the butane, sending my body into a blaze.

"From the moment I first saw you, Iris…" He places his hands on either side of my face. "You have been completely…" His eyes scan my lips. "And utterly…" He pulls me in closer. "*Insufferable.*"

Twenty-Four

IRIS

I've never been closer to him than I am at this moment. Watching the rise and fall of his chest, breathing in his air and trying to process the equal amount of rage and desire that pulsates through my veins.

Fuck, I want him—I want him badly. But nothing about our relationship has been easy. So why should I let this? If Dakota wants me, then let's see just how much.

"You really think you know me, don't you?" I forcibly push against his firm chest, leading him to take a step backwards. "Do you think I'd want to go and be with Sean right now?" I irritably scoff. "I walked out on him, Dakota. I walked out on him because I couldn't stop thinking about you," I confess as his legs meet the edge of the bed. "Do you even remotely understand just how frustrating that is? Thinking about you, despite the anger you pulsate through me?"

Dakota breathes in deeply yet remains silent—he doesn't have to say anything. The evident erection between the two of us tells me I'm lighting that same fire in him as well.

Dakota eyes follow my movements as I gravitate towards the waistband of his boxers as my fingers dance along the outside of the seam, teasing him slowly. Doing so much, all the while doing so little.

"I refuse to be the first one to cave here, Foster." I glare at him expectantly. "Care to concede?" Our lips hardly brush against one another—an action that's sending me into an absolute fit of anguish. He says nothing as I divert my touch upwards and tug away at his t-shirt.

Willingly he lets me undress him, and I hardly have to nudge him so that he falls back onto the bed. A single breath would've just knocked him over, and all at once, I know I've got him right where I want him.

"You wanna know what I've come to learn about you, Dakota?" I mutter as I straddle his waist but refuse to allow my center to make contact against his.

"What's that?" His is voice is a low growl.

I lean down to whisper into his ear. "That you're nothing but a sore loser whose only way of dealing with things is to be an asshole."

Dakota scrunches his lips as one while I slowly unzip the top part of my dress. "Must be hard to be at another's else's mercy…" I unclip my bra. "You know, push your ego aside and let someone else win something for once." I discard it to the side, taunting him as my breasts fall onto my chest.

Dakota's brown eyes darken while I watch him do everything in his power to avoid looking directly at what I know he wants—me.

"What?" I tactfully turn his chin upwards, with a kiss of my teeth. "Don't pretend like you haven't seen them before." I smirk, while slowly grazing my lower body against his, prompting him to not so subtly clench either side of the bedsheets as he resists every urge I can see flashing between his eyes.

I'm on a total fucking high from this, but why hasn't he conceded yet? I'm pulling out all the stops here.

What more can I do?

An idea comes to mind.

"On second thought." I pull back despite my reluctance. "Maybe you're right, Dakota. Maybe I should just go back to Sean," I taunt, reaching for my bra as something happens in his face.

His eyes narrow.

His brows tighten.

His scowl pierces my very being.

But I don't care—I keep going.

"Sean doesn't have any opposition against touching me." I officially remove myself from his lap. "So, thanks for warming me up…I guess I'll just be—"

Dakota flips us around so that his body hovers over the top of mine. "Don't you dare leave."

I bite down on my lip as I feel his weight on top of me. "Then make me want to stay."

He crashes his lips into mine.

After all this time, finally, I'm tasting him. Feeling him—being all that he's thinking about. I hadn't realized that deep down, maybe that's all I've ever wanted.

The kiss deepens, and I'm not sure what's more euphoric, how his lips fit perfectly with mine or how he's surrendered not only to the battle we were just in, but the one we've been facing from the moment we met.

"Fuck, Iris," he mumbles against my mouth. "What are you doing to me?"

My breath hitches as I speak. "The better question is…what are you going to do to me?"

Dakota's eyes roll to the back of his skull as he groans. "You have no fucking idea all the things I want to do to you." He sucks on my neck so hard that a wince escapes my lips. "But, if you think I'm going to be the only one here to yield, then guess what, princess, you're sadly mistaken. I'm going to make you beg for me."

My body aches as he runs his mouth down my chest, finding comfort over my left breast as he kisses along my nipple while toying with the other. It's blissful torture as he swaps sides, so much so that I release an audible moan—one that I forcibly tried to hold back from.

"Holding out on me?" Dakota licks the taste of me from his lips.

I can barely open my eyes to look at him. Why? Because I know that the second I do, it will be game over.

"Well then," Dakota carries on. "I see how it is. Let's see how headstrong you really are then, *Iris*."

The sound of my name rolling off his tongue is enough to send a wave of heat to my core as he pulls down on the remainder of my dress and plants slow, delicate kisses between my inner thighs.

"I'm not going to give you a single thing unless you tell me you want me to touch you," he taunts as his hands graze over my center. "You hear that?" His fingers trace the outline of my panties, gently slipping in and out of the seam. "You're. Getting. Nothing."

I start to stammer like a fool—he's ridden my mind of any and every thought but him. I can feel myself starting to cave, but somehow, the desire to lose to him still remains more potent than his touch.

"I wonder what you taste like." Dakota pulls my panties to the side, now humming against my inner thighs. The vibration makes my legs quiver as I continue to deny my body of everything I want from him. "I bet you're so fucking sweet…" His tongue hardly touches my clit before he pulls back. "Please, Iris?" he urges me again. "Just let me have a little taste."

I'm weak.

"Dakota…" I choke on his name.

"Yes, baby?"

"Please…" I beg. "*Please.*"

It's all I can keep on repeating, considering saying anything else would be far too difficult right now.

Dakota brings his face back up to mine yet is smug enough to carefully leave one of his hands securely between my thighs. "*Please?*" he teases with a devilish smirk. "I'm so sorry, baby, but I'm not quite sure what you're asking me. What exactly is it that you want me to do?"

Christ, I've seen this smirk before—it's one I once despised, but now crave above all else. The forbidden fruit to all my temptations. "Touch me," I beg. "I want you to touch me, Dakota.

I want you to touch me now!" I demand.

He bites down on his bottom lip as he lowers himself back. "All you had to do was ask," he spreads my legs wide and dances his tongue along my clit.

I'm left running my hands through his hair, tugging on his dark locks as the heat rises to my face. "Oh God, Dakota." A build-up in sensation haunts me below, and after a few minutes I'm crying out, "I'm close…I'm so close."

I'm seconds away from releasing against his tongue when he pulls back.

"What the fuck?" I practically shout in annoyance. "Why did you stop?"

Dakota looks me in the eyes as he wipes the corners of his mouth with his thumb "See how that felt?" he taunts. "Feeling so close. So, on edge but not getting what you want. Well…that's how it's been with you, Iris," leans back in close. "That's how it's always been."

I brush my hands across his stubbled cheek, frazzled beyond belief. "What…what are you even saying to me right now?"

Dakota releases a thoughtful breath as he assesses my face. "I didn't mean what I said earlier, Iris," he admits. "I don't hate you. The truth is…" His eyes divert as he shyly talks to the pillow, "I've always hated how much I wanted you. How you've driven me insane. He's back to looking into my eyes.

I flip us around so that I'm back on top, a place that I feel much more comfortable being. "So, instead of dealing with that, you decided that you'd torture me this entire time? You made me hate you just so that you wouldn't hate yourself?"

His cheeks turn into a flush shade of red. "Hate from you, was better than nothing from you."

I swallow deeply, until my hands find their way towards the front of his jeans—an article of clothing I'm left stunned has lasted this long.

"I don't hate you either," I simultaneously reveal my own truth as I pull down on his pants.

"You don't?" He sucks in a breath.

I shake my head. "I don't…" Next comes his boxers as I reveal his erection that's been aching to come free. "I…" I stroke his swollen tip, guiding my head downwards. "I've always just hated what you make me."

"And…what do I make you?" he croaks, his head falling back into the pillow—eyes firmly shut.

"*Vulnerable.*" My mouth connects with his tip as I gently bob my head up and down, taking my sweet dear time as it becomes my turn to call the shots again.

Dakota shows no reluctance when it comes to holding back from the moans that escape his mouth as I take him deeper, tighter, faster.

"Oh, Iris," he whimpers as I feel him begin to twitch between my lips. He's close. I was close, but no one is getting what they want just yet. I pull back.

"Fuck," he groans out in utter frustration, pinning me down onto the bed. "God, just let me fuck you," he practically begs for more.

"Oh, I don't know," I tease, pulling away my panties, the final remaining material left between us. "Maybe you can if you ask me *nicely.*" Taunting him with his own familiar words has somehow become my favorite thing in the world.

"Don't be fucking a brat!" Dakota hisses between his teeth.

I grasp behind his neck, pulling him down. "Don't fucking tell me what to do."

The way he grumbles beneath his breath is enough to make me want to forget all of this suspense and let him get right into it, *literally*, but he beats me to it.

"Fine," he surrenders. "Can I fuck you...*please?*" he submits himself. "*Please* let me fuck you. Let me fuck you unlike anyone has ever fucked you before. I know what you need Iris, so let me give it to you."

I stroke his tip, carefully lining him up with my entrance. "And what do I need, Dakota?"

He runs his tongue on the inside of his cheek. "Sounds like you'd like to find out, baby, but...I've asked nicely." He runs his thumb along my bottom lip. "Now it's your turn."

Feeling the way he's so close to pushing himself inside of me is enough to make me regret starting this begging fest. I'll tell him whatever he wants to hear as long as he continues to slowly ease his way in.

"Dakota..." I begin "Please...can you fuck me—"

"Shit." Dakota pulls out filling me with absence and not his length before I can finish my sentence. "We can't."

I sit up on my elbows in annoyance. "Are you seriously kidding me right now? I'm tired of playing this game with you, Dakota! What more do you want me to say? I want you. I've wanted you since I first saw you all those months ago. It was never Sean. Sean was just a distraction. A distraction that clearly didn't work. So please, don't make me keep begging. I want you. I need you."

"Iris." Dakota kisses my forehead to ease my frantic state. "Relax, okay? I just needed to put a condom on. Although…" He cockily puffs out his chest. "That just boosted my ego beyond belief."

I playfully roll my eyes at his comment. "Just hurry up." I demand. "I can't wait any longer."

Quickly Dakota scurries to grab a condom, taking his sweet time as he slides it down his length. "Holy, shit, Dakota. You're so slow! Do you even want to have sex with me, or should I go back to—"

"Don't you *ever* repeat his name again," he cuts off my taunting yet meaningless words as he re-lines himself between my thighs, his tip meeting my entrance. "I'm going to fuck you until the only name you know is *mine*. I'm going to fuck that little attitude right out of your mouth."

"All I want is you," I ease his jealousy by planting tender kisses along his face as he slowly enters me. "It's only you…" my voice is replaced by a moan—one I don't hold back from.

"That's it." Dakota thrusts that much deeper. "You only moan like that for me," he commands. "You hear me? Only me."

"Dakota," his name escapes my mouth like it was made to fall from my lips, as he sends my body into overdrive.

"*Fuck…*" His forehead leans against mine as the heat radiates between the two of us. "I knew you could be a good girl when you wanted to, Iris."

My eyes are transported to the back of my skull as suddenly, his pace quickens and in this moment I'm confident I'm in heaven, despite my preconceived idea that sex with Dakota would've been my own personal hell.

"You can take more." He tells me.

"More?" I barely have a chance to question as lifts one of my legs so that it hangs over his shoulder, leading him to thrust that much deeper.

"God, Iris." He lifts my other leg up so they're both at the mercy of his broad shoulders. "You see what you're doing to me." He continues his pace. "You see how badly I've fucking needed you."

"I'm…I'm close," I manage to choke out, between the gasps escaping my chest and the pressure that builds up between my thighs. No one has ever made me orgasm from intercourse alone before—no one has brought me to this point of no return like Dakota.

"I'm…I'm almost there." Dakota releases my legs from his shoulders as they wrap securely around his waist.

"Dakota…I…" My body twitches beneath his, falling limp as my nails dig into his back, scratching from the top all the way down to the bottom of his spine.

He grunts as I feel him come undone inside of me, until finally, he pulls out and falls to my side.

"That was…" He shakes his head in utter disbelief. "Fuck…. that was…*fuck*."

I scoff, a smile looming onto my lips as I stare up at the ceiling. "*Fuck*, is definitely right."

A moment passes by before I feel Dakota caress along my

A Recipe for Disaster

cheek. "Are you okay?" he asks softly. "Do you need me to get you anything, baby?"

I turn to face him, overwhelmed by the fact that we just had sex, and not just any ordinary sex. The best sex I've ever had in my life.

Well, that was unexpected.

"I'm okay," I admit. "Trust me...I'm more than okay."

"Tell me..." Dakota circles his hand over the top of my core. "Did you..." His devious smirk makes it difficult for him to finish the remainder of that sentence. "Finish?"

I'm reluctant to give him the satisfaction but can't help myself. I nod my head in disbelief. "Yeah," I tell him. "I actually did."

Dakota now breaks into a full-on grin. "I thought you did. But I couldn't quite tell over all that noise," he playfully remarks.

I bypass his comment, even though he was just *way* louder than I was. For once, I'm not in the mood to fight as I rest against his chest. "You know, that's never happened to me before," I nervously toy with my hands before peering up at him.

His eyebrows flex together. "Sex?"

I roll my eyes. "Don't flatter yourself, Foster. You didn't just take my chastity belt," I tell him. "That's been gone a long time. I was trying to say that I've never orgasmed from penetration alone...ever. That was the first time."

He seems impressed with himself for a moment, before his mood switches to apologetic and weary, as if he's thinking of something.

"What?" I read into the look on his face. "Why do you look like that?"

"I feel bad." He stares down into my eyes, and I can't quite tell what he means by those three words.

"Bad? Why do you feel bad?"

"Because." He frowns. "How could you ever sleep with someone else ever again after being with such a sex God like me? I feel sorry for you." A playful smirk closes out the sentence.

"Shut up." I push against his chest, even though I'm surprised that he's even been able to hold back from his sarcastic nature this long.

"I'm joking." He laughs, pulling me snugly back into his embrace. "But seriously, I do feel bad about something."

"Now, I can't tell if you're being serious or not." I raise an eyebrow in question. "What could you possibly feel bad about after what just happened?"

Dakota intertwines our hands as one. "I feel bad for how I've been on your case these past few months," he confesses. "The truth is, I never meant to upset you. I just…never really knew what to say to you."

"Oh, Dakota." I shake my head, sitting up and tucking the duvet into my chest. "I think you've always known exactly what to say to me. You've always known what makes me tick."

"True." He's confident as he says it. "But deep down, I knew I could never just be friends with you—that would've been way too tempting."

"So, being my enemy was better?"

He runs his thumb along my cheek. "So…I was something to you?"

I scrunch my nose as I shake my head. "Oh, you're something, that's for sure."

"A sex God?" He throws the title out there.

"A mediocre sex God," I lie, unwilling to boost his ego any more than I already have, my eyes landing back onto the tattoo on his wrist. "Tell me…do you have any more secret tattoos I should know about?"

"Well…" He hovers himself back over the top of me. "How about you explore my body and find out, while I attempt to promote myself to advanced sex God?" he murmurs against my lips. "Does that sound good, baby?"

I bite down on my lower lip to suppress a smirk.

"It sounds perfect."

Twenty-Five

DAKOTA

"Dakota!" Iris shouts from the bathroom, and immediately I go running. After the night we just had, I'm surprised I still have any energy left. But when Iris calls, you'd be stupid not to run.

"What's up? Are you okay?" My voice is frantic as I reach her, taking in the way she's perched over the counter, analyzing her neck as she drags down on her skin.

"Couldn't you have tried to be a little bit gentler?" she grumbles as she looks at me through in the reflection of the mirror, dabbing some makeup onto her neck in an attempt to hide the remnants of last night. All the while, I'm trying my best to recall whether or not that love bite was the result of the first, second, third, or...*never mind.*

"And you would've liked it gentle?" I tease as I pace my way over to the sink, prompting goosebumps to rise to her skin as she shoots me a playful glance in the mirror. "Yeah." I smirk in amusement. "That's what I thought."

Iris rolls her eyes as she continues to blend the product into her skin, while I wrap my arms around her waist, kissing the other side of her neck.

"Hey, hey, hey." She laughs, brushing off my touch. "No more! You've done enough."

"Excuse me?" I pull back, meeting her eyes. "Need I remind you that you aren't innocent here, either."

She cocks a brow. "What are you talking about?"

I step back and turn around, pulling up my shirt to reveal the deep red scratches along my back. The ones that are only a result of her ridiculously long nails.

"Oh my gosh." She does an absolutely terrible job of hiding the fact that behind that dainty hand that's flown to her face there is an abundance of laughter.

She's sick for laughing, yet her laughter is infectious, boisterous, slightly obnoxious, but unquestionably beautiful—the most perfect sound in the world.

"Aw, Dakota," she pities me between giggles. "I didn't realize…I'm sorry."

"No, you're not." I scoop her into my arms and place her on top of the sink, perching myself in-between her thighs, my new favorite place. "You're an animal, woman," I whisper, our foreheads now pressed together. "My animal…"

My words are enough for our lips to seemingly fall back together just like they did all night long as she tosses the concealer to the side.

This is a dream.

"Okay…no more." She brings me back to reality as she gently pushes against my chest. "We're done."

"What?" I pout as if I'm nine years old and back at the pumpkin patch. "Why not?"

"Because…" She jumps down from the counter, planting her feet firmly on the ground. "We've still got a competition to finish, and I've still got a championship title to win, remember?"

"Oh, I haven't forgotten, alright." I follow her out of the bathroom, watching as she throws on her chef's jacket and lifts her hair into a messy bun.

"Ugh…" I fall back onto the bed. "You're so fucking hot. Do you know that?"

Iris shoots me a suggestive smirk. "I think you might have reminded me once or twice last night."

I groan in blissful annoyance. "How am I supposed to focus today after last night? How am I going to be able to focus on anything ever again?"

She walks over to meet me at the bed and plants herself on my lap, making it virtually impossible to process anything else. "I guess you'll just have to try. But for now, hold onto those thoughts for my celebratory night tonight," she teases. "After all, you'll be sleeping with the winner."

"You're such a smart ass." I can't help but flip her around so that I'm back on top.

"Dakota…stop…" She giggles as I plaster her face with kisses. "Seriously, we've got to go! The competition is starting soon."

"Just five more minutes," I whine. "Please."

She sits up ever so slightly with a look of intrigue. "Is that enough time?" She tucks a strand of hair behind her ear.

"Baby, five minutes is all I need." I inch down her body, reaching for the button on her jeans when a knock comes through the door, pulling us both away in unison.

A Recipe for Disaster

"Who's that?" Iris looks up at me in confusion. "Did you get room service?"

"No." My brows crease. "Did you?"

She shakes her head. "Go check," she urges me.

"Now?" I ask.

Another few knocks come through the door.

"Yes, now."

I let out a sigh of frustration. "This better be fucking good." I walk towards the door to peer through the peephole.

"Who is it?" Iris calls out in question yet the sight that stands in front of me leaves me speechless.

What the hell is he doing here?

"Take a guess," I as I stare at Sean, who's pathetically stood on the other side of the door. Fuck him, I should open this door just so that I can slam it shut in his face.

"I don't know? Housekeeping?" Iris guesses.

"Wrong," I announce. "It's Sean."

"Sean?" She immediately sits up and marches her way over, propping up on her tiptoes to peer through the peephole. "Why is he here?" she demands.

"I don't know. Let me answer it and I'll find out." I reach for the handle, but she objects.

"No. Don't."

"Why not?" I argue. "I want to see what he wants."

Another few knocks come through the door again. "Dakota?" Sean calls out my name. "Are you there? Can we talk? Please?"

Iris shoots me a look that says *don't you dare open the door, Dakota*, but I don't listen—I've never been good at listening, and so,

I swing open the door, prompting Iris to tuck herself into the bathroom so that she's out of sight.

"Hey, Dakota…" Sean speaks as he sheepishly shoves his hands into either pocket. "How's it going?"

My eyes narrow in on him. I'm not doing the talking here, he's at my door, after all. Instead, I impatiently fold my arms across my chest, waiting for him to speak.

Visibly picking up on the un-amusement plastered across my face Sean releases a pained sigh. "Listen, man," he attempts. "What I said to you yesterday…that was an asshole thing for me to do, and it wasn't fair. You made your way into this competition because you're a talented chef, and my feelings towards Iris shouldn't have come in between that. And for that, I'm sorry."

Am I losing it, or is Sean Dellan, culinary expert, competition tycoon, and egotistical idiot—an added part on my end, apologizing to me?

Me?

I drag out the apology, only because the stress in his eyes gives me a slight boost myself, before I grant him a faint nod, which in guy-world, universally means that not only have I accepted your apology, but I want to move past this conversation as quickly as possible.

Usually, I'm not so forgiving, but right now, I have no other choice but to be considering Iris is listening in on every word that comes out of his mouth. I didn't once mention Sean's threat to her. I couldn't have. If she barely believed me when I said I saw him and Colbie kissing, how would she have believed that he'd threatened to eliminate me?

A Recipe for Disaster

"Have you spoken to Iris at all?" Sean breaks the awkward silence between the two of us. "It's just…I've been trying to find her all morning and I can't seem to."

I'm tempted to reach for her in the bathroom and pull her in for a kiss to prove to him that I've done much more than just talk to her this morning with my lips, but I sike myself out of it. "I'm sure she's closer than you think," I slyly settle on as my response.

The sound of Iris snickering from behind me is enough to make me chew on the inside of my cheek to suppress the laughter, one I quickly have to drop as Sean peers back up from the ground. "You two are close, right?"

Do you mean was I balls deep inside of her last night? Then yeah, I'd say we're very close.

"I'd say so…" I opt for instead yet grow defensive. His shenanigans with her are done…*over*. Besides, he's delusional to think that she'd give him another chance, let alone that I'd ever let him. "Why? What's it to you?"

"Well, she walked out on me last night while we were about to…never mind." He shakes his head. "I guess what I'm trying to say is that I didn't get a chance to apologize properly to her. So… if you see her, can you tell her I'm sorry?"

Little does he realize that his half-assed apology has already been received, but even then, so, I have to be the bigger man as I respond, "sure. I'll let her know."

"Thanks." He's back to standing nervously as there's this dreadful silence between us. "I uh…better get going. But good luck today, and this time…I mean it."

I grant him a final affirming nod before I close the door and turn back around. Iris wastes no time re-emerging in my direct line of view with her hands on her hips and her eyes narrowed in on me.

"What?" I play innocent with a shrug of my shoulders. "Why are you looking at me like that?"

"*'I'm sure she's closer than you think,*'" she imitates my voice. "'*I'd say so?*'" She laughs. "You really think you're a comedian, don't you, Dakota?"

"I mean, you seem to think I am." I smirk as I walk past her, pulling my arms through my chef's coat.

She playfully rolls her eyes before she meets me, helping me to do up the buttons, when suddenly a frown falls over her lips.

"What's wrong?" I can't help but feel an aching pang of concern whenever Iris's face drops. "Why are you sad, baby?"

"What exactly was Sean talking about?" she pries, meeting me with glazed eyes. "What did he say to you that he needed to apologize for?"

"It was nothing." I make an immediate attempt to mitigate the situation. I can't stand talking about Sean for another second longer.

Iris glares at me once more, visibly unamused at the vagueness of my answer. "What did Sean say, Dakota?"

Nothing quite makes me cave like the sight of her bottom lip jutting out in frustration—if she and I were in a courtroom together, I'd have no chance of lying. Her face alone is enough to make me spew out the truth. "He just saw us looking at each other at yesterday's competition and got jealous. That's all." I miss out on the most crucial detail.

"Yeah, I could see that," she states the obvious. "But what exactly did he say to you?"

"It's not a big deal, Iris," I tell her, finishing up the last of my buttons. "Don't worry about it, okay? Let's just focus on the competition. That's what's most important right now."

I attempt to brush past her, but she places a hand on my arm. "Dakota," she groans out my name like she did all night long. "Can you just tell me, *please*?"

"Fine…" I intertwine our hands. "The truth is, I called him out for what I saw between him and Colbie on the boat, which obviously, didn't go down well. And to cut a long story short, he basically said that 'if I knew what was good for me in this competition, I wouldn't accuse him or tell you anything.'"

Iris pulls back at my words, jaw slacked. "Dakota…that's serious! He threatened to eliminate you?"

"Iris." I run my hands down her arms to calm her. "A threat is when you actually get intimidated by something. I didn't give a single fuck, baby. Do you think Sean had me stressed? Worried? Fuck no, I was more upset with the way he was treating you!"

She shakes her head in refusal. "We should tell the committee," she suggests. "Get him removed from the panel. He's in no position to be abusing his power like that. In fact, I'm going to go right now…"

"Iris!" I have to stop her as she marches her way towards the door ready to kick up a fight. "No one is reporting anyone. It's not worth it. Please baby, don't worry about him."

I know that my attempts at assuring her that Sean is the least of our concerns is pitiful. She's not convinced one bit, but still, she's no longer tugging to break away from my grasp, instead, she settles into me.

I'll take what I can get.

"How could you say that, though?" she furrows her brows. "Don't you care, Dakota?"

"Of course, I care." I wrap my arms around her waist as I press my forehead against hers. "But truthfully…I care about something else more."

My confession is enough to make the fury fade from her blue eyes and with a faint nod of her head, there she is—the girl I've fallen in for, and the girl who above all things, is a determinist at heart—*my chef.*

She bites down on her lip to suppress a smile, prompting me to release her from my embrace, rest assured that she's not going to sprint off and run to the committee. "You get ready, okay?" I tell her. "Focus on you."

She nods. "I'll be out in a second."

"I'll see you then." I go to escape the room, only as the door starts to close I'm halted in place as she shouts, "Dakota, wait. You forgot something."

She joins me in the hallway as I search for what I could have possibly forgotten when suddenly she clutches onto the neck of my jacket and pulls me down for a kiss.

Right…how could I have forgotten?

I'm not sure how much time passes by with our lips pressed together, but all I know is that as she releases me she's breathless, smirking in devious delight as she backs into the room, closes the door behind her, and leaves me virtually stunned.

A Recipe for Disaster

Now, as I walk down the hallway, I'm left replaying the moment in my mind. It's virtually impossible to hide this cheesy grin on my face—the worst part, I'm now standing amongst a crowd of people waiting for the elevator. Clearly no one wanted to be late for today's competition…well, except me.

"Hey, Foster!" a voice shouts, breaking me free from my escalating thoughts—it's a good thing, considering I was seconds away from having to suppress another, less controllable part of myself.

"Hey, Tim!" I recognize his face from some of our conversations earlier on in the competition. He's from California if I recall correctly, where he owns a mom-and-pop style coffee shop. Tim and…the name escapes me as he guides his way over.

I'd never been one to make friends easily—but maybe that was because I'd never found the right crowd. But now, as I'm surrounded by people that share the same aspirations, goals, and talents as me, it's hard not to.

"How's it going?" Tim finally reaches me, patting my back. "Are you excited for today?"

I nod my head in agreement. "Definitely, and you?"

"Without a doubt." He smiles enthusiastically. "Though…" He leans in slightly. "Did I catch you swooning the competition, or what?"

My stomach drops.

Shit.

Iris and I are about as discreet as Colbie and Sean—a terrible pairing to be compared to, might I add,

The last thing I need right now is the gossiping voices of

others pulling both of us off track. Iris needs to focus. I need to focus. Nothing can stand in the way of that.

"So, tell me, Foster, is there something going on between you and *red* or what?" Tim's attempt at using a code name rather than just saying "Iris" is obsolete, considering Iris is the only red-head in this entire competition.

As he awaits my response, I quickly assess my options.

Option one: tell him the truth and insist he doesn't say a thing. *Or.*

Option two: deny, deny, deny, until all of this is over.

"You know, I always thought you two hated each other…" Tim continues to go on, despite the fact that I haven't said a single thing, and like magic, a third option comes to mind: play into the facade.

"You know what they say." I meet his eyes as the elevator doors open and the crowd makes its way inside. "Keep your friends close, but your enemies *closer*.

Twenty-Six

IRIS

"Excuse me…sorry…" I push my way through the all-consuming crowd that floods the lobby, panting out of breath after running down six flights of stairs.

There was no other choice. I was seconds away from joining the crowd of people in the elevator, when I overheard the poisonous statement escape from Dakota's lips.

"You know what they say. Keep your friends close, but your enemies closer."

It was a statement unlike I'd ever heard before. When I first overheard someone probing him about our canoodling, I couldn't help but escape into my own internal sense of panic wondering what Dakota was going to say.

How would he react?

Would he tell him the truth?

The truth.

Had our truths been different this entire time?

Was all of this…*fake?*

I'm distressed by the sheer number of questions that circulate through my mind. Nothing is making sense anymore. I can hardly tell my right from my left. Up from down. Good from bad.

How could Dakota do this to me?

How had I let him?

"Keep it moving!" A voice demands in front of me—granting me some sense of direction amidst this crowd as I continue to shuffle forward. Step by step, I silently pray that for once in this whole competition, I'll be assigned a station as far away from Dakota as possible.

"Could you move forward, please?" the voice repeats with more urgency, prompting me to lift my head up as I take into account the gap that has since formed between myself and the check-in table.

"I'm so sorry." I scurry forward, attempting to get my head into the game. I need to focus. Nothing will surmount the feeling of finishing this competition with a bang and forgetting that this week ever happened. That *he* ever happened. Yet, as I approach the check-in table, the face that greets me takes me back to where this all began.

"Beth?" I say in disbelief, overwhelmed by her presence—her warm smile.

"Iris." Her eyes light up in delight. "Is that you? Oh my goodness, what a surprise."

"What are you doing here?" I can't help but wonder.

"I'm working for the competition." She gestures towards the vest on her shirt that reads "The Culinary Committee of the United States". "It's so great to see you, Iris," she says my name with assurance, and I'm surprised that she remembered. But truthfully, how could she have forgotten? My showdown with Dakota was one for the books.

A Recipe for Disaster

Dakota.

I can't even string together a few thoughts without being struck with the ache that everyone around me only reminds me more and more of him.

"How are you, hon? What's new?" Beth props her hands on either side of her face.

Oh, Beth. Not much is new in my world besides since the last time I spoke to you, I nearly hooked up with one of the judges of this competition and then ultimately slept with my supposed arch-nemesis. You know, the one I had a full-on brawl with in front of you. So, a typical week. Really.

I stifle a sarcastic laugh. "Oh, nothing new here…" I opt for instead. "I'm just surprised to see you, that's all. It's been months."

Beth shoots me a soft smile, dimples forming in the hollows of her cheeks. "I've been working behind the scenes lately," she explains. "Processing paperwork and whatnot. But how could I turn down a trip to Miami, right? Especially the finals, which, frankly, I'm not surprised to see you in at all."

I peer up from the form she'd handed over to me, struck by her words. "You're not?"

"Of course, I'm not." She waves her hand. "I've always known that you were a tough competitor, Iris, and frankly, an even stronger woman. You don't take anyone's shit. That's what I like about you."

Her words force the corners of my mouth to lift in a smile, an action that somehow I'd forgotten that I was capable of doing.

Tough competitor.
Strong woman.
Not taking anyone's shit.

It's the first time this whole trip that someone has reminded me of exactly who I am—who I've always been, and why at this moment, I refuse to allow myself to be swallowed up by this mess.

Iris Hammond came to Miami for a reason, and she's not leaving this competition today without that title—*I don't care if it kills me.*

"Oh, Beth…" I place the forms before her. "You have no idea how much I needed to hear that right now."

"Well, don't you forget it." Beth winks, replacing the forms in my hands with my assigned workstation number: 30. "Is there anything else you need from me?" she continues. "Don't you also fill out an allergy form or something like that?"

As Beth closes out her sentence, I see Dakota fall into my line of vision, making a bee-line towards the check-in counter. There's a smile on his face as approaches me yet all I can see are the words *deja vu*—it's funny how history has a way of repeating itself.

"Wait," Beth speaks as Dakota shoves his way through the crowd. "Is that…Dakota? Oh, my goodness. What are the odds? Do you remember him, Iris?"

Oh, Beth, if only you knew just how hard he is to forget.

"Iris!" Dakota calls out my name—blissfully unaware just how much hearing him say it is breaking me by the second. "I've been looking for you."

"You guys…are talking to each other?" Beth looks at me in disbelief—confusion evident all over her face. "Are you guys together—"

"Thanks for everything, Beth." I refuse to play into Dakota's little act a second longer as I cut Beth short and break away from the table. "It means a lot."

"Iris?" Dakota shouts as I push my way through the crowds and race into the venue, knowing damn well that if I keep up this pace, he'll have no chance of reaching me.

DAKOTA

I'm bodied by crowds of people as I call out her name yet Iris continues to shove her way through the crowd. "Iris?" I attempt once more. "What's wrong?"

I'm left dumbfounded at her icy gaze—in contrast to her heated touch not ten minutes ago.

Did she not hear me?

But she looked right at me.

Is she trying to focus?

But she didn't seem to mind the occasional distraction this morning.

I'm left with no ulterior resolution to soothe my mind other than the fact that I know this girl, and I know more than anyone that that look on her face means she's mad.

But why?

My mind races as I clutch a hold of my wrist, attempting to channel my thoughts. If Dallas were here, he'd know exactly what to do. There was a reason why he was the one in the long-term relationship and not me.

"Well, I'll be damned," a voice chimes up. It's one that sounds awfully familiar in the strangest way possible. "I knew it was you.

Dakota Foster, live and in the flesh."

I lock eyes with the woman sitting down in front of me. Her smile grows by the second as I analyze her face, her eyes, and the look of complete adoration smitten across her cheeks.

"Why do I feel like I recognize you?" I speak, making her face fall slightly flat. Clearly, I have no idea how to talk to women today. "Have we met before?" I cautiously do some backtracking.

"Oh c'mon, Dakota." She folds her arms across her chest. "Surely your memory isn't that bad." She points to the name tag on her vest, and immediately it hits me.

Beth.

Shit.

My fingertips graze alongside my temples. "Beth," I say exasperatedly. "How could I forget? Of course, I remember you," I admit, even though I only remember Beth because she was present at one of the most impactful introductions of my life—one that I never thought would lead me here.

My attempt at revoking my initial forgetfulness works as a smile rises to her cheeks. I mimic her expression but take a second to peel away, looking back towards the crowd, desperate to catch another glimpse of Iris instead.

"Looking for someone?" Beth shoots me a suggestive look, handing me the check-in forms to fill out. Yet again, I've managed to bypass the line. "You know…" she admits. "I'm not surprised at all."

I tilt my head in confusion, accepting the papers from her grasp. "Surprised about what?"

"You and Iris." She cocks a brow as heat rises to my cheeks.

A Recipe for Disaster

"I kind of always pictured you two together, if I'm being honest."

God, what is up with today? Sure, Tim saw Iris and I kissing—but Beth? Are we really that obvious? Panic starts to set in as I'm reminded that option two needs to come into play.

Play dumb.

"I don't know what you're talking about." I do an absolutely terrible job of acting as though Beth's words didn't just prompt my heart to skip a beat.

"Don't try and fool me, Dakota." Beth rolls her eyes. "You do realize I process all the forms for each competition, right?"

I furrow my brows. "So?" I question. "What's that supposed to mean?"

Beth stares me down. "It means, don't think that I haven't noticed that for every competition you two compete in together, two allergy forms always come in for Iris Hammond."

My eyes go wide.

"At first, I thought there was a processing issue, but after further investigation, I realized that one form was always in her handwriting, and the other always looked awfully similar to *yours*. Does that ring a bell, Dakota?" She cocks a brow, visibly chuffed by her detective abilities.

If my cheeks were warm before, by now they're absolutely on fire. I've always kept that a secret. When I first overheard Iris request an allergy form from Beth, I knew that I'd also fill in another, just in case. I'd never wanted to take any chances.

I look at Beth in shock. She knows she's got me. "Can we please keep that a secret?" I whisper, shooting her a straight look. "Promise?"

Beth softens her shoulders, tilting her head to the side. "Did something happen?" she pries. "Iris didn't seem like herself."

"What do you mean?" I choke out. "Did she say something to you?"

Beth shakes her head. "She didn't, but I could tell that something was up."

"Did she seem like she was avoiding me?" I can't help but wonder if Beth picked up on that too.

"I mean, if you're asking, did I just watch her practically run away from you? Then yeah, she's trying to avoid you."

My heart sinks. Leave it to me to fuck things up without even realizing it.

"Shit." I rub my head in defeat, an action that makes Beth release a long-drawn-out sigh as she takes the forms back from my hands and shuffles through a stack of numbers on her right. "You know…I shouldn't be doing this," she confesses, placing a number in my grasp. "But here. Take it, and don't speak a word about this, you hear? That's my terms for your promise."

I peer down, seeing station number 35 rest in my hand. "What's this?"

"I switched your station," Beth reveals. "Now, you're directly across from her. A place it will be hard for her to avoid you from," she says with a radiant sparkle in her eyes. I think Beth might be a hopeless romantic at heart. "Make things right, Dakota. Whatever that may be. I'm rooting for you."

"Thank you," I say wholeheartedly. "Really…thank you."

She nods. "Oh, and Dakota?" She stops me in my tracks as I attempt to step away. "Do you mind filling out that allergy form

A Recipe for Disaster

for Iris? For the first time…she forgot."

Twenty-Seven

IRIS

"Competitors!" Sean shouts into the microphone. "This is the moment you've all been waiting for. Welcome to the grand finale of The Art of Cooking Competition!"

An overhaul of cheers rocks the room around us, and it's not just from the remaining fifty competitors, it's from the live audience that now watches over our every move—no wonder the lobby was so busy.

I can feel the pure anticipation as it rattles through my chest. I should be joining in on the excitement, jumping up and down and twirling like a certified idiot because getting to this stage of the competition has always been a dream of mine. But instead, here I am, trapped in an endless game against my mind and body. My mind tells me to stop looking directly ahead at Dakota—yet, my body proves that the task is impossible. I catch wind of every diminutive movement he makes, especially now as he brushes his hands alongside his apron in a slow and controlled motion.

Little does he know that he's thoroughly torturing me as I fantasize about his touch while reminding myself that none of it was sincere. I'm pained by the thought. Haunted by the memories. Remorseful that I'd let us get to this point.

A Recipe for Disaster

There's a moment where Dakota and I catch each other's gaze, and before I can turn away, I watch as his eyes drop. He takes advantage of this opportunity as the perfect time to mouth, "what's wrong?"

I ignore him as I swiftly turn back towards the stage, my ponytail swaying to the side as I swallow deeply. Yet, in my attempt to shift my attention away from one crisis, it lands on another, as my eyes catch those of Sean's—who clears his throat and brings the microphone back up to his lips.

"This is the first round of a series of challenges you will complete today. After each round, a number of you will be eliminated, leaving us with the top ten contestants. The top ten will then battle it out for the chance to win The Art of Cooking Competition, be named America's Ultimate Dining Experience and a cash prize of $100,000! Are we ready to get started?"

Subtly I join in on the applause, hopeful that it will drown out the way my hands are shaking in nervousness. I didn't think I'd make it here—and now that I have, I'm left with an overwhelming sense of imposter syndrome that I know I have to shake.

"Like in the grand finales past, you will be tasked with creating a three-course meal—a hors d'oeuvre, a main, and a dessert. This time, however, we're bending the rules. We'll be doing the same competition, but in *reverse*. In order to wow us into the next round of the competition, you'll need to start by mastering a hand-crafted dessert."

I release a controlled breath. *Okay, dessert—I know how to make dessert.* I'm no Lore Llyod, but when you've spent half a decade in a kitchen with one, you naturally pick up a thing or two.

Lore.

If only she knew what had taken place these past few days. I can't help but wish she were here, yet at the same time, I'm left wondering that if she had been, would everything have still transpired with Dakota? Would we have still managed to find our way to one another?

The thought alone irks me—and I'm not quite sure which part hurts the worst. The ache of being so close yet feeling so far away from him, or the thought that he and I were only one hiccup away from never coming together. Even if none of it was true, Dakota sure has a way of making you feel like you're falling in love.

Love.

I add the word to the list of things I'm trying to forget—but it's an emotion that will forever be ingrained into my heart, like a sad poetic melody.

"But here's the catch," Bruno picks up where Sean left off. "You aren't going to just be making any ole' dessert. That would be too easy." He moves the microphone from one hand to another as a smirk rises to his thin lips. "This is the finals, after all."

His cryptic ulterior words leave me twiddling with my thumbs in nervousness. How many more curve balls will be thrown my way before I strike out?

"In order to successfully complete this challenge, you will be tasked with replicating a dessert of *our* choice, solely based on a *taste test*."

"A taste test?" I faintly repeat under my breath.

"That's right!" Colbie responds as if she could hear me

A Recipe for Disaster

question the challenge. The reality is, I should be questioning her choices with Sean. I want to tell her to abort mission. He's not worth it. But right now, I'm holding onto my vow to leave both Sean and everything else in the past and focus on the present.

"We want to test the limits on not only your abilities as a chef but your palette too. This time around, when it comes to acquiring points, you will not only be awarded on presentation and taste, but, you will also be awarded on the likeliness to the original dessert."

At the same time as Colbie chimes back in, servers walk over to each workstation where they gently place a silver tray on the table.

"Being placed in front of you is the dessert that has been selected for this first round of competition," Bruno explains. "As soon as the timer starts, uncover the lid and dive right in. You will have a few minutes to taste the dessert and make some notes before we take it away. After that, you'll have an hour and a half to replicate it to the best of your ability.

As I digest the instructions, I can feel Dakota staring over at me. This time I actually listen to the lingering voice in my mind and refuse to entertain his glare. Apparently, he's more concerned about figuring out why I'm jaded than listening to the rules.

"Does everyone understand?" Sean jumps back onto the mic. The room seems receptive, and without wasting a second, Sean jumps back onto the mic. "Good! Because your time...starts... now!"

As the timer kicks off, I rush towards my workstation and lift the lid from the tray. Without needing a second glance I can tell that the dessert that rests in front of me is a chocolate mousse. That, or some sort of mocha infused flavor—just based on the brownish tint alone.

But there's no point in wasting my time when it comes to playing an internal guessing game. This is a taste test, after all, meaning that the only way to find out the mystery flavors of this dessert is to taste it.

I reach to my right where I lift a spoon and dip it into the layered mousse. Immediately the silverware is coated with a light layer of cream and delicate chocolate swirls. A sight that's enough to electrify the eyes in anticipation.

When it comes to anything I eat, competition related or not, typically, I'll opt for a smell test. Sometimes I find that my nose can be more robust than my palette. But with the clock ticking just ahead, I'm reminded that there's no time to analyze the aroma of this dessert. Instead, I place the spoon directly between my lips, licking it clean so that not a single trace is left behind.

For a moment in time, I close my eyes—turning off any other senses that aren't nearly as important. I need to allow my palette to work into overdrive. Give my brain a chance to process the flavors…or dare I say *flavor*.

The flavor that rests on my tongue is unlike the sugar rush you'd hope for when it comes to a sweet treat. Instead, this flavor smacks me right in the gut as it slides down my throat, and an immediate rush of panic kicks in.

This is bad.

DAKOTA

A Recipe for Disaster

I'm a troubled man, with troubled thoughts, and right now, I'm left wondering whether or not I need to thank Beth for her interference between Iris and I or curse her name into existence.

Standing directly across from Iris with her cold shoulder and daunting glare—reminds me of the Iris I once knew, not the Iris I know. *My Iris.*

But her disdain is nowhere near powerful enough to stop me from staring at her—thinking about all the possible things I could've said or done for her to have flipped her switch. I'm so distracted that I hardly heard the instructions for this first round of competition.

Instead, I've been left piecing together what I can, that being that I need to taste and replicate something. From the outside the task may sound easy, but in reality, it's much more challenging than you'd imagine.

With full transparency, I dislike a good portion of the judging panel—Bruno excluded when it comes to my vengeful hate, but between the three of them, they have by far tested my limits as a chef.

I take pride in the fact that my palette is strong, that's why I've been able to catch onto Iris' nature so quickly, I can taste the displeasure. But with all that aside, I can honestly say that I've never tried to replicate a dish entirely based on taste. The task alone always seemed too daunting, pointless, yet now it feels almost impossible when I can rid this worry that lingers on my lips. There's no way to replace it with anything else.

Get it together.
Stop ruminating on this.

There's a voice in my mind that forces me to focus. That reminds me that I need to remember the facts.

Before there was Iris, there was a dream, a hope, a goal to take The Closed Cook to the next level—and inclusive of that was the desire to make Dallas proud. From the moment I arrived in New York City that's all I ever wanted.

But now, as I stand adjacent to her, my mind forces me to think otherwise. Perhaps dreams can change—evolve. Perhaps something, or someone that you never imagined could be your dream, becomes that overnight. I've come to learn that the best dreams aren't the ones when you fall asleep. *No.* Those always come to an end. The best dreams happen when you're awake—when you're living in one.

I'm left rubbing my wrist in comfort in an attempt to calm my unsettled breathing as I take into account the fact that not only has the countdown begun, but I've already wasted 30 seconds standing in thought.

Shit. I stumble ahead, reaching for the spoon that rests in front of me and gently lifting the tray to reveal a bite-sized dessert. One that I waste no time sinking my spoon into before I place it into my mouth.

As the taste dances along my tongue, suddenly, the flavor translates to my mind, prompting my head to shoot up and my eyes to widen in disbelief.

All at once I'm left looking across the room as a deep-rooted sense of fear flooding through my body as I watch Iris reach for the sink behind her, grab an empty glass and fill it up.

Her frantic commotion catches the attention of those around us. "Are you okay?" I hear someone shout, yet she hardly looks over as the water fills the glass, and she takes a massive gulp.

It doesn't seem to help. I can see her grazing her shaken hand along her throat in discomfort. I break free from behind my station. "Call an ambulance!" I shout desperately. "Call an ambulance!"

The crowd comes to a stand-still.

"What?" I catch the attention of the judging panel as they frantically make their way off the stage and rush in my direction. "What's wrong?"

"The dessert," I announce loudly. "The dessert had peanuts in it. Iris is allergic—"

A gasp radiates through the audience, cutting my sentence short as I catch the tail-end of Iris declining to the ground.

"We need a medic now!" Someone cries out as I race over to her side, helping to support her weak frame.

"Iris," I speak as she starts coughing...choking. There's a sense of panic that washing all over her face.

"My pen," she barely croaks. "Dakota...I..." She looks into my glazed eyes. "I need my *EpiPen*."

"It's coming, baby," I try my best to soothe her as the first aid crew rushes over. "You're going to be alright. I promise—"

"Move, please!" The medics reach her side, signaling for me to pull back as Iris's lips turn into a faint shade of blue, her breathing so pained and frail.

"She's going into anaphylaxis shock," the medic declares, and his words scare me half to death.

I can't lose her.

I've lost the most important person in my life, for fucks sake, don't take her from me too.

I don't know who I'm pleading with, all I know is that the medic is frantically grabbing a blue pen from his colleague's hand as he injects it into Iris's outer thigh.

A whimper escapes her mouth as her eyes start to flutter. "Iris!" I shout, crawling my way back over to her side, as she grows distant. "Iris…can you hear me?" I mumble as her eyes slowly come to a close. "*Iris!*"

A Recipe for Disaster

Twenty-Eight

IRIS

"*Iris!*" a voice calls out to me, but it's no longer Dakota's. I'm transported away from this world, and as I open my eyes, I realize that I've entered another. "*Iris, dinner is ready!*" The same voice speaks again, and without having to second guess, I recognize who it is and where I am.

"*Coming, Mom.*" I see my five-year old-self come racing down the hallway—my red curls bouncing with each step.

I start to piece together exactly what's happening. "Is this…" my voice trails off. "My dream?"

"*Dex!*" Mom calls out. "*Dexter, come join us at the table.*"

"Dad?" I try to speak, but he can't seem to hear me as he walks right past me and heads into the kitchen, kissing my childhood self's forehead as he takes a seat.

This can't be…I'm having the same dream…no…this is different. I'm not five years old and reliving it. No, this time, I'm here. Watching this all transpire as an adult. It's an out-of-body experience—an experience that I know all too well.

"*Here you go.*" Mom places Dad's dinner in front of him. He looks up at her in adoration, paining my heart. "*Thanks, hon.*"

Mom takes a seat beside Dad, and just as I anticipate, her fork plants straight into her mashed potatoes. Because—

"*Mom always eats carbs before protein.*" Dad smiles over at me as I watch myself strut my way over to the oven and slowly scoop some food onto my plate.

"*Iris, don't forget your vegetables,*" Dad calls out before I can even make my way back over to the table, balancing the plate with two hands.

I laugh faintly at the image of my sassy self playfully rolling my eyes at him while stomping my way back over to the oven, attempting to scoop some peas onto my plate. Yet, amidst all of this, my attention is drawn back onto Mom. This time, I see her differently than I had before. Her head is still down, but she's twiddling her thumbs in her lap. She's nervous…anxious… stressed. She knows what's about to happen. She must.

"*So, anything exciting happening at school this week?*" Dad eagerly smiles over at me.

"*Yeah, actually.*" I perk up with a toothless grin, prompting Mom to lift her head. I'd never noticed her weak attempt at a smile until now.

"*We're doing this really cool experiment in science class, and on Friday, there's a class trip to the Statue of Liberty! And then*—"

All at once, my voice is cut off mid-sentence, and I'm no longer hovering over the dinner table. Now, I'm standing beside the sink, watching Mom collect the last of the dishes.

Now we're at this part.

"*Wanna watch a movie?*" Dad proposes as I eagerly stand up from the table.

"*Yes!*" I jump up in delight. "*Can we watch a superhero movie, Dad?*

A Recipe for Disaster

Please?"

"*Sure thing, my sweet girl.*" My heart skips a beat, hearing him repeat my nickname. Now that I'm in my mid-twenties, he hardly says it anymore—only the odd time, like on a birthday or when we're having a heart-to-heart. Little did he know how much of an impact it would have on my life at the time.

"*Let's go!*" Dad gestures for me to follow him out of the kitchen and into the living room. As I do, I'm reminded of what is about to come next.

"*Wait, Iris,*" Mom calls out, a weariness in her voice. A part of me wishes I could stop this from happening. Protect the innocence of my younger self as she stares up at the woman I once admired, loved, and cherished. Completely unaware of just how much things were about to change.

"*Yes, Mommy?*" I speak softly.

I can't tell what's worse, watching this transpire in front of my eyes or re-living it, knowing the outcome.

"*I...*" she stutters, just like how I remember. "*I just want you to know that I love you. I will always love you. You know that, right?*"

"Then why are you about to leave?" I whisper, only she can't hear me. This is a dream, after all.

"*I know, Mommy.*" My small frame pulls her into a tight hug, one that, again, she hardly reciprocates. "*I love you too.*"

A dampness fills my eyes, and my vision goes blurry. I can't watch this anymore. How can I wake up from this...why can't I wake up from this?

"*Iris,*" Dad shouts from the couch, remote in hand. "*Get your butt in here!*" The opening chords to the movie cause me to turn my head back. *"The movie is starting!"*

"Go," she tells me as I'm released from her grasp for what I hadn't known would be the very last time. *"Go, watch your movie with your Dad."*

I do as she instructs, taking a few short steps back before she stops me. *"And Iris…"* I turn my head at the sound of her voice. *"Just always remember what I said, okay?"*

"Okay, Mom…I will."

My childlike self rushes into the living room and onto the couch with my dad, prompting the dream to flash forward again. Only now, we're approaching the worst part.

Standing in the hallway, I catch a glimpse of my mom as she makes her way quietly down the stairs with that same suitcase in her hand, leaving me to wonder, how could she do this? Why would she do this? We were a family. Didn't we mean anything?

"Mom?" my frail voice catches her attention. I stare into my weary eyes, knowing first-hand just how many questions are going through that little mind. *"Where are you going?"*

"Iris, I…" Mom nervously pauses by the front door, looking back at me before she swallows hard. *"I'm sorry,"* she mouths, her hand connecting with the doorknob as she twists it open.

Here it comes.

I anticipate the final moments of this dream, seeking comfort in knowing that it'll be over soon. Yet, as the door swings open, things start to feel real. Like, I'm no longer in a third-person point-of-view. Now, as I feel the cold air connect with my skin it's as if I'm here.

"What's happening?" I look around the room, taking in the

fact that no one is there.

My five-year-old self is gone.

Dads gone.

And now, it's just me and Mom whose body halts in place. She's no longer racing towards her car.

What is going on?

"Mom?" I speak, only imagining that she can hear me at this point, but somehow she turns around, meeting me with those blue eyes and stares directly at me.

"Iris," she whispers, and hearing my name come out of her mouth feels like poison. *"You're all grown up."* The directiveness of her words causes a single tear to fall down my cheek.

I stand in silence, wondering how in the hell all of this is all happening. But I need to push that aside. This might be the only time I'll ever get to ask her the only question I've ever wanted to know the answer to. "Why are you doing this…why are you leaving us?" my voice is soft but demands an answer.

My mom shakes her head, visibly ashamed before she goes virtually silent, and that's when things suddenly start to make sense.

My mom can't formulate an answer, because frankly, she never gave me one when she left.

For far too long, I've allowed myself to be swallowed up in the hopes of a truth. A clear and direct explanation as to why she couldn't stay, when I could've been using that time to find my power in knowing that I don't need an answer to move on… to *let go*.

At this moment, as I watch her stand in front of me, I'm

reminded that although she's about to walk out of my life, so many people are about to walk into it. It's a peace that somehow settles my soul, and for the first time ever, I stand my ground and let her go.

"You—you aren't going to come after me?" Mom visibly realizes that my body is still, and that, unlike the million times my five-year-old self has run after her in these dreams, now I'm an adult. Now I've decided that I'm no longer going to chase her. Not anymore.

"No," I say—a simple, single syllable that manages to re-write everything. "I'm letting you go, Mom," I tell her with assurance. "I'm letting you go."

As the words escape my lips, there she reappears, five-year-old Iris, watching me as she stands by my side with watery eyes, pushing away a few tears.

I look down at her, kneeling by her side. "You can let her go," I tell her. "Things are going to be okay…you can let her go."

Twenty-Nine

IRIS

"Iris."

I open my eyes to the same sound as when I closed them. Now, as I lift my head up from a pillow that rests below my neck, I'm no longer looking into the eyes of my five-year-old self. No. Now, I'm looking into the eyes of a man who, six months ago, I'd never dreamed of waking up to.

"Dakota?" I groan out in discomfort as the exhaustion pulsates throughout my body.

"It's me," he says. "I'm here, baby." Not only can I hear the sense of relief in his voice, but I can see it written all over his face. Despite his tired eyes and untamed look, Dakota intertwines a hand with mine, brushes a few strands of hair out of my face and gently plants a kiss on my forehead. "Thank goodness, you're okay," he desperately whispers against my skin. "I was so worried about you, Iris. So worried."

My mind escapes me for a second as I try to take in my surroundings.

Pristine white walls.

A blue gown that covers my body.

An IV in my arm.

Even through my disorientated state, I come to the conclusion that, shit, I'm in a hospital.

"What happened?" The two words feel as though they're being cut by a thousand knives on their way out—I've never felt so parched in my life.

Dakota doesn't have to say a thing, all it takes is one look into his eyes for the repressed memories to come flooding back in.

The competition.

The dessert.

Peanuts.

I must've had peanuts.

I groan out at the reminder of the piercing sensation in my outer thigh from the jab of the *EpiPen*, all before the world went dark and I time-warped into the past. I feel like I've lived a whole other life since then. I haven't had a reaction in years. Nor have I had one where I actually fell unconscious. I attempt to peer around the room for a clock of some sorts, but give up and lie my head back in defeat.

"Iris?" Dakota's expression turns weary as he leans in closer, breaking me free from my mind. "Are you okay? Do you need me to get the doctor? You know what…" he hardly gives me a chance to respond before he's come to a conclusion himself. "I'm getting one." He leaps up from the bed. "I'll be right back."

"No," I say with all my might, stopping him in place as now, the questions start to race.

How could this have happened?

How come I was served peanuts in the first place—

Reality comes crashing down on me, like the bitch it is…*shit.*

A Recipe for Disaster

"Don't you also fill out an allergy form or something like that?"

Beth's words torment my mind on loop, as I come to the stark conclusion that the one thing I always make sure I do, I didn't.

"This is my fault," I admit, shaking my head in disbelief. "God…I shouldn't have forgotten." My hands fly their way up to my face, pulling down on my skin. "I can't believe this."

"Hey…" Dakota sinks back down onto the bed, pulling both of my hands back. "Don't say that," he scolds me, though his voice remains tender. "This is not your fault, Iris. You hear me? It's not your fault."

I shake my head in disagreement. There's no way he can convince me otherwise. I had a responsibility, and I didn't do it, no one is to blame here but me. "Yes, it is, Dakota. How would they have known? Nobody else knew."

There's a silence before he meets my eyes. *"I knew."*

The two syllables catch me off guard, and despite lying down in a hospital bed, I feel as though I stumble back at his truth. "You…" I can hardly formulate a sentence. "You knew? How?"

Dakota sucks in a deep breath, holds it there for a second and then releases a long-drawn-out sigh. "Do you remember the day we met, Iris?" Dakota asks a question that I know must be rhetorical in nature. As if I could ever forget the day the two of us met. It's as if it's an archived memory in my mind—one that I know will last me a lifetime. "When you were signing in at that first competition in New York City, I overheard everything you said to Beth, including when you mentioned your allergy."

I attempt to speak, but I'm speechless.

Is this all starting to make sense? Now that the memories are coming back, and this revelation is fresh in my mind, I can't help but focus right back onto what Dakota had said earlier: *"You know what they say. Keep your friends close, but your enemies closer."*

My blood runs cold.

Was Dakota responsible for this?

Was this his plan all along?

Learn my kryptonite and use it against me?

I feel sick.

"You…" I attempt to muster enough momentum to sit up, pushing up on my forearms until I realize that my body has absolutely no strength at all. I go limp in response as I collapse back onto the bed.

"Hey, hey…" Dakota prompts me to lie back down. "You need to rest. Your body has been through a lot. You've been through a lot; you need to take it easy."

I shake my head, refusal all over my face. "I can't believe that you would do that to me, Dakota!" My voice is weak, but I start to shout. "I could've…I could've died!"

I catch him furrowing his brows before I look away, an action that prompts him to reach his hand up onto my cheek and pull me back. "What…" he stutters in utter disbelief. "What in the world are you talking about?"

I met his face with somber eyes. It's hard to be so angry when deep down you're just sad…*hurt*. I attempt to shake him off me but am unsuccessful, I crave his touch. "I heard what you said, Dakota." My voice is a whimper as I hold back from the tears. "Keep your friends close, but your enemies closer," I recite back to him, prompting his face to fall flat. "So, you can stop pretending.

A Recipe for Disaster

I know that this was all just a part of your act."

Dakota releases his touch—and for a split second, as he swallows deeply, I'm certain I've caught him red-handed. But I'm wrong. There's a genuine pang of betrayal that flashes through his brown eyes that completely catches me off guard and swallows me whole.

"Are you being serious right now?" Dakota shakes his head in disbelief, standing up from the bed. "Is that…what you think I've been doing this whole time? Pretending?"

I can hardly muster up enough strength to raise my voice, despite how badly I want to. "What am I supposed to believe?" I interject. "That's what you said, Dakota! That's what I heard you say!"

He refutes the thought with a shake of his head.

"You knew my kryptonite, Dakota," I can't stop spewing these words from out of my mouth. "So, congratulations. I hope you're happy."

He stands in silence, and for a moment, I debate whether or not he's about to keep fighting or storm out of this room. A part of me wants him to. A part of me wants him to walk out of my life and never come back—but he doesn't. He brushes his hand along his forehead, and despite the way he's pacing back and forth, he sinks himself back down onto my hospital bed, this time, clutching onto my hands with a profound sense of urgency.

"You, Iris…" I'm forced to gulp back my anger as he says my name. "Have always been *my* kryptonite."

I pause, suck in a breath, do anything in my power to not completely burst into tears and fold into his embrace. He makes everything so difficult. I need to stay mad at him. I need to be mad at him, but his truth keeps on going.

"I never would've let anything happen to you," he tells me without an ounce of hesitation. "And when I found out about your allergy that first day we met, regardless of how much you supposedly 'hated me', I made sure that every competition we were in together, they knew. You may have forgotten to fill in the form for this competition, Iris, but I didn't. I never have. The committee knew. This was their fault…their mistake, so please… you have to believe me."

"You…you did that for me?" is all I can manage to say, my voice full of judgment as I'm overcome with a round-about of emotions on what's real, and what's fake. "I don't understand. Why would you?"

He looks at me, eyes full of concern, before he leans in close. "Because Iris, I…I love you."

Silence.

I have no words.

He loves me?

"I don't…" I start to speak. "I don't understand."

"You don't need to understand," he says with sincerity. "But you do need to hear these words as I say them to you. You're right. I did say, 'keep your friends close, but your enemies closer.' But I didn't mean it, Iris. I was feeding into the facade. I wanted to save face. I didn't want anyone gossiping and distracting you away from today. I mean that. You have to believe me." He caresses delicately along my cheek. "I know we've had our up's and down's, Iris, but from the moment I first laid eyes on you, I knew you were different. You made me feel things no one has ever made me feel before, and that infuriated me. I didn't know a single thing about you, but you already held the power to consume every thought, feeling and nerve ending inside of me. And then I got to know the woman you are. This irrevocably beautiful, perfect, smart, driven, talented, funny, strong, passionate woman that only drove me that much more insane. And before I knew it, the infuriation soon turned to infatuation, Iris, and I tried so hard to fight it, I did. But I failed. I failed so miserably, but you want to know what? I don't care. I don't care, Iris, because nothing, absolutely *nothing* will ever be more infuriating than not telling you how much I'm in love with you. I love you, Iris. It's you. It's always been you."

I'm resting my forehead against his before I know it, feeling an insane level of guilt wash over my already tired frame. How was I foolish enough to believe that this all was fake, when the look in Dakota's eyes has never looked more real. Dakota's seen me. He's always seen me. Perhaps longer than I've ever seen myself.

"Dakota, I…" I'm so embarrassed. "I'm so sorry." I hardly have the right words to dismantle my accusations. "I should have never accused you of anything. I didn't mean it…I'm so sorry."

Tears begin pooling from my eyes, but Dakota settles me back. "It's okay, baby." He brushes away my tears before he pulls me into his chest. "It's okay. Don't apologize. If anything, I should be the one apologizing to you."

"To me?" I sniffle against his shoulder. "For what? What are you talking about?"

Dakota averts his gaze, staring to the floor as he nervously twiddles his thumbs. "You're not entirely wrong, Iris," he admits.

"There is something that I have been lying to you about since we first arrived here."

My stomach drops. "What?" I watch as he rubs up behind his neck, clearly trying to stall from spewing whatever it is on his lips.

"Lying about what, Dakota?" I prompt him yet again, snapping this time. "Tell me, now."

"The hotel." He mumbles. "I lied about the hotel."

The hotel?

"You messed with our reservation?" I assume, completely confused as to what exactly he's trying to confess to. "You booked us both to stay together?"

"No, no!" Dakota raises his hands in defense, before scooching back in closer. "That genuinely was the hotel, Iris, I swear! I'm referring back to that first night. Remember when you went to the bar with Sean and threw me your purse?"

I faintly nod, recalling the memory.

"When you were talking to him, your phone wouldn't stop ringing. At first, I didn't answer, but eventually, I pulled it out of your bag. It was the hotel you were on the cancellation list for. When they said they had an opening, I realized just how far away it was from the venue, and then it dawned on me—I couldn't let you travel all the way there and back every day. It wasn't right. So, I told them that you were no longer interested, meaning, that you'd be staying with me instead. I felt bad about it the second I did it, Iris. That was your choice, not mine. But I wanted things to be fair…I wanted you to be okay."

Dakota's truth—a truth that deep down only meant that he was saving me from the headache of the daily commute from Fort

Lauderdale to Miami—something that, with full transparency, I'd despised the thought of anyway. Sure, at the time, staying with him was *not* ideal. Should he have let me make my own choice? 100%. But would I change a thing? Absolutely not. Because everything in this moment has led us here—led him to saying those four not-so-simple words to me.

"Please…" Dakota begs for a response as he assesses my face. "Say something."

Despite the monologue in my mind, I hadn't realized that I'd been virtually silent this whole time, though my answer to everything is clear as day. "It's you, Dakota," I admit. "It had always been you. You're the only person in this world that I could loathe while still finding a way to be entirely in love with. I love you, Dakota. I do."

Dakota's face turns into a bright shade of red, a bashfulness in his eyes before I'm safely tucked back into his arms, basking in this moment. "You know…" I admit, staring up into his eyes. "I always thought that we'd be a recipe for disaster."

Dakota tucks both sides of my hair behind my ear, practically speaking against my lips. "Maybe you're right," he admits. "But you wanna know what? We've both never been one to shy away from a challenge…now, have we?"

I'm seconds away from kissing him when a keyword in his sentence electrifies my mind and forces my eyes to widen. I pull back.

"Challenge…competition," I mumble beneath my breath. "Wait, what happened with the competition, Dakota? Please tell me you won, or at least gave the other competitors a run for there money." My words are as quick as they are frantic as his eyes start to wander.

"About that…" He rubs behind his neck. "I came in the ambulance with you, Iris. I needed to make sure you were okay."

I raise a suspicious brow. "So, you were eliminated?"

"I withdrew."

"Dakota." I let out a pained sigh, drawing out his name. "You didn't. You quit? But what about the prize? The title—"

Finally, he crashes his lips into mine. His lips are like sugar, and I'm melting on the tip of his tongue. I never want this moment to end. Maybe this is what that feeling was between us on the day we first met. Not frustration. Not anger. *Love.*

I'm overwhelmed by the gesture. After putting everything ahead of myself in my life, for the first time, it feels like someone has put me first. "I don't know what to say." I'm at a loss for words.

"You don't need to say anything," he tells me. "I don't expect you to."

"But I want to," I retort. "I know how much this competition meant to you. How much making your brother proud meant to you. And the fact that you put all of that aside for me…" I shake my head. "You didn't have to, Dakota. You could've won."

The glimmer in his eyes is unlike anything I've ever seen before. "I did, Iris," he murmurs against my lips. "Everything I've ever wanted is right here in front of me. I won, Iris. All along, I just never knew it was your heart that I was fighting for."

I have to gulp down the disbelief that he could ever feel this strongly about me. "You…you mean that?"

A Recipe for Disaster

He scoots himself even more onto the bed. "From the moment I arrived in New York City, I decided I wanted to be the best in Brooklyn. But now, I know that being the best in Brooklyn means being with *you*."

"Dakota, I—"

"Shh," he hums against my lips before finding his way to the nape of my neck. "Let's just enjoy this, okay? No more talking."

I stifle a laugh as his warm breath plants tender kisses along my skin. "But who won?" I refuse to drop this topic of conversation so easily—despite how entrancing his lips are.

"Tavern House," he mumbles into my neck. My eyes roll to the back of my head as I release a huff of frustration.

"Seriously?"

Of course the resturant that ended up winning was there's. It only lights a fire in me that much more—one that Dakota seems to reciprocate.

"Don't worry." He runs his hand along the soft part of my cheek. "We'll take them down together someday. I just know it." His hand now travels down my neck as he leans back in for another kiss.

It's impossible to cling onto this conversation now with him so close, but still, I can't help but ask, "Dakota Foster, are you really trying to seduce me while I'm in a hospital bed?"

He pulls back with that same devilish smirk on his face. The one that I'm in love with. "Why? Is there something else you'd like me to do?" he playfully remarks.

I allow a smile to break through my lips as I reach for behind his neck and find some strength to pull him back in.

KATE LAUREN

"Just shut up and kiss me, *jerk*."

A Recipe for Disaster

Thirty

IRIS

It takes 24 hours before the hospital discharges me, and its hardly enough time for both Dakota and I to race back to the hotel, gather our things and catch our flight—the same one back to New York City.

As we reach JFK, Dakota insists on taking care of my suitcases. He's hardly let me lift a finger since we'd left the hospital. I can't complain though. It's quite comical watching him juggle four suitcases as we make our way out of the airport terminal and into a taxicab that waits out front.

"Dakota?" I catch his attention as he lifts our suitcases into the trunk—momentarily losing my train of thought as his arms flex beneath his t-shirt.

He slams the trunk shut, snapping me out of it as he reaches to open up my car door. "Yeah?"

I pause before stepping inside. "You know, I haven't told anyone from home what happened."

"Isn't that what we were supposed to do?" He looks down at me in confusion, likely thinking back to the NDA we both had to sign before the competition.

I shake my head. That's not what I was trying to allude to.

"What I mean is that I haven't told anyone that we're coming back...*together*."

"Which means?" Dakota subtly bites down on his lower lip as pulls me in close, wrapping his arms around the low of my waist.

"Which means..." I'm left choking on the suggestive thoughts that his touch evokes, "that—"

"Hey! The clock is running here you know." I'm interrupted by the taxicab driver who rolls down his window and shouts at us with that familiar New York impatience.

"Then this should be easy money for you," Dakota snaps back, both his face and voice full of annoyance before he shoots me a soft stare. "You were saying, baby?" He changes his tune.

My heart flutters hearing him call me that as I suppress a smile and toy with the neck of his shirt. "It means that they're definitely going to be shocked when they see that not only are you trailing in behind me, but that we're together now."

His face hovers inches away from mine as he whispers. "So, that means we're official then?"

I playfully roll my eyes, pecking his lips. "We're official, alright." I pull back. "Officially crazy that we're doing this."

"Oh, what's the big deal?" Dakota closes my door and works his way around to the other side. "It's not like anyone knows me." He buckles in his seatbelt. "It'll be like we just met on the trip."

I suck in a breath, shooting him a stare that makes his head tilt in confusion. "*Iris?*" he says my name expectantly. "What haven't you told me?"

"Well..." I twiddle with my thumbs. "Let's just say that my past hatred for you may have translated towards the rest of the staff at The Sweet Red," I attempt to sugar-coat my words—although, there's no real pleasant way to tell someone, "oh, by the way, everyone at home hates you."

"Wait...did you say The Sweet Red?" The cab driver butts in, whipping around from the driver's seat. "I know The Sweet Red. It's my favorite place to eat in all of Brooklyn!"

"Good." Dakota tosses him a hundred-dollar bill. "Because that's where you're taking us." He closes the window that separates the cab, before darting his attention my way. "So, what you're saying is, everyone at your restaurant hates me? Is that it?"

Yes.

"They don't hate you, per se," I'm having a hard time suppressing a playful smirk. "They just don't particularly like you, that's all." I shrug nonchalantly.

Dakota's face is stoic before his lips curl into a devious grin. "And whose fault is that?" He dances his fingertips along the bare of my skin. "A certain redhead, perhaps?"

My cheeks match the color he infers. "Perhaps," I admit. "But, once they see that that's no longer the case, they'll change their tune. Trust me."

Dakota stifles a laugh, shaking his head as he brings my hand up to his lips. "How do you know that they're all going to be waiting for you anyway? A bit presumptuous now, don't you think?"

"Not at all," I disagree with his claim. "Lore and everyone at the restaurant knew that I was flying back in today, and one thing about Lore is that she's big on surprises."

"But—"

"No, buts." I place a finger against his lips, before drawing his face into mine. "Let's just enjoy these last few moments before the chaos begins. Besides…" I murmur. "I have something else I'd rather those lips be doing right now."

"Surprise!" I hardly take a few steps in through the doorway of The Sweet Red before I'm greeted by an overwhelming mixture of cheers and noisemakers, just like I'd expected—which is why I had Dakota wait outside until I give him the cue to come in.

Everyone's here—Susanna, Dad, Travis, Melody, Lore, Elias. Even Auston, who patiently awaits with a bouquet of red roses in his hand.

Well, this is about to get really awkward.

"Iris!" Lore is the first to reach my side, pulling me in for a firm hug. Clearly, she's feeling much better since the last time we spoke. "Welcome home!" she cheers before dropping her voice. "Did you win? You know you can tell me, right? I promise my lips are sealed."

"I—"

"There she is!" Susanna and Dad are quick to beat me to a response as they pull me into their embrace. "Our culinary girl." Susanna smiles from ear to ear as she places her hands on either side of my face squeezing my cheeks like she's done since the moment Dad first introduced me to her. "Look at you. Doesn't she look great, Dex?" She turns to my dad. "She's got this glow to her…don't you think?"

Dad nods in agreement, planting a tender kiss on my forehead. "You look beautiful, *sweet girl*."

My heart softens with the phrase as Travis guides his way forward. "Miss me, Cliffy?" He jokingly opens his arms wide. Little does he know that I'm receptive to his embrace and pull him in for a hug, prompting Susanna to join in too.

"Um, okay…can someone call an ambulance?" Travis requests. "There is something *seriously* wrong with her."

He awkwardly pulls back, shooting me a confused stare which prompts Susanna to burst into laughter. "What?" I protest hands now on either side of my hips. "Can't I give my *mom* and *brother* a hug?"

It takes a second for the words to register—and when they do, I can see the pure level of shock wash across not only Susanna and Travis's faces, but Dad's too. I think he's waited a long time to hear me say those two simple words, and now that they've been said, it's almost as if it's heals a piece of him, too.

"Aw, come here, sis." Travis pulls me back in for another hug, dragging Dad in too. "What happened? Did Miami make you all soft?"

"Miami made me realize what's most important in my life," I murmur into their embrace. "And I'm just so thankful for you guys. I hope you know that."

"Oh, Iris," Susanna whispers into my ear, with a careful caress of my hair. "We know. We've always known."

We stay together as a family for a few moments before Melody butts in, gently tapping me on the shoulder. "Um, Iris…" she mumbles, "I hate to interrupt this moment, but why is *he* here?"

I waste not a single second before I pull away from my family's grasp, watching as Dakota steps inside the restaurant without a care in the world, pulling our suitcases in from behind him.

"I told you to wait for my cue!" I snap, marching my way forward. "What part of that didn't you understand?"

"You were taking too long," Dakota protests, raising both hands in defense. "Plus, it's cold out."

I roll my eyes, folding my arms in a huff. "I told you to put a sweater in your carry on."

"But it was so hot when we left?"

"Yeah, but now we're on the other side of the country and it's—"

"I'm sorry," Lore speaks and somehow, I've forgotten that everyone is still listening to our conversation. "What the hell is going on? What is *he* doing here?"

Dakota flashes the dumfounded group a playful wave accompanied by a head nod. I push his hand down in response—now is not the time to be sarcastic.

"This is the infamous Dakota?" Auston places his bouquet of flowers to the side, taking an aggressive step forward.

"*Infamous?*" Dakota smirks proudly. "Hm, I quite like that."

"Shush," I nudge him, taking a step towards the group. "I can explain—"

"No need," Auston cuts me off, fired up beyond belief. "What the hell do you think you're doing here?" Auston cracks his knuckles, craning his head from side to side. "You want me to punch him, Iris?"

A Recipe for Disaster

"No, of course not—"

"Punch me?" Dakota seems to find the threat amusing as he snickers. "I'd like to see you try." He takes a cocky step forward.

Auston's face turns into a dark shade of red as he charges his way forward. "Oh, I oughta—"

"Stop!" I shout, placing a hand against his chest to hold him back. "You're not punching anyone. You hear me?"

The space is silent before I see Lore break away from the group and take a step forward. "Do you want me to punch him, Iris?"

"What?" I shake my head in concern. "No, I—"

"I can kick him if you like." Melody joins in.

Travis nods. "Me too! I did karate camp for three summers, I'm a certified master."

"Enough!" I shout, interjecting everyone's obscure willing acts of violence. "No one is punching, kicking or going 'certified master' on anyone, okay? Dakota's here because I asked him to be!"

There's got to be at least ten seconds of silence before finally Travis speaks back up. "Okay, now someone *seriously* better call an ambulance. She's completely lost it!"

"Is this a joke?" Melody whispers to Lore. "Surely, this is a joke, right?"

"It's not a joke." Dakota takes a commanding step forward, prompting everyone to cower back. I can't blame their reaction I've trained them to be this way. "Nothing about how I feel for her is a joke..." He wraps a comforting arm around my waist as I nestle in beside him, staring up in adoration. "Nothing at all."

The room gasps in response.

"Lord have mercy, is this baby brain? Or are you all seeing what I'm seeing right now?" Lore places a hand on her forehead.

"I think I'm hallucinating." Melody joins in on the melodrama.

"Listen," I scan the room. "I know it's hard to believe, but Dakota and I..." I peer back into his deep brown eyes. "We're together now. Okay?"

My words don't appease the jaws dropped along each person's face. "As in, you're standing together or you're together *together*?" Auston asks in disbelief, brows furrowed in concern.

I raise my hands in annoyance. "What is wrong with you all? Why is this so hard to believe?"

I knew the group would be shocked, but I didn't think they'd be in quite such denial. What more do we need to prove here?

"You know what?" Melody calls out, prompting everyone's attention to fall on her. "If you're actually together, then kiss him!"

She looks around the room, everyone smirking as if they're ready to catch me in a lie. The Iris before Miami would've never kissed Dakota, but little do they know that the Iris post-Miami is hardly able to stop.

"Okay." I waste no time reaching for either side of Dakota's t-shirt and pulling him in for a long and drawn-out kiss—one that takes Dakota by surprise as much as it does the entire room.

"Holy shit..." I hear Lore mumble, prompting both Dakota and I to peel back from one another in a fit of laughter. "How many chapters did I miss?"

"Oh," Dakota speaks, drawing me back in. "You all have no

idea."

DAKOTA

"Could we uh, maybe…get some privacy, *please*?" Iris requests, considering her entire family, friends, and what appears to be a scolded ex-lover continue to stare over at us in sheer disillusion.

I flash them an awkward smile until one by one, they clear their throats, mumbling an absurd amount of words in disbelief under their breath as they disperse.

"Well…that went…*well*," I can't help but sarcastically remark at that less than conventional "meet the family". Iris did say that they hated me—and, she was right.

She always is.

"They'll warm up to you." She nestles her head against my chest. "I promise…I'll make sure of it."

I plant a tender kiss on her forehead. "There's no need to reassure me, baby," I tell her as she peers up at me. As she does, I can't help but get lost in counting the number of freckles that cascade along the bridge of her nose, and throughout her cheeks.

How did I land this girl?

"But I do," she insists. "They don't hate you, Dakota. When they get to know you, they'll see what I see."

"Iris…it wouldn't matter even if they did hate me." I smile down at her, delicately brushing my hands through her hair. "You wanna know why?" I kiss the tip of her nose.

She scrunches it playfully in response, batting her eyelashes.

"Why?"

"Because…" I attempt to rid any space between the two of us. "Having someone hate me has never stopped me before. In fact…" I lift her into the air, wrapping her legs around my waist. "Sometimes… it's the start of something beautiful."

She rests her forehead against mine. "I couldn't agree more."

As we bask in this moment together, I'm reminded of just how privileged I am to be holding this girl in my arms. Six months ago I arrived in New York City with nothing but a dream. But now, here I am, holding a dream in my arms. There's nothing better than this.

"Now…" Iris speaks as I gently place her down. "Enough of all this sappy stuff. Care for a tour?" She raises her hands into the air, prompting me to break free from my internal dialogue and take a moment to assess my surroundings.

I never would've imagined that I'd ever step foot into this place, let alone be offered a tour of it. The Sweet Red sure as hell looks a whole lot different when you're not sneaking a ten-second glance at it through the window. This restaurant screams Iris. It's her, and without a doubt, I can see just how much she's put her heart and soul into every piece of this place.

"Where should we start?" she prompts me, reaching for my hand. "Anywhere you're interested in seeing first?"

"The kitchen," I tell her with certainty. "After all, we've got to get back to work if we want to make it into The Art of Cooking Competition next fall, don't we?"

She shoots me a playful stare. "Dakota Foster…" She guides her way back to my side. "I have never loved you more."

Epilogue

IRIS

Five Years Later

They say people come into your life when you least expect it. Boy was that the case with Dakota. He came rolling into my world like a hurricane but lit up my skies like a rainbow. I guess that's how life works, isn't it? Sometimes the most beautiful of things can emerge from the most turbulent of times.

Now, with Dakota by my side, I'm no longer afraid of the uphill. In fact, I crave the incline, the *challenge*. Those moments in life where you embrace change because regardless of the outcome, you know that when someone loves you with all their heart, nothing in this world can surmount that.

"Hey, Iris!" Lore calls from across the kitchen, her pregnant belly making it difficult for her to maneuver between workstations. Frankly, I don't know how she does it. Lore is a total super mom. She's on baby number three and never ceases to amaze me with just how much she can accomplish.

"Yeah?" I respond, lifting my head up from my clipboard. "What's up?"

"I think your in-laws just got back," she informs me, gesturing ahead. "I just heard the front door chime."

"Already?" I question, brows furrowed as I look down at my watch, realizing just how quickly time has passed by. They left at nine o'clock this morning, and now it's already half past five.

I waste no time exiting the kitchen and making my way into the dining room, spotting Dakota's parents—Nancy and Paul, or should I say, my *mother and father-in-law*.

"Hey, guys! How was your day?" I smile in delight. They're both here on a one-week trip to New York City—though I'm certain they love it here so much that they're going to stay. They've got an incentive now.

"Oh, Iris, dear." Nancy pulls me in for a hug. "Our grandson is an angel, a complete and total angel. We had the best day! Didn't we, Paul?"

"We certainly did." He nods enthusiastically. "We went to the park, walked along the pier and even told the little man all about the history of the Hudson River. Did you know that the Hudson never freezes around New York City? Because—"

"Mama." My name is called out at the perfect time, interrupting what was about to be one of my in-laws' in-famous American history lessons—Dakota was undoubtedly right about that one.

"We'll tell you about it another time." Paul smiles as he bounces his grandson in his arms. "Go to Mommy," he instructs, handing him over to me as I pester his face with kisses.

"He's going to be a real smarty pants, you know!" Nancy sings his praises. "I mean, look at him. Eight months old, and he's already talking!"

A Recipe for Disaster

"Mama...Mama," he babbles, melting my heart each time he says it. There's no greater feeling—especially considering he said it before Dada.

Take that, Dakota.

After we found out that we were having a baby boy, Dakota and I debated for months on what we should name him. But ultimately, we decided that there was only one name that would suit our son—one that made the most sense.

Brooklyn.

Of course, Dakota's parents were ecstatic that we unintentionally kept the American city names in the family. They loved Brooklyn, and in my eyes, it sure beat out some of their other alternative options like Eugene and Memphis. I fear for our next baby and what American city they'll be named after—I mean, we can't stop the trend now.

Brooklyn was perfect. Not only is it where Dakota and I built up our own respective restaurants. But it's where we've opened up our own, *together*—right smack dab in the middle on Orange Street, naming it another name that only seemed fitting.

The Sweet Cook.

I guess we have both Isabella and The Art of Cooking Competition to thank for that one.

Speaking of which, two years after Dakota and I opened The Sweet Cook, we received an invite back to the competition. It was on that trip, and following the day that we won the grand prize together that Dakota decided to pop the question in the most Dakota way possible—while suspended in the air on a parasail.

I'm not quite sure how I managed to rope myself back into

that one, but the tears as we descended were certainly that of joy and not of fear.

We got married a year later, along the beachfront in Miami where not only did we run into Randy from that first boat trip, but he somehow ended up DJing our wedding reception. After all, he did have good taste in music.

Granny and Grandpa from the resort also managed to *swing* an invite. No pun intended. How, you may wonder? At some point in the wedding planning process, Dakota took it upon himself to seek the two of them out in the phone book. He thought it would be hilarious to have them show up—little did he think they actually would.

In the five years we've been together, I've learned that Dakota's notorious for playing pranks, especially on me. At my bachelorette party, he secretly convinced Lore to invite a stripper named Sebastien—reminiscent of my conversation with Beth on the day we first met.

Like always, Dakota's plan soon came to a demise when I found out about his shenanigans and shut it down. The "no climbing on tables" enactment has still managed to find its way into our new restaurant—Beth made sure of that.

As for Colbie and Seen—*Sean*—they ended up being a hot celebrity couple for the first few months that followed The Art of Cooking competition. That was until they fizzled out and had an extremely public breakup. Turns out Sean isn't the commitment type—*shocker*, and Colbie isn't the open relationship type—who would've thought? Needless to say, the two weren't invited back as judges after their fooling around got exposed to the culinary committee. It's crazy how things end up working out for the best, isn't it?

"Aw, our sweet Brooklyn boy," Nancy and Paul coo as they tickle him in-between my arms. "Give Grandma and Grandpa a kiss before we go." They plant a series of kisses on his chubby cheeks. "Oh, I just want to eat you up!"

Somehow Brooklyn finds his way back into his grandma's arms as he giggles with each and every kiss.

I'll admit, he really is scrumptious. My little boy's got red hair just like his mommy, but the temperament of his daddy as he tries to squirm out of his grandma's touch. He's now clearly had enough of this intense affection.

"There's my boy!" I hear Dakota call out from behind me, re-emerging from the kitchen while Travis trails in tow. The two of them are now best buddies. *Lucky me.*

"Did you guys have a fun day?" Dakota takes Brooklyn into his arm, wiping a smudge of lipstick off his cheek, before he plants a kiss of his own. "Hi, buddy."

"That we did!" Nancy and Paul say in unison. "In fact, we were just telling Iris all about it. Oh, hey, Travis…" They smile as he joins the group.

Travis waves in response. "How are things?"

Travis is all grown up now. He's the same age as I was when I first met Dakota, and as the years have gone by, my brother has proved to me that he can be trusted to do much more than just to close up shop. Now, Travis is not only the manager, but dare I say the lead when it comes to The Sweet Red.

Dakota and I knew that the only way we'd be able to prioritize opening up an establishment together was to get as much support in our respective restaurants as possible. That's why Dakota appointed Auston to be the head chef of The Closed Cook. After all, we kind of owed him one after he unintentionally caught Dakota and me mid-action while re-creating a particular freezer dream. *Whoops.*

"Walk us out?" Dakota's parents request.

Dakota agrees before turning to face me. "Ready to call it a night?" He plants a tender kiss on my cheek.

I smile, nodding in agreement as I follow my family outside of the restaurant, stopping for a moment to admire it. In the past five years, it's crazy how much we've accomplished, but this is only the start. There's so much more to come, and I can't wait for what lies ahead.

"Hey, you coming?" Dakota asks in question given that my eyes are fixated onto the plaque that's secured on the brick of the main entrance. It that reads:

> *In Loving Memory of Dallas Foster. Brother, best friend and our honorary first customer.*

There's a sense of warmth that floods my heart every time I read those words. The truth is, I know Dallas is proud of Dakota right now...I know that with every ounce of my being.

"I'm ready." I pull my eyes away, jogging ahead to plant a kiss onto his lips, brushing over the tattoo on his wrist before our hands intertwine as one.

"Why are you so smiley?" Dakota places Brooklyn into his

A Recipe for Disaster

stroller, nudging me playfully as we walk down the street in stride.

"I'm just thinking," I admit.

"Thinking about what?"

"How we're not half bad for a recipe for disaster, now are we?" I joke, prompting him to come to a standstill as he pulls me in and looks into my eyes, and at this moment I'm certain I've never been more in love with this man than I am right now.

"Not bad…" He leans in for a kiss. "Not bad at all."

KATE LAUREN

A Recipe for Disaster

KATE LAUREN

Acknowledgements

Considering I can't cook to save my life, I only thought that it would be fitting to write a rom-com all about two-chefs, makes sense right?

I hope you enjoyed my take on enemies-to-lovers, and fell in love with Iris and Dakota the way I have as I wrote this story. As my sophomore novel, I couldn't be prouder to show you all sides to my writing. This book means the world to me, and who knows, maybe it's inspired you to go to New York, Miami or hell…enter a cooking competition of your own.

Either way, thank you to each and every person who made this book possible, and to those of you who have taken the time to read it. Welcome to the family—I'm so happy to have you here.

About The Author

Kate Lauren is a "certified fangirl" whose passions include writing contemporary romance novels, using suggestive innuendos any chance she can get, and subliminally tying in Taylor Swift song-titles into her books.

Based out of Toronto, Canada, when Kate's not daydreaming about which fictional character she'll create next, you'll find her with her friends, family and husband—or nose deep in her next novel.

Follow Kate on IG - @theauthorkatelauren

Graphic Illustration by Jessica Lynn Draws

jessicalynndraws.com

KATE LAUREN

Printed in Great Britain
by Amazon